Two-Headed Alligator
By Iphigenia Strangeworth

**A HellBound Books LLC
Publication**

Copyright © 2025 by HellBound Books Publishing
LLC
All Rights Reserved

Cover and art design by Kevin Enhart
For HellBound Books Publishing LLC

No part of this book may be reproduced, stored in a
retrieval system, or transmitted by any means,
electronic, mechanical, photocopying, recording or
otherwise without written permission from the author
This book is a work of fiction. Names, characters,
places and incidents are entirely fictitious or are used
fictitiously and any resemblance to actual persons,
living or dead, events or locales is purely coincidental.

www.hellboundbooks.com

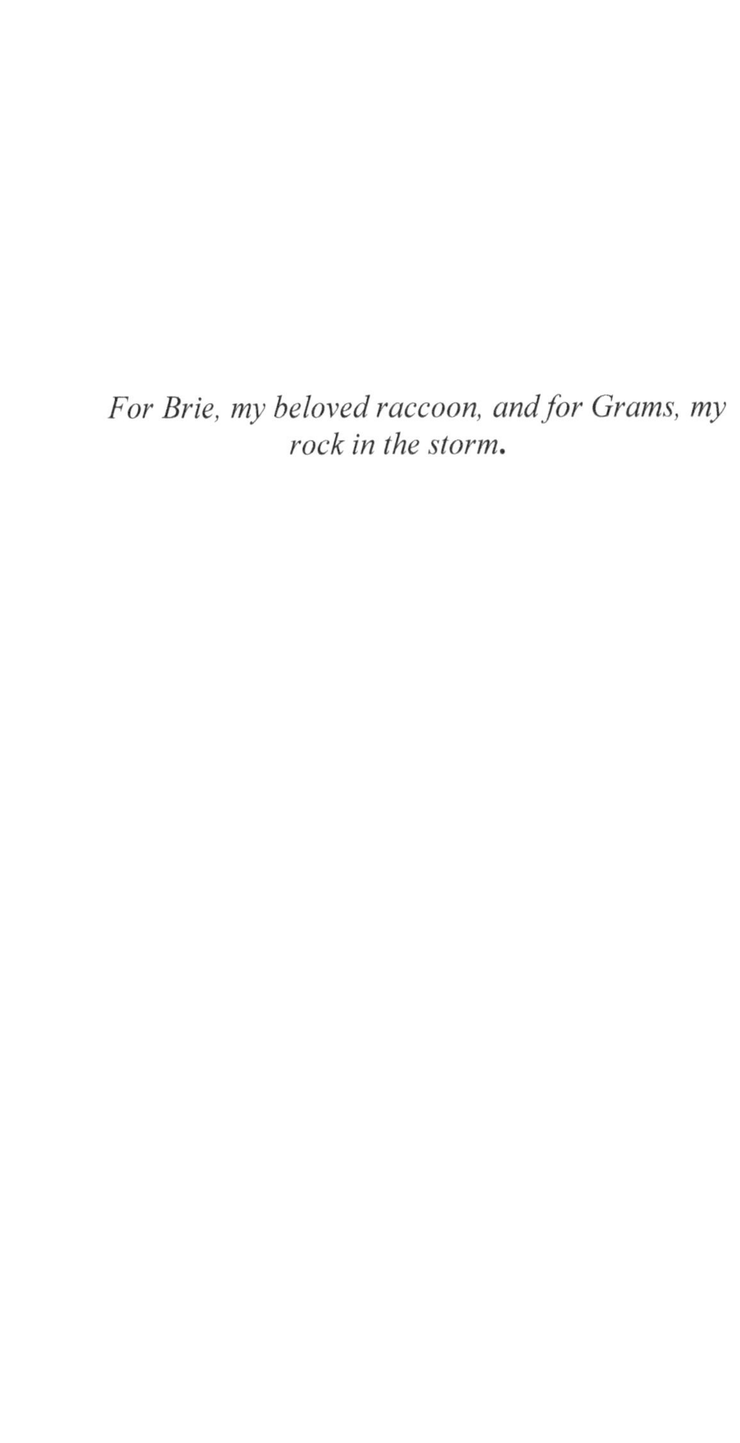

For Brie, my beloved raccoon, and for Grams, my rock in the storm.

Acknowledgements:

As always, thank you to Grams for supporting my writing. This is the story you consider my least disturbing, and I'm glad I wrote something that didn't give you nightmares for once. When you were driving me to the airport for my most recent "let me move across the country on a whim" adventure, you told me that you had a conversation with a friend in which she said "I know you love all your grandchildren, but [Iphigenia] is your heart." You paused for a moment and then added, "Be careful with my heart." Grams, you are my heart, too, and you have inspired me to live my life to the fullest. I am blessed beyond words to have you in my life, and I love you with all my heart and soul.

Thank you to my dear friend Brie for your kind words of encouragement, your endlessly entertaining stories, and for bringing a little more whimsey into the world with your marvelous pet names. You are an incredibly talented writer and artist and an amazing friend. Give He Who Screams a kiss on the head from me.

Thank you to my parents for telling me all about your exciting trip to the UK that I wasn't invited on. Sounds like it was super fun. Glad I got to experience that vicariously.

Thank you to Aunt Kathy for being your wonderful, overwhelmingly positive self. We all look forward to reading your beautiful, eloquent messages, and we are all in awe of your ability to stay sane while giving so much of your time and energy to causes you are passionate about.

Thank you to Maeve and Abby, my oldest friends, for continuing to put up with my nonsense.

Thank you to everyone whose research contributed to this book: Alice Dreger, author of *One of Us: Conjoined Twins and the Future of Normal*, Sarah Miller, author of *Violet & Daisy: The Story of Vaudeville's Famous Conjoined Twins*, and Joanne Martell, author of *Millie-Christine: Fearfully and Wonderfully Made*.

Thank you to James Longmore, Xtina Marie, and the rest of the wonderful team at HellBound!

And finally, to Ken Walker, a retired male gynecologist who felt the need to write a deeply ableist article about the birth of craniopagus conjoined twins Tatiana and Krista Hogan, calling their existence a tragedy and bemoaning the monetary cost of allowing severely disabled people to live- how much are you contributing to the economy now that you're over a hundred years old? How much is your healthcare costing taxpayers? Judging human beings by how much you think they are able to benefit society is an awfully bold position for a man who some might say has lived much, much too long.

Disabled people have as much right to live as anyone else, regardless of the severity of their disability. Physically deformed people are just as human as anyone else, regardless of the severity of their deformity. To anyone who draws a line in the sand and appoints himself arbiter of who is and is not human: remember, if you live long enough, you will one day be one of those "useless" disabled people "wasting resources". Remember, you could be hit by a car or suffer a stroke at any moment. You would do well to remember that the only thing separating you from the people you consider subhuman is an accident of birth.

Contents

Prologue

Our last name is Gardner, but everyone in town called us the Garden girls for three reasons.

Number one: our mother had a rose garden that she tended to obsessively, and which our father became even more obsessive over after she died.

Number two: our sister, Rose Red—whose real name is Alice—threw a massive temper tantrum when we were referred to as such, screaming that our name was *Gardner,* not *Garden,* and could never really explain why the misnaming bothered her so much.

Number three: it would have been impolite to call us the freakshow family.

The three oldest Garden girls were Tiffany, Diamond, and Alice. They have always been called Tiff, Dia, and Rose Red. The youngest and, formerly, the most extraordinary were Deirdre and Desdemona, always known as Arcana and Dezy. We were extraordinary only by virtue of being conjoined twins, joined at the chest and sharing one heart between us. Thoracopagus twins are among the most common types of conjoined twins, but we were the only known pair to survive into adolescence, making us a medical anomaly and international curiosity.

Doctors speculated that our unusually long life was due to two factors.

Number one: we were female. Females are, on average, both weaker and hardier than males; weaker in the sense of physical strength, hardier in the sense that we can survive longer and harsher conditions. Fat-storing patterns and temperature regulation makes us better equipped to survive famines and extreme weather, and because we are more durable in general, most conjoined twins who live past infancy are female.

Number two: Desdemona had sacral agenesis, a severe deformity of the pelvis and legs (and a condition not quite as rare as conjoined twinning). If you looked at her fully clothed, you would think she had no lower body at all, and the optical illusion had been known to make old ladies faint in church. She was also born with only one arm. Because there was simply less of her to require blood, the twins' shared heart may have been under less pressure.

We faced each other, always, and usually slept with our foreheads pressed together, but when Deirdre walked, Desdemona tucked her chin against her twin's shoulder so she could actually see where she was going. As an obvious consequence of our condition and the way our bodies were built, Deirdre had complete control over our lives. Desdemona did not get a say in where we went or what we did, and because she had lived her entire life in Deirdre's arms, being carried where her sister wanted to go, she never thought to complain or wish anything was different.

Looking at us from the neck up, you would see two identical girls facing each other, staring into each other's eyes, one grinning mischievously and one frowning in anticipation of whatever her sister was about to do. Looking at our full bodies, you would see Desdemona's underdeveloped legs on either side of Deirdre's waist, Deidre's arms supporting Desdemona, holding her close, our chests merged together and Deirdre's strong legs holding us both up.

We are no longer extraordinary, because one of us is dead. I won't tell you which one; Tiff loves stories, and she told us you should never spoil the ending before you get there. Our story isn't very exciting, and if it weren't for the alligator farm, I would tell it like this:

Once upon a time, a woman who loved her rose garden more than her children died giving birth to thoracopagus twin daughters. The doctors wanted to cut them apart, but their father refused, hoping they'd both die. He named them Deirdre, which means broken-hearted, and Desdemona, which means ill-fated. Much to his disappointment, the twins survived infancy, then childhood, and he was beginning to think he'd be stuck with them forever when their shared heart finally began to give out. At sixteen, the twins agreed to the separation surgery that had been pushed on them all their life, and one of them died on the operating table. The end.

There was one thing, though, that made our lives worth talking about. The trip to Louisiana, the alligator farm, the two-headed alligator and the two-headed girl, the famous- or infamous- dead conjoined twins. Dicephalic parapagus versus thoracopagus; one very, very rare but carrying a higher chance of survival, the other accounting for 75% of conjoined twin cases but carrying an almost 0% survival rate if the twins aren't separated.

So I'll tell you our story, because Florence and Sage Labelle made it interesting. I still have their diary and little Liliana's memories, so I'll include those where it seems relevant, but I can't cut straight to the interesting part. I have to tell you our story, first.

Chapter One

We lived in a fairytale house, with a fairytale garden, ten minutes away from a fairytale river. It was a little white cottage high up in the mountains, and our mother's roses grew in perfect neat order all our lives. Daddy didn't care about anything except the roses; consequently, he had the most beautiful garden in all of Arkansas and the most resentful children in the entire country, if not the world.

When we were born, Tiff was six, Dia was four, and Rose Red was two. Our parents planned the gaps like that, wanting us to be close enough in age that we could play with each other but not so close there were multiple infants in the house at once. Rose Red could walk and, unfortunately, talk by the time we were born. According to Tiff, her favorite words were *no, mine,* and *stop.* We used to say that never really changed, but Arcana said it loudly and Dezy just whispered it.

Every member of our family had a different version of our birth story, and if you asked us, we'd each tell you something different, too. Arcana would say, with a proud glint in her eyes, that the doctors gave us an hour to live. Dezy would say, talking to the wall behind you more than you, that we were lucky to have lived this long.

"I don't remember our birth," she said once, apologetically.

"Nobody remembers their birth, stupid," Arcana laughed. Dezy, who could do very little to get back at the sister who ruled her life, dug her fingernails into Arcana's shoulder and winced right along with her. We felt everything the other felt, so pinching and hair-pulling never got us very far.

Tiff told us, with a bright, proud smile, that she may have saved our souls from Hell. That was how she always put it, even when Rose Red yelled that she was being overdramatic. "Mama believed in home births," she'd sigh, "and, honestly, she probably would've been totally fine if she'd gone to a hospital. Dia thinks all that kind of hippie thing is cool, but personally I always think you should err on the side of caution. Modern medicine exists for a reason." (Tiff would know all about that. She's in medical school now, which might be cutting ahead a little, but it doesn't really matter. Tiff being in medical school hasn't changed our lives at all.)

"Anyway, her water broke in the kitchen while she was making dinner, so Daddy rushed her into their bedroom to have you. Isn't that gross? Giving birth in the bed where you *sleep?* There's a rubber sheet down, but still, ew. It took almost a whole day in labor before she finally had you, which was weird, 'cause the rest of us were all born within a few hours of her water breaking. That should've been the first sign something was wrong. Y'all were born normally, but you tore her open all the way from here to here." Tiff spread her legs and traced a line from her clitoris to her anus for demonstrative purposes.

"I was in the room with the midwife, and I'm probably the reason she didn't kill you both on the spot. She screamed when she saw you, so I grabbed you, still all wet, and wiped you off. I cut the umbilical cord, too. She ran off to get Daddy, who took one look at everything and called 911 right away, but our mom had already bled out by the time they arrived. While we were waiting, the midwife said y'all were gonna die soon, you *had* to, so I baptized you myself. I'd seen the preacher do it to Dia and Rose Red and figured I could do as good a job as him. After the ambulance came, y'all were in the NICU for months, but you made it through!"

Dia's version of events was very, very different. "Mama's water broke in the rose garden," she'd say, closing her eyes dramatically, "and she barely had time to stumble in the house before y'all were born. She bled out before the midwife even got here, and the last thing she said before she died was, 'These are my girls? They're miracles!' She held y'all on her chest even though you were gross, like newborns are, kissed the tops of your heads, and passed away. Then Tiff baptized you."

"You were born on June twentieth," Rose Red offered, "and Mama died right after. Tiff baptized you with tap water, but it doesn't actually mean anything because she's not a preacher or a priest."

The only time we asked Daddy about our birthday, he just got a faraway expression and, without looking at us, murmured, "It was the worst day of my life."

"Well, we know for sure that Tiff baptized us," Arcana said drily after we'd collected everyone's input. "No idea what the hell else happened, though."

In the NICU, several medical decisions of varying importance were made on our behalf, mostly by the midwife, Margaret Trimble, an old woman who almost certainly never had any intention of killing us. First, it was decided, with the help of our father, that we would not be separated. "God made them this way," Margaret snapped when the doctors pressed the issue, "and men must never interfere with God's plan."

"What if they die?" the doctors asked her.

"Are they dying?"

"They will be."

"Separate them when they start dying, then. They're not dying now."

Second, Margaret had to fight the pediatric surgeons to get them to fix Desdemona's most immediately apparent problems—namely, bladder exstrophy and an imperforate anus. In layman's terms, her bladder had developed outside her body, and she did not have a normal anal opening. Margaret would later learn that both of these conditions are common in babies with sacral agenesis, but at the time she figured God was giving us multiple trials and was determined to help us overcome them.

The doctors gave her the runaround for several hours, muttering that they weren't sure, it could be dangerous, they'd never seen a case like ours, before finally admitting that, because Desdemona was the less developed twin, they didn't want to waste resources on her. The only surgery they were willing to perform was a separation surgery to save Deirdre's life. Margaret responded, with a sweet smile and her best Southern belle accent, "Now, sir, you took an oath to do no harm, and until the twins *have* to be separated, you have no reason not to help this poor girl. My father left me quite an inheritance, which, being a simple woman, I've left completely untouched right up 'till now. If you let this child die without reason, not only will I sue this hospital into oblivion, I will make sure every news outlet in the country knows what you did. My family has friends in high places, as you know."

He did not know this, because it wasn't true, but Margaret spoke so confidently—and, incidentally, was right about the doctor's oath—that the surgery was scheduled. Desdemona's bladder was put back where it belonged, she had a permanent colostomy, and six months later the twins were cleared to go home. Margaret, who had started coming around to watch the older Garden girls, ordered the local preacher to our house and had him baptize us properly, much to Tiff's annoyance.

Daddy didn't really get out of bed until our first birthday. It was Margaret who made him get up. It was Margaret who was responsible for most of the functionality in our house. According to family legend (and, because all of our sisters agreed on this, we figured it must be true), she threw his door open, marched to the window, ripped the curtain down and said, "Your wife's roses have grown wild."

Margaret kept us alive those first few years. Our older cousin Jewel started living with us in the wake of our mother's death, but she was remarkably unhelpful in pretty much every conceivable way. With Margaret's help, though, we were alive, happy, as healthy as we could be. She also, with some unwanted help from Rose Red, taught Deirdre to walk.

There's a home video of our first steps, a home video that Dia would post to her Instagram account years later, much to our fury and humiliation. It's a grainy video taken on Daddy's old camcorder, very shaky because Tiff was holding it. We were over a year old but, due to the sister hanging from her chest, Deirdre had yet to crawl like a normal child. Instead, she got around with an awkward sort of crab walk/shuffle, scooting on her butt until she reached whatever she wanted. Sometimes, but not often, she reached what Desdemona wanted and grabbed it for her.

"Come here," Margaret says in the video, and Deirdre blinks at her, peering over her twin's shoulder. We move our heads to face each other, Deirdre gurgles something incomprehensible, and then she starts to awkwardly pull herself forward, but Margaret holds up a hand. "Not like that. Stand up. Up, now!"

"Up?" Deirdre repeats, confused. Desdemona isn't talking yet. Desdemona will not talk until she's almost two years old.

"Like this." Margaret stands, wincing at the resistance from her old knees, and takes a few steps forward. Deirdre stares blankly, then laughs at the assumption we could ever manage that. "You've got this, honey. Put your arms around your sister,carry her, and walk."

"Up," Deirdre laughs.

That's when Rose Red runs into frame, scowling, grabs Deirdre under the arms, and yanks her suddenly to her feet. Both twins shriek in fear, but Rose Red doesn't let go. Instinctively, Deirdre wraps her arms around Desdemona's waist and, in an attempt to get away from her big sister, takes a wobbly step forward, then another. When Rose Red takes her hands away, she stays standing.

Margaret did not scold Rose Red for grabbing us, although we always thought she should have.

Growing up, we went to the doctor at least once a month. It didn't take long for us to realize we were different from everyone else—our sisters, obviously, did not have twins sprouting from their chests. In addition to the most apparent conditions, Deirdre suffered severe migraines that left the twins bedbound for days on end, Desdemona experienced frequent and intense nosebleeds, and both of us had endometriosis. Desdemona was completely incontinent; Deirdre was not, but had a lot of accidents, which she always blamed on her sister. Desdemona allowed this, and everyone except Rose Red politely pretended to believe her. Both of us had mild asthma that, miraculously, got better as we got older.

We were not allowed to engage in any kind of strenuous activity. Rose Red, who tended to shelter us, would have preferred we always use a wheelchair to get around, but everyone else encouraged Deirdre to walk. The awkward way we were conjoined meant Tiff had to help us with things most people take for granted; bathing, changing clothes, changing

Desdemona's colostomy and catheter bags, tying shoes, making our bed, cleaning our room. She never complained about these tasks.

"I've got some news, ladies," Margaret announced, sitting across from us at the kitchen table when we were five years old. Arcana had a deck of tarot cards spread out in front of her and was arranging them by color while Dezy made a My Little Pony trot through the air behind her. We had already received our nicknames by then- Arcana loved tarot cards from the moment she got her hands on a deck, and Desdemona was just too long to say.

"We're going to Hollywood?" Arcana asked hopefully. She'd wanted to be a movie star for a week, making it her longest lasting career goal yet.

"Not quite, but you *are* going to school with your sisters."

"No, thank you," Dezy said politely.

"I don't like that news," Arcana said, less politely, but not rudely. No one was rude to Margaret.

"I thought about homeschooling y'all, but I just don't think I'm able to come out here every day," Margaret said sadly. "It's important that you get a quality education."

"Why? We won't live long enough to use it," Arcana pointed out.

"Don't talk like that. The two of you are already a medical miracle, a gift from God, and I know you're meant for great things," Margaret said fiercely.

"Yes, ma'am," we chorused, because we knew better than to argue when Margaret started talking about gifts from God.

"Who's homeschooling?" our cousin Jewel asked suddenly, ambling into the kitchen. Jewel was a glamorous young woman who bleached her hair blonde, wore a fur coat all winter long, and was completely fucking useless as a guardian. We worshipped her.

"No one. I thought about it long and hard, prayed on it, and I can't think of any way to schedule it right," Margaret sighed.

"What, for the twins?"

"Who else?"

"Rose Red's having a hard time in school." Her perceptiveness surprised us.

"Her grades are perfect," Margaret said, clearly as shocked as we were that Jewel had actually noticed something about one of us.

"Sure, but everyone hates her. She's a little tyrant." Jewel chuckled.

"How do you know that?"

"I read her report cards," our cousin shrugged.

"*Why?*"

"Aren't I their guardian, pretty much? Lord knows their daddy—"

"Not in front of the twins," Margaret hissed.

"We already know," Arcana muttered under her breath.

"I don't think public school's a good idea," Jewel continued, as if she had any experience in childcare or education. "They'll get bullied, for one thing, and those places are full of germs. It can't be good for their immune systems."

"Maybe a private school, then? I'm sure we could scrape together the money somehow, find a scholarship program or ask for donations…"

"How 'bout I just homeschool them?"

"You have no background in teaching."

"I went to school," Jewel countered.

Dezy moved her head so we could look each other in the eyes. Pressing our foreheads together, mouthing a few words, we quickly came to a decision—being homeschooled by our fancy cousin, with her long acrylic nails and overdone eyeshadow, sounded impossibly *cool*.

"We wanna be homeschooled!" we cried in unison. Margaret, who had been halfway through a list of reasons Jewel should never be let within twenty feet of a curriculum, deflated slightly. Jewel grinned triumphantly.

Jewel was, surprisingly, not a terrible teacher. She was unorthodox for sure, but she believed children couldn't learn through rote memorization and went out of her way to make learning fun. "I sure couldn't memorize shit," she laughed, throwing away the lesson plans Margaret printed off at the library. "Y'all know the alphabet, right?"

"Rose Red taught us," Arcana said, shuddering. Rose Red's favorite games were anything that let her be in charge of as many people as possible, so we often ended up playing classroom (with her as the teacher) and house (with her as the mother). Tiff and Dia, being older and possessing longer, less clumsy legs, managed to escape her tyrannical games more often than not, but we were not fast enough to run away from her.

"We know the whole alphabet," Dezy added quickly. We hadn't been allowed to stop playing classroom until we could both recite the whole thing without mistakes.

"Perfect! And how many words can you read?"

"We know our names."

"Off to a great start, then."

Jewel believed Dick and Jane books were an archaic torture method, so she taught us to read with Dr. Seuss, quickly moving on to fairytales once Arcana got the hang of reading. Dezy was always slow on the uptake, and it didn't help that she only had one arm. In order to read, she had to ask Arcana to position herself very carefully so that Dezy could rest a book flat on a table and slowly turn the pages. This required Arcana to sit still with her back against a hard edge, so she only did it when she was feeling especially generous, which didn't happen very often. Had Jewel been a real teacher, she would have noticed Dezy's struggles and slowed down the curriculum; because she was just our overzealous cousin, she cheerfully moved on to math, which confused Dezy even more.

Please don't think Arcana was cruel. How would you feel in her place, a conjoined twin growing out of your chest, carrying your sister's weight around every second of your life, sharing every breath with her and knowing she was shortening your life? Maybe she was a little selfish, but she loved Dezy, she was never, ever intentionally mean to her. She just wanted to live her own life, and Dezy was, by design, largely unable to stop her.

Both of us loved stories, and Arcana made up for leaving her sister behind academically by reading to her every night she could. It became a ritual, Arcana leaning over Dezy's shoulder to read from a huge book of fairytales, often reaching to pet her hair, smiling as Dezy nuzzled at her neck, sighed contentedly and fell asleep in her arms. When Arcana was incapacitated by a migraine, Tiff took over bedtime duty, arranged us gently in bed and, in a low, low voice so as not to worsen Arcana's headache, told us a story.

Tiff's stories were a mishmash of half-remembered fairytales starring all of us Garden girls in the lead roles. We became conjoined Rapunzels, Dia was Sleeping Beauty, Tiff was a frog princess, and Rose Red was, rather unflatteringly, the Queen of Hearts. It was not hard to imagine Rose Red on a throne, ordering people beheaded for fairly minor infractions. She always wanted to be a princess for Halloween, her pink, poofy dresses clashing horribly with her frizzy red hair. We all had red hair, although Dezy and Tiff's hair faded to auburn as they got older.

Jewel knew next to nothing about history and science, so our education in those subjects consisted pretty much entirely of visiting museums. We had to drive quite a ways to see them, journeys which necessitated Tiff to come along with at least two changes of clothes. Jewel fainted at the sight of blood and had what she called a "sympathetic stomach", meaning she vomited when she saw other people throwing up. It went without saying that she would not be cleaning up any other bodily effusions.

Our first trip to the nearest science museum—which was, in fact, two hours away—was also, in some ways, our first trip out of Eureka Springs. We had been to a great many hospitals and specialists, but we had never actually been out in *public,* not even to go to the grocery store. Dia's friends had seen us and spread rumors about the freakish conjoined twins, and we were somewhat famous with certain groups of people just for being born and surviving to age five, but we did not go into town. Arcana wanted to; Dezy did not. More importantly, Margaret and Daddy did not want us to.

"Are we *allowed* to go this far?" Arcana called from the backseat. Dezy was half-asleep on her shoulder but jolted awake at her question.

"Probably!" Jewel chirped.

"You said Margaret was fine with it," Tiff chimed in suspiciously.

"She totally is. It's important that you two get an education, right?" Jewel asked, meeting Arcana's eyes in the rearview mirror.

"Does she even know?" Tiff asked.

"Yeah," Jewel said flippantly, which we all knew meant *I'll tell her later.*

The science museum was massive, not as big as some hospitals we'd been to, but impressive to the eyes of sheltered kindergarteners. We were so enthralled by the building itself, the little exhibits just inside, that we failed to notice how we were being stared at until we heard a woman's shrill voice crying, "*Don't* push my child!"

"He can't just walk up and touch them," Tiff said, calm but firm, and Arcana turned to face the little boy (actually, a boy older than us) who had, indeed, clearly come up just to touch us.

"What *is* it?" he asked. Dezy stiffened in anger, and Arcana burst into tears, immediately wishing Jewel had never brought us here.

"Don't cry!" Tiff yelped. Dezy rubbed her sister's back soothingly, sighing in relief when she heard the rude woman's heels clicking away across the tile floor. Arcana squeezed her like a teddy bear, legs on the verge of collapse, and Jewel scooped us both into her arms.

"I wanna go home," Arcana wailed, drawing even more attention to us. Dezy glowered at everyone who turned to look, baring her teeth like a dog.

"There's a lot you could learn here," Jewel said softly. Having already bought our tickets, she was reluctant to leave. "Plus, you can't stay home forever, sweetheart. You need to get used to people staring."

"I want to stay," Dezy said. She moved her head to look Arcana in the eyes and repeated, "I want to stay."

It was already rare for Dezy to begin a sentence with *I want,* and as we grew older, it would become much, much rarer. For all her pushiness, Arcana was always moved when Dezy dared to state her desires so plainly, and while she sometimes ignored her anyway, she submitted to her that day.

It wasn't immediately clear that we were conjoined twins, but a closer look told you we were *something.* Margaret made all our clothes, and as children it was just the same dress repeated in different colors over and over again. She made a long, billowy dress with a very wide neck hole, two sleeves for Arcana, none for Dezy. It looked like Arcana was carrying Dezy, which she was, but if you paused to stare, because that was an unusual sight, two little girls sharing a single dress with one carrying the other, if you stepped closer and were taller than us, you would see that our chests grew into each other.

Despite Arcana's crying fit and the nosebleed Dezy had all over our dress on the way home, we counted our first official outing a success.

After the museum, Jewel started taking us to the grocery store in town, then Margaret took us to church. Rose Red, who believed our education was too unstructured, wanted us to attend school, but everyone, even Margaret, firmly agreed it was a terrible idea.

We quickly learned that we just had to shut everyone else out when we left the house. Eureka Springs is a gorgeous, gorgeous town, probably one of the prettiest in America, but it's also entirely a tourist town. This is both a good thing and a bad thing. If, like Dezy, you're the type to look on the bright side, you might say that a tourism industry based around natural beauty and old-fashioned charm means Eureka Springs will never change and will always put more resources into keeping nature pretty than other Southern cities do.

If, like Arcana, you're inclined to pessimism, you might say that a tourist town is not the best place to be the world's oldest living thoracopagus twins. With our increased presence in town, Eureka Springs became known for the natural springs, the preserved historic buildings, the Crescent Hotel, and us, Deirdre and Desdemona Gardner, the freakshow act who just wanted to be left alone in the grocery store.

Personally, we always thought the Crescent Hotel was more interesting than us. It was supposed to be the most haunted hotel in America, which, to girls who had never seen a ghost but lived our entire lives together, was much more novel than conjoined twins.

"Do we have spaghetti?" Jewel asked, frowning over a box of noodles. She never made grocery lists.

"I think so," Arcana offered, squirming so her back wouldn't be pressed up against the hard metal grating of the shopping cart. We liked to sit in the cart; we thought it made us slightly less noticeable.

Someone walking by stopped to stare at us, and Dezy pressed her face into Arcana's neck, tightening her arm around her.

We actually had a very happy childhood. It was as normal as it could have been, given our condition, and looking back on it now I can really only think of a few bad memories, mostly people staring at us in public or other kids making nasty comments. Life was pretty perfect until we turned fourteen.

There was some tension, though, of course, and Daddy was the biggest source of it. He never actually tried to kill us, but he hated us for being alive. Margaret and Tiff said this wasn't true, but Jewel and Dia, who were always more honest, said it was. Rose Red, who never told a lie in her life, also said it was true, which was an absolute confirmation that our father hated us.

Daddy refused to take care of us at all. If Margaret hadn't come around so much and roped Jewel into moving in with us, we probably would have died. Tiff did her best, but she was only six years old when we were born and couldn't even reach the stove, plus Daddy stopped buying food or getting out of bed at all, so even if Tiff had been a superhuman genius we all would have starved.

Tiff took care of us, but when we were ten, Arcana started complaining. "We're not babies," she whined, pushing Tiff's hands away as she tried to wash our hair, "we can do it ourselves!"

"Dezy can't," Tiff pointed out.

"Sure she can, she's got one hand. Lots of people only have one hand. Here, Dezy, wash your hair like this." Arcana started scrubbing at the shampoo in her hair one-handed to demonstrate, and Dezy copied her, a perfect mirror image.

"And how are you planning to wash the rest of yourselves?" Tiff asked, unamused. "You have to be really careful with Dezy's stoma, and you can't see it."

"I'll be careful!" Arcana snapped.

"I think it's better if I help Dezy, at least." A lot of careful repositioning went into bathing Dezy, who quietly accepted it and didn't complain when Tiff moved her tiny, twisted legs like she was a doll, urged Arcana to stand so she could see our stomachs better, and generally poked and prodded us until we were clean.

"You can do it yourself, right?" Arcana asked Dezy, who hesitated.

"Not on my… not on this side," she said, tilting her head to where her missing arm should be. She could never tell the difference between left and right.

"I'll do that side, then."

"I'm also worried about you slipping and hurting yourselves," Tiff said.

"We won't!"

"I think it's best if I help you with this," Tiff repeated, and we knew we were just going in circles. Arcana pouted for the rest of our bath, muttered bitterly when Tiff had her stand still so she could re-insert Dezy's catheter and give her a fresh colostomy bag, two tasks Arcana knew, but would not admit, she couldn't do.

"I'm tired," Dezy announced after our bath.

"Well, I'm not," Arcana said, so Dezy rested her head on her sister's shoulder and fell asleep while Arcana played high school with hand-me-down Barbies. Dezy learned very quickly how to fall asleep in the most inconvenient situations imaginable, because Arcana often refused to stop playing when she was tired.

It started with complaints about bathtime, but it certainly didn't end there. Obviously Arcana realized that it wasn't easy to navigate life when you always had your arms around another person, but she was determined to be as independent as our sisters. (Dezy's independence was not mentioned, which was fine, because she had no real desire to be independent anyway.)

"We can do it alone!" Arcana shrieked, trying to grab the dress from Tiff. "We're ten years old, we know how to get dressed!"

"Go for it," Tiff said with a sigh, obviously tired of arguing. Arcana grabbed the dress with both hands and tried to get it over our heads, struggling to adjust around Dezy, who sat still and occasionally reached to lend a hand. After several minutes of useless squirming, Arcana dropped the dress and started crying, fell down on her back to kick her heels against our mattress. We slept on our side, but Arcana liked laying on her back, liked the comforting weight of Dezy on top of her. Tiff worried that it was bad for our heart.

"Arcana?" No response. "Deirdre?" Tiff tried, sitting next to us to stroke her hair. "I'm sorry, sweetheart. It's okay to need help. Dezy needs more help than you, and she doesn't mind it, do you, Dezy?"

"No," Dezy said quietly.

"I just want to keep you two safe and healthy."

Arcana sniffled and didn't speak, then reluctantly sat up so Tiff could get us dressed. She practiced dressing ourselves every day for weeks until she could do it unassisted, but was content to let Tiff help us with everything else. Clothes, for whatever reason, were where Arcana drew the line.

Somehow, Margaret convinced Jewel to sleep in the twins' room when she moved in. As we got older, Arcana complained more and more about her presence, but Dezy liked having her there. Knowing an adult was around to check on us, to monitor our breathing, made her feel much safer.

"We should have our own room by now," Arcana whispered in the dark. We slept on our side, our heads so close together that our lashes brushed each other's cheeks, and whispered low enough that Jewel couldn't hear us. It helped that she fell asleep as soon as her head hit the pillow and snored loud enough to wake the dead.

"It's dangerous," Dezy responded, sucking on the ends of Arcana's hair.

"No, it's not. We're totally fine."

"What if we die in our sleep?" That was Dezy's biggest fear, going to sleep and just never waking up.

"Then we die in our sleep. Jewel can't do anything about it."

"If we start breathing funny—"

"She'll never hear it. There's no point to having her here at all!"

"I feel safer."

"I don't," Arcana huffed, but she dropped the issue for the time being and fell asleep, as she always did, holding Dezy's hand.

Daddy stopped going to work not long after we were born. Tiff says CPS probably would have gotten involved if Margaret hadn't stepped in. If CPS had taken us away from her, if Daddy wasn't our guardian, they almost certainly would have had us separated. Daddy refused to sign off on it, hoping our joint heart wouldn't be able to support us both; ironically, it's only because he wanted us dead that we lived so long together.

Because we had no money, and because our grandparents weren't willing to help us (our mother had been estranged from her parents, and Daddy's parents hated us as much as he did), Margaret made a choice Tiff never forgave. We didn't like it, but as we got older we started to understand why she'd done it. Every news outlet in the country was clamoring to report on us, thoracopagus twins who'd survived past birth, and Margaret, with Daddy's permission, cut a deal with one of them. Between the documentary money and Margaret pitching in whatever she could, we had enough to get by until Daddy finally went back to work.

Chapter Two

Our sisters went to the river every day in summer, every summer, all summer long. We went with them, but weren't allowed in the water. Sometimes Arcana stuck her feet in when no one was looking.

"Why can't we get in?" she'd whine, watching our sisters enviously from the bank.

"Because you can't swim, and the water isn't clean enough for Dezy. You could get in a pool, maybe, but the doctor told Margaret that people with catheters can't swim in rivers and lakes."

"Then I'll just wade in and keep her outta the water, duh."

"You could slip. It's just rocks here, the bottom's uneven."

"I won't slip. Dezy trusts me, right?" Arcana met her sister's eyes, pleading, and Dezy nodded placidly as always.

"No, Deirdre." When Tiff used our real names, it was serious. Arcana huffed and sat down gingerly in the grass, bitterly watching our sisters cool off while we were stuck there sweating, but eventually forgot to be angry and started whispering to Dezy, pleased that they couldn't hear us.

"I saw a photo of a horse with a mermaid tail," she began, grinning wickedly. Dezy, sensing that Arcana was about to play a trick on her, shook her head firmly.

"That's not real," she said.

"Yes, it is. I *saw* it. In a *photograph,* not a drawing, okay?"

"I didn't see that."

"I saw it over your shoulder."

"What's it called?"

"A horsemaid."

"You're lying!"

"No, I'm not! It's totally real! You can ask Dia."

"Dia lies, too!"

"She doesn't! I promise, it's super, super real!"

Our summer memories take place almost entirely at the river, blending into one long, picture book perfect day in our minds, sunlight streaming through the leaves to blanket us in pretty shadows, our sisters laughing and splashing in the river, Arcana making up fantasy creatures that Dezy always wanted to believe in. Summers were perfect until we turned fourteen, and Mr. Smith moved in down the road.

His name wasn't really Mr. Smith. We never knew what it was. If it was up to me, I'd keep talking about our childhood forever, about how adored we were, about Tiff's overprotectiveness, Margaret's unconditional love, how fun Jewel and Dia were, how Rose Red cared for us in her own strange way and showed it by bossing us around. I don't want to think about the horrible things that happened to us or our loved ones, not when I'm lying in a hospital bed without my twin. But if I gloss over the bad things, our story is just *we had a great childhood and then one of us died, the end,* which isn't a story at all.

Mr. Smith's house used to be occupied by a very old woman whose name we also didn't know. Dia knew all the neighbors—she had a baking phase in middle school, made so many treats Jewel said we couldn't eat them all on our own and had to go door to door giving them away. We weren't scared of the neighbors, but we didn't trust them. Dezy wanted to like them; Arcana was scared they'd turn on us, so she refused to even try.

The old lady died, and her grandson found her the next day. "It's good he found her so soon," Rose Red told us at the dinner table. "Lots of old people die alone and their bodies aren't found for a long time."

"Not while we're eating," Jewel said, scandalized.

"We should go to her estate sale," Dia suggested. "She had some cool shit."

"Don't swear!" Rose Red shrieked.

Her grandson organized the estate sale, which we attended only after Dia promised us the old lady had an enormous collection of old teddy bears. Tiff was interested in her cookbooks, Dia in her clothes, and Rose Red just wanted to see the things she'd liked and kept. "It tells you a lot about a person, looking in their room when they're not there," she insisted.

It was mostly neighbors who showed up to the estate sale, so no one was too horrified by our presence, but a few people stopped to stare at us, particularly the old women's son. He'd never seen us before.

"Are you… what…"

"They're thoracopagus twins," Rose Red said primly. "They're conjoined at the chest and share one heart, and they're the oldest living thoracopagus twins in history."

"Shut up, Rose Red," Arcana snapped. We hated how easily she shared our medical information.

"He asked!"

"You don't have to tell people everything they ask about!"

"I'm older than you!"

"No fighting," Tiff interrupted, smoothly pushing us apart from each other. "Look, here's the teddy bears Dia was talking about, aren't these cool?" She turned us to the side so we could both look, and Dezy squealed in delight, making Arcana wince.

"Don't scream in my *ear!*"

"It's so cute," Dezy cooed, holding her hand out for the bear. Tiff gave it to her, and the fight with Rose Red was forgotten as she wandered off to look at something else. When we tried to pay for the teddy bear, the old woman's son told us to take it for free.

A month after the old woman died, Mr. Smith moved in. We were fourteen, like I said, but we acted a lot younger. Arcana was stubborn as a mule, and tended to ignore problems until she couldn't anymore. While Dezy was very naive and, admittedly, not the sharpest tool in the shed. Neither twin was very introspective, but Arcana at least knew what the word meant before Tiff explained it to her.

Jewel still lived with us, because Daddy was still, for the most part, totally useless. Tiff had gone to college with the intention of being a doctor; she didn't know what kind yet. Dia was about to graduate high school and had almost a million followers on Instagram. Rose Red was on track to be valedictorian and universally hated by her classmates. Margaret was getting older and coming over less. Arcana didn't want to be separated, but she was starting to get frustrated by her lack of privacy limiting her ability to masturbate, which had become very interesting to her with the onset of puberty. Dezy had no interest whatsoever in masturbation and worried about anything that might increase our heart rate.

We met Mr. Smith the day Rose Red came home from school in tears.

"What's wrong?" Dezy asked immediately, reaching out to pat her head. We were about the same height as her by then.

"My essay," Rose Red moaned, wiping frantically at her eyes. "I worked *so hard* on it! It's not fair!"

"Somebody tore up her history essay," Dia said, sounding very unsympathetic.

"Are they gonna get in trouble?" Dezy asked.

"I think they got detention," Dia shrugged.

"But I worked *so hard!*"

"You can print it out again," Dia told her.

"It's not *fair!*" Rose Red punched the wall, then screamed in pain and clutched her fist to her chest. The twins looked each other in the eyes and silently agreed to leave her to her hysterics, because there was no comforting her when she got this way.

When we were kids, Rose Red used to throw herself on the floor and scream at the top of her lungs, kicking her heels against the ground, and you couldn't make her stop until she wore herself out. She never wanted anything material, she just wanted us to do what she said, and she lost her mind when she couldn't get her way. Everything in Rose Red's life had to be perfect.

The day Rose Red came home crying, we went out to the garden, where we liked to play princesses. Dia and Rose Red thought they were too old to play with us anymore, but Tiff would join in when she came home to visit. We could still hear Rose Red crying from inside as Arcana trotted over to the biggest rose bush in the garden and sat down carefully to scoot underneath to the dark, shadowed spot where we could be alone.

"Where'd we stop last time?" Dezy asked, reaching to gently press the tip of her finger against a thorn, not hard enough to hurt.

"The knight was coming to rescue us."

"Who does the knight look like?"

"A movie star."

"Which one?"

"A cute one," Arcana said, annoyed at the questioning. Neither of us was good with famous people's names. "So, we're stuck in our tower, right? And this is our tower. Now the knight's coming to save us, and she's—"

"The knight's a girl?"

"Yes."

"Knights have to be boys."

"No, they don't. Ours is a girl. So she's coming to rescue us, okay?"

"Okay," Dezy said, trying to pick a rose and succeeding only in grabbing a fistful of rose petals, which she set about tucking into Arcana's hair.

We ended up scurrying around in the garden, running from imaginary threats—as close as Arcana could get to running, anyway—and would have stayed out for hours if we didn't notice the eyes on us. Dezy, always looking backwards, saw him first.

There was a stranger standing right at the garden gate, watching us.

"Arcana," Dezy hissed. "There's a guy."

"What?" Arcana turned, blocking Dezy's view, and gasped when she saw the man. "Who are you?" she called, rather rudely.

"I'm your new neighbor," he said. "I came to introduce myself. Are you… what are you two doing? Are you carrying her?" He had a strange, clipped accent and spoke very fast. He was very short and very, very skinny. We couldn't tell how old he was.

"Yeah," Arcana said. She didn't say we were playing princesses; it would have sounded too immature.

"Why?"

"She can't walk."

"Why are wearing the same dress?"

"Why don't you mind your business?" Arcana countered, tired of his questions.

"*Deirdre,*" Dezy hissed, but her sister ignored her and hurried inside, where Rose Red was still crying on the floor. It had been almost an hour since she got home from school.

"I didn't like his voice," Dezy said that night.

"I didn't like the way he looked at us," Arcana agreed.

"He never told us his name," we said in unison.

We started calling him Mr. Smith, because we had to call him something—he wouldn't leave us alone. Not *us* as in the twins, *us* as in the Garden girls as a whole, but we suspected it was the twins he was interested in. The day after we met him in the garden, there was a knock on the door. It was a Saturday, so Rose Red was studying in her room (she spent most of her free time studying, which we were all grateful for as it meant she couldn't bother us so damn much) and we were playing in the living room, having been scared out of the garden for a while.

"I'll get it!" Dia yelled. Jewel was still asleep, but Dia had become our caregiver in Tiff's absence, so we were generally awake at the same time as her.

"We know!" we yelled back.

"Who d'you think it is?" Dezy whispered, watching the door over Arcana's shoulder.

"A Mormon," Arcana said boredly. No one except missionaries knocked on our door, and if it was Margaret, she'd just let herself in.

"Hello!" Dia chirped, throwing the door open to reveal the man from the garden. Dezy gasped and poked frantically at Arcana's shoulder.

"It's that creepy guy from yesterday," she hissed. Without looking, Arcana scrambled to her feet and escaped down the hallway, where he couldn't see us, but stayed right there to listen. We fell silent, stroking each other's hair as we always did when we were stressed, foreheads pressed together.

"...to meet you," Dia was saying. In our hurry to get away, we'd missed his name again. "We don't get a lot of new people up here, but there's lotsa out-of-towners downtown during tourist season."

"Well, I don't want to be an out-of-towner," Mr. Smith laughed. "It's a beautiful place, isn't it?"

"Oh, yeah. Arkansas's one of the prettiest states in the country, honestly, but nobody knows it and we like it that way." We could hear the grin in Dia's voice. "Keeps Yankees from coming down here and raising all the prices."

"I guess I *am* guilty of being a Yankee," Mr. Smith said, laughing. He laughed a lot.

"That's the accent," Dezy muttered.

"It's ugly," Arcana sniffed. "If he's gonna live in the South, he needs to learn how to talk right."

"What brings you here?" Dia asked.

"She's too polite," Dezy whispered.

"Just tell him to leave!" Arcana agreed.

"Oh, you know, this and that. Work, mostly."

"What do you do?"

"I do a lot of things, most of them online, all of them boring. Right now I'm working for the parks and rec department, so I'm actually going into an office every day, even though I really could do it from home."

"So you're going into town a lot? Have you seen the Crescent Hotel?"

"Only from a distance."

"It's haunted," Dia said confidently. "Beautiful building, though."

"I don't believe in ghosts, I'm afraid," Mr. Smith said.

"You will," Dia told him.

"I look forward to it! Now, what was your name again? I'm sorry, I'm terrible with names…"

"Diamond."

"That's a beautiful name!"

"Thanks."

"Now, two of your sisters… maybe I'm wrong, but I was walking by your house yesterday, and I'm not sure what I saw, exactly…"

"Don't tell him," we whispered, but Dia, of course, didn't hear us. She probably would have told him anyway even if she *had* heard us. Margaret used to say that Dia loved the sound of her own voice.

"Oh, Deirdre and Desdemona! They're conjoined twins." She said this very casually, as if conjoined twins were just an expected part of life that you might encounter anywhere.

"Is that right?"

"Yep. Actually, they're the oldest thoracopagus twins in history—they share a heart."

"That's incredible."

"Pretty cool," Dia chirped. Our sisters found our condition a lot more interesting than we did.

"I've never met conjoined twins."

"Most people haven't, but they're honestly just normal girls. And they're really different from each other too. Desdemona's quieter and Deirdre's more assertive. I mean, that's probably 'cause Desdemona can't walk, so Deirdre just kind of takes her places."

"I don't mind," Dezy said softly. Arcana smiled at her.

"It must take a lot of cooperation to live like that," Mr. Smith said thoughtfully.

"Not really. They just do whatever Deirdre wants."

"Do you have any other sisters?"

"Yeah, Tiffany and Alice, but Tiff's away at college. I'm about to graduate, too, actually, but I'm not really into school, so I'm not sure what I'll end up doing. Probably just working in town somewhere so I can keep taking care of the twins for a while."

"And who do you girls live with? I assume you haven't been raising yourselves?"

"Our dad, technically, but he's pretty out of it, so mostly our cousin Jewel and this lady Margaret from town. We're pretty much on our own now, though. I mean, I'm an adult."

"Still, you must be awfully busy with school. I'm sure it's…"

Arcana walked away, bored, and slipped into Rose Red's room to bother her. "Don't." Dezy muttered.

"It's fun," she responded, giggling.

Later, we'd all realize that Dia shouldn't have talked to Mr. Smith so openly, that at eighteen she should have known better than to just chat with random strangers who showed up on our doorstep, but we were all sheltered. Eureka Springs isn't a big city, and we lived a ways outside of the town, on a street that had always been safe. Mr. Smith didn't seem dangerous. Maybe I'm making him seem shadier than he did because I know what happened.

Around the time Mr. Smith moved in, Arcana became obsessed with the alligator twins. She'd always been interested in other conjoined twins, particularly Daisy and Violent Hilton, but something about the alligator twins caught her attention in particular. Dezy thought it was mean to call them that, but that was how people knew them.

"You wouldn't like it if people compared us to an animal," Dezy told Arcana firmly. "They had names."

"Yeah, but most people don't remember their real names," Arcana said with a shrug. She was doing a tarot reading for herself, another, another, over and over again. Dezy thought they didn't really mean anything but Arcana, though she wouldn't admit it to anyone else, believed she could see into the future at least a little bit.

The alligator twins were Florence and Sage Labelle, Cajun conjoined twins raised on an alligator farm just outside of Welcome, Louisiana. They got the nickname because a two-headed alligator hatched on their father's farm shortly after they were born, and they kept it as a sort of pet all their lives. Back then, some people in that part of Louisiana still believed in witches, and they called the two-headed alligator the twins' *familiar*.

It was a famous story, not just among conjoined twins. It made international news, and Arcana could see why. It was horrible and fascinating, like a train wreck you couldn't look away from. Dezy thought it was *just* horrible and didn't want to think about it at all. The story published in newspapers was that men started going missing in Welcome, and the suspicious townspeople, who had always hated the twins, whispered that they had to be responsible for the disappearances.

Creepy girls with hundreds of alligators on their property (because it was *their* property, their father died when they were eighteen and passed it on to them—convenient timing, the townspeople said) made perfect villains. Men kept disappearing, no bodies were ever found, and one night—the twins' twentieth birthday—a group of locals went up to their house to demand answers. They said they found the girls covered in blood, one of them hysterical, one of them eerily calm, neither of them able to speak. Taking this as proof of guilt, the men in the group forced them outside, stripped them naked, wrapped one end of a chain around the back of someone's truck and the other around the calm twin's neck, and dragged them down the road until they were dead.

Someone took a photo of their corpse lying face down in the dirt, their skin so torn up you could see their intestines spilling out around them. Dezy always got sick looking at it.

No one in Welcome would say who, exactly had gone up to their house. No one would say who grabbed them and forced them outside, no one would say who tied them to his car, no one would say anything to the cops. Some people thought the local police may have been there. After their murder, a local man bought the alligator farm at a heavy discount but fell into one of the pools and was torn apart. His widow, who insisted the house was haunted, couldn't sell the property after that, so she just left it there to rot.

The alligators multiplied.

Men kept going missing.

Welcome isn't quite a ghost town, but the population has declined sharply since 1949, when the twins died. It seems to be mostly old women there now. The Labelle mansion is still standing, even though no one's lived there in decades.

"Why do you like this story?" Dezy asked, frowning at the Wikipedia article Arcana was poring over.

"'Cause it's *cool.*"

"People died, Deirdre."

"It's still a cool story, though, right?"

"No. It's just sad. Nobody knows who murdered the twins?"

"Nobody knows what happened to the men, either." Arcana grinned at her sister, who reluctantly smiled back. "You think they killed 'em?"

"Maybe. They were all bloody when the townspeople found them, right?"

"Yeah, but the police searched their house after they were dead, and they didn't find anything incriminating."

"What?"

"They didn't find any evidence to prove the twins did it."

"I hope they did." Dezy announced. "Otherwise, they just died like that for no reason."

"It doesn't say it in the Wikipedia article, but a couple kids went missing, too."

"Alligators probably ate them. What the hell do you farm alligators for?"

"Leather and meat. And I bet you could sell their skulls." Arcana waggled her fingers dramatically. "Maybe you use their bones for voodoo! It's Louisiana, right?"

"I don't know anything about voodoo. Except what we saw in *The Princess and the Frog.*"

"Yeah, I don't think that's super accurate."

"I hate that story," Dezy said softly. "Do the twins have graves?"

"They have a mausoleum, since you can't bury people in Louisiana. It's a tomb, with their bodies inside this big stone building."

"Creepy. This whole stupid story is way too creepy."

"Alright, alright," Arcana said, patting Dezy's back. "Don't freak out."

"What happened to the two-headed alligator?" Dezy asked after a minute.

"I dunno. The article doesn't mention it again."

Chapter Three

When Arcana stood up too fast, Dezy got black spots in her vision, but when Arcana had her migraines, Dezy didn't feel a thing. If you squeezed Dezy's hand, Arcana felt it too. Dezy could tell when Arcana was tired and warned her to rest, but she rarely listened. When Dia was little, she liked to pinch Arcana and ask Dezy if she'd felt it, a game that stopped when Arcana stomped on her foot and threatened to tell Margaret.

Mr. Smith's arrival coincided perfectly with Rose Red's increasing social difficulties. That was what Margaret called them, anyway. Dia said she was a cunt and Tiff thought she was autistic. Jewel said she needed to loosen up a little, but since Jewel thought *everyone* needed to loosen up a little, we all took her advice with a grain of salt.

"So how's school going?" Arcana asked, a little cruelly, when Rose Red came home with tears running down her face again.

"I'm at the top of my class," Rose Red said immediately.

"Cool. Why are you crying, then?"

"Everybody laughed at me in gym," she sniffled, "when we had to change clothes. They said I'm fat, but I'm *not!* I'm not fat, am I?"

"No," Dezy said.

"You're kind of chubby," Arcana said. Rose Red started sobbing louder and ran downstairs to her basement room, slamming the door behind her.

"That was mean," Dezy snapped.

"She totally flipped her shit 'cause we interrupted her yesterday," Arcana said. "We were literally just asking if she wanted dinner."

"That was still mean." Dezy remembered how Rose Red had lost it, screaming at us for distracting her from her schoolwork until she was red in the face, but she thought our sister was just stressed and didn't want to hold it against her. Rose Red was very sweet when she wanted to be.

For example: every month, when our endometriosis had us curled up in bed, crying in pain, Rose Red brought us chocolate cookies and hot tea, sympathetically saying it ran in the family and we should get hysterectomies as soon as we could. She helped us with our schoolwork and, if we played by her rules, she was a good playmate. She would still play teacher with us sometimes. Rose Red was our only sister who never talked about our mother.

Rose Red was excelling academically but falling behind socially. Dia was saving up her allowance to buy a cute pair of shoes for graduation. Jewel was planning a surprise party for her but not hiding the surprise very well at all. Daddy was a ghost in the garden. Margaret's knees were giving her trouble. The twins were feeling lonely, starting to fantasize about going to public school (Dezy) and getting a girlfriend (Arcana). Eureka Springs was a safe town. On our street, at least, we didn't lock our doors until the first murder.

It was an unusually warm day, and we were sitting on the couch, Arcana reading a book while Dezy dozed off on her shoulder. She was tired—she hadn't slept well last night, but no one believed her when she tried to explain why.

"I woke up to a sound like a creaking floorboard," she said nervously, "and I saw a person's shadow on the wall. I couldn't move enough to see what was happening, but there was a breeze. I think the window was open."

"You're crazy," Arcana said lightly.

Dezy didn't tell her the next part for fear of being mocked—that she'd heard a weird, distinct clicking noise. It had probably just been a weird dream.

Arcana was halfway through her book and Dezy had just fallen asleep when Dia ran into the living room, panting. "Holy shit!" she yelled, startling both of us to awareness. "Did you guys see the news?"

"No."

"This girl I go to school with is missing. Well, a girl Rose Red goes to school with, really."

"Did she get lost in the woods?" Arcana asked, turning and pulling her legs onto the couch so we could both look at our sister's scared/excited face.

"No, that's the weird part. Her parents left her home alone last night and she was gone when they came back. Her name's Celeste, and she's a total goody two-shoes, just like Rose Red, so she wouldn't have run away. *And*—" Dia snickered, trying not to smirk, "—she's fat and ugly, honestly, so there's no way she's with a guy."

Dia was always nice to us, never mocked us for our condition or complained about helping us, but we disagreed on her treatment of other people. Dezy thought she used up all her kindness on us, while Arcana thought she probably talked about us behind our backs. She, unlike Rose Red, was very, very popular, which Dezy figured had to count for something. ("People don't like you if you're mean. She might gossip to us, but she can't be mean at school or people wouldn't like her anymore," she often insisted. Arcana thought she didn't understand how high school popularity worked.)

"Are people worried?" Dezy asked, wide-eyed.

"Yeah. She's probably fine, though. I bet she's at a friend's house." Dia raised her eyebrows in mock surprise. "Maybe she's pregnant! Ran off to get an abortion, y'think?"

"It's kinda scary, her disappearing," Dezy said anxiously.

"Aw, she'll turn up. Nothing ever happens around here," Arcana assured her, patting her twin's back. Dezy, biting her lip, did not reply. "I'll do a tarot reading about it, if you want?"

"Sure."

Because she only ever used the major arcana, Deirdre's tarot readings tended to be dramatic, and the one she did for Celeste was no exception. We sat staring at the three cards— reversed World, upright Tower, and upright Death—for a second before Arcana laughed and shuffled her deck, then fell silent when she drew the same exact cards in the same exact order.

"That's not literal," she finally said, tapping the Death card.

"The Tower's bad, too, though," Dezy said softly.

"It doesn't really mean anything," Arcana said, quickly putting her cards away.

Celeste did not return to school the next day, and Dia stopped laughing about her disappearance.

"I'm scared," Rose Red said softly, fidgeting with the edge of her blouse. "I really like Celeste."

"You do?" Dezy asked, stunned.

"You have *friends?*" Arcana asked.

"We eat lunch together. Sometimes. She's nice, and people give her a hard time, too. She's really smart."

"She'll be okay," we said. Dezy reached to pat Rose Red's hair but fell short, so Arcana reached out to do it instead.

Dezy heard the clicking noise again that night. She didn't tell anyone in the morning.

Later, she'd find out Arcana had heard it, too.

A week after her disappearance, Celeste's body was found in the woods. The back of her skull was caved in, and the coroner said she'd been dead less than twenty-four hours.

Rose Red did not take this news very well.

"It's alright, baby," Margaret soothed, holding Rose Red's head on her lap and stroking her hair, murmuring a lullaby while our sister sobbed into her skirt. "You're gonna be alright. Celeste is in Heaven now, okay? She lived a good life, it doesn't matter how short someone's life is, it still has meaning. She had a good life, she was a good girl, and she's gone home to Jesus. You'll see her again one day."

"She was *murdered*," Rose Red wailed, and Margaret hushed her again.

"They weren't *that* close," Dia said. She had been slumped on the couch with dead eyes since we read the morning news, and the twins both suspected she was trying to distance herself from an unimaginable tragedy.

"Still, I bet it's hard to know somebody and then they die like that," Dezy argued.

The coroner said Celeste's ankles were slit. He proposed that whoever kidnapped her had been hiding under her bed and cut her Achilles tendons when she walked close enough. Her house was in a more rural area, which explained why no one heard her screaming. All the Garden girls, and probably everyone else in town, started checking under our beds every night.

Maybe it should have scared us, sent us running off to our rooms, but the untimely death of a girl just a little older than us made us eager to experience life more fully. We'd always known we could die at any time, we knew our shared heart would give out one day, so we started asking Jewel to take us to the library once a week.

"We could meet more people," Arcana said hopefully.

"It's good to get out of the house," Dezy added.

Jewel took us, but she stayed in the same aisle as us the entire time, never letting us out of her sight for a moment. She was more attentive than she'd ever been before, and Arcana hated having her around, always watching. Dezy liked it, often reached to hold her hand while we walked through the library, ignoring everyone staring at us.

We met Loreley Washington and Risa Burke at the library almost as soon as we started going. We shouldn't have talked to them, but at the time, we had no way of knowing that. We still thought we were essentially ordinary girls, and we had no idea that we were interesting enough to watch.

We didn't hear the clicking very often anymore, but Dezy still though she saw a shadow on the wall sometimes, very late at night.

"I've got it!" Loreley snarled, reaching as high as she could for a book on a shelf just barely above her head. Risa stood back, arms crossed, an irritated frown on her face while we quietly pitied Loreley, then hated ourselves for it. We didn't want people to pity *us*, after all, and she was honestly better off than we were.

Everyone in town knew about Loreley Washington. She was an athlete in Tiff's class, a track star with a full ride to college, until the car accident that killed her sister and left her paralyzed from the waist down. Risa was hired to take care of her, and everyone whispered that her parents always loved her sister more, that they thought the wrong daughter had died. It was another story Dezy didn't like to think about.

"You don't got it," Risa drawled after a minute, watching Loreley strain to reach the book.

"Shut up," Loreley snapped.

"Here," Arcana said, grabbing the book and handing it to her. Loreley opened her mouth to yell at her, then realized who we were and fell silent.

"Thanks," she finally said, looking from Arcana to Dezy and back again. "Deirdre."

"You can call me Arcana."

"I go by Dezy."

"Arcana and Dezy," Loreley said quietly. "I'm Loreley. Uh, thanks again…" She didn't seem to know quite what to say. Nobody ever did when they first met us.

"No problem."

"I'm Risa, not Lisa," Risa added.

"Nice to meet you both. What are you reading?" They were talking only to Arcana, because she was facing forward. Dezy didn't mind being excluded, generally content to just play with her sister's hair and daydream.

"It's called *The Haunting of Hill House*. It's by Shirley Jackson, she wrote 'The Lottery'?"

"Never heard of her."

"Famous author," Jewel commented, scanning the shelves for romance novels.

"Dezy doesn't like ghost stories, and I don't read much fiction," Arcana said.

"It's a good book." Loreley giggled nervously. "And it's not exactly a ghost story. You never find out if Hill House is really haunted."

"Maybe I'll check it out sometime."

After that, we saw Loreley and Risa at the library all the time. They started waving to us, inviting us to sit and read with them, and we went home giggling that we had *friends*. Loreley seemed cool, older and worldly, and Risa laughed constantly, but never at us. Arcana wanted to marry Loreley.

"I've never met conjoined twins before," Loreley commented, twirling her hair. "I didn't think I'd get used to it so fast."

"We've never met another set of conjoined twins," Dezy offered.

"We're one of a kind," Arcana said, grinning, "or two of a kind, depending on how you count it. I read a lot about other conjoined twins though, have you heard of Daisy and Violet Hilton?"

"No."

"They were vaudeville stars, and they were in a couple movies, *Freaks* and *Chained for Life*. They were joined at the hip—literally, I mean—so they didn't share any major organs. They were performers for most of their lives, but then their manager abandoned them in North Carolina, and they ended up getting jobs at a grocery store. They stayed there for the rest of their lives, and then—"

"I hate this part," Dezy interrupted. Arcana covered her ears.

"Then they got the Hong Kong flu and died alone in their apartment. Daisy died first, and Violet died somewhere between two and four days later. She never called for help."

"Oh," Loreley said awkwardly.

"She's obsessed with awful conjoined twin stories. Like the Labelle twins. The alligator twins," Dezy muttered bitterly.

"I know about them," Loreley said, nodding. "Never heard of the Hilton sisters, though. That's awfully sad."

We dreamed about the Hilton sisters sometimes, about what Violet must have felt, alone for the first time in her life and connected to a corpse. We always wondered why she didn't call for help, and landed on the same conclusion every time: if someone had found them, they would have separated them. Like us, she probably preferred to die with her sister, no matter how long it took.

"Did you hear about Celeste?" Risa asked, playing with her cross necklace. Loreley was not religious; Risa went to church every week. Risa was nineteen years old and had started working for the Washington family as soon as she graduated high school. Her only relevant experience was taking care of her dying grandfather, but Loreley loved her. Dezy thought Loreley was *in* love with her; Arcana refused to believe that.

"Yes," we said. Dezy didn't want to talk about the murdered girl, but she knew Arcana did, so she stayed quiet.

"Our sister knew her. Rose Red. Well, her real name's Alice," Arcana said.

"I remember her," Risa said, snickering. She stopped laughing when she saw the expression on Arcana's face. (Dezy, with her back to the group as usual, did not see the expression but knew Arcana was glowering.) "How's she, uh, how's she doing?"

"Bad," Arcana said flatly. "She was getting bullied, but now people just kind of avoid her, since she was friends with Celeste."

"That sucks."

"She's grieving," Dezy whispered, quiet enough that only Arcana heard.

"I wonder who did it," Loreley murmured. "Probably someone from out of town, right? Nobody here would…?"

"Had to be," Arcana agreed.

"For sure," Risa said.

Dezy didn't respond.

Shadow on the wall, but no clicking.

"How many guys went missing?" Dezy asked. Arcana was reading about the Labelle twins again, a more in-depth biography this time.

"It says sixteen men, in a tiny little town," Arcana responded, whistling through her teeth. Dezy, who couldn't whistle, tried to copy her and only managed a pathetic hissing intake of breath.

"Were any of them actually near the alligator farm?"

"Nobody knows. Most of them were married men, and they told their wives they had to go deal with a family emergency or they'd been called in to work or they were drinking with their friends, something like that. Some of them just didn't come home from work."

"They told their wives they were leaving?"

"Mhm."

"And went… where?"

"Nobody *knows,*" Arcana repeated.

"If sixteen men went up to this house outside of town, somebody must have seen."

"Exactly." Arcana moved to press our foreheads together. "So maybe the twins were totally innocent."

"Why were they covered in blood, then? And one was hysterical?"

"Florence. Florence was the hysterical one. They put the chain around Sage's neck."

"I hate this story," Dezy repeated, moving her head away.

"If they didn't do it," Arcana continued as if her sister hadn't spoken, "who did?"

"Maybe the guys all went up to the alligator farm to meet their secret mistresses and fell in the pools," Dezy suggested. "Just like those missing kids, right?"

"We don't know alligators ate the kids. Plus, there were fences, you couldn't just walk right up to the water. Some people say the twins did, though. There were rumors that they swam with their pet, the two-headed alligator."

"That's made up."

"Maybe."

Arcana would not shut up about the Labelle twins. Dezy knew she was doing it to distract herself from the dead girl our sister had sort of known, so she didn't complain.

Shadow.
Breeze.
Click.

"Let's start locking our window from now on," Arcana suggested cheerfully. Jewel had started locking the doors after Celeste's murder, but she hadn't thought to lock the window, since it was too small for an average-sized man to crawl through.

"Oh. Yeah, good idea," Jewel said. She was putting an egg in a glass of water to see if it was still good; if it sank, she said, that meant it was safe to eat.

"Why?" Dezy asked her sister quietly.

"Just in case."

We didn't admit it to each other, but we knew we'd both heard the clicking noise and felt the breeze.

Chapter Four

The first time we went to Loreley's house, Dezy noticed an old track team photo on the living room mantelpiece. "Is that you?" she asked, rather stupidly.

"Yep," Loreley responded.

"Who else would it be?" Arcana muttered.

"I hate those old photos," Loreley said with a forced laugh.

Arcana picked the photo up and stared at it, holding it so Dezy could see, too. A younger Loreley stood front and center, grinning, hands on her hips and a cocky expression across her face. Dezy was struck by how strong her legs looked, since we'd only ever known her after the accident. Loreley used to be leanly muscular, but she'd been very, very skinny—unhealthily so—since we'd known her. Her unused legs were like sticks, and we'd watched Risa lift her carefully, afraid to hurt her. She wore long skirts all the time.

Arcana's gaze was drawn to a short girl standing off to the side, the only girl in the photo with hairy legs. She had a buzzcut, and her head was lowered so we couldn't quite make out her face. "Who's the girl with the buzzcut?"

"That's me," Risa said.

"No way!"

"Yep."

"We didn't know y'all knew each other in high school."

"Well, we weren't close." Risa shot Loreley a knowing look, and Loreley averted her eyes, murmured something we couldn't hear that made Risa laugh. "It's in the past, honey. But, yeah, I was just a year behind her, and there's only one school in town, so…"

We were both burning to ask if it was weird, taking care of someone you'd gone to school with, but we managed to hold ourselves back. After all, we hated people asking questions about our own medical issues.

"It was a few years ago," Loreley said, sounding unusually anxious. "We really… I mean…"

"People change," Risa said. She touched Loreley's shoulder lightly, smiling, and Loreley swallowed hard.

"Yeah," she muttered.

Risa was not the world's greatest driver, but we didn't complain. We got the impression she didn't have a lot of friends; all she wanted for her birthday was to hang out with Loreley and us. "So she wants to do her job, pretty much," Dia said when we told her we'd been invited out to lunch.

"She really likes Loreley," Dezy said.

"I think she really likes getting paid. Her family's trailer trash, y'know."

"Don't be mean."

"Do y'all need anything before you go?"

Risa picked us up ten minutes before she'd said she would. "Can y'all sit in the back? Loreley gets carsick," she said apologetically. "And I was super hungover this morning, so I've already cleaned up puke once today…"

"That's fine," we said, giggling. It was our first outing with friends, and neither of us could contain our excitement.

"I'm just gonna swing by Loreley's house, pick her up, and then we'll go have a picnic in the park," Risa said cheerfully. The windows were still rolled down, and Margaret had left most of the windows in our house open while she cleaned, so we all heard Rose Red screaming something inside.

"Ignore her," Arcana said quickly.

"What's her problem, exactly?"

"She's still upset about Celeste, and she's always been… uptight."

"She throws tantrums," Dezy said.

"Little old for that, huh? And isn't she, like, super smart?"

"She's just kind of weird," we said defensively, in perfect unison. Risa dropped the subject.

At Loreley's house, we stayed in the car so as not to scare her parents and watched Risa ring the doorbell. The Washington family had a nice house, an old Victorian mansion; Arcana whispered that she wanted to live somewhere like that one day. With the windows still down and Risa having parking very close to the front door, we saw and heard everything, clear as day.

First, Loreley's mother answered the door. She looked young, but her hair was grey—we'd heard she went grey in her twenties, dyed it constantly until the car crash, at which point she gave up on hair, makeup, fashion, and God. "Risa," she said, smiling stiffly.

"I'm here for Loreley, ma'am," Risa responded, so painfully polite we knew it was fake.

"She's here. Give me a second." Mrs. Washington disappeared back into the house, then returned pushing her daughter's wheelchair. Loreley preferred to push herself— had apparently insisted on a manual wheelchair for that very reason—but she didn't protest having her mother's help. She didn't seem to be paying any attention at all, actually. "Have a good day, baby." Mrs. Washington said something else, too quiet to make out, and kissed the top of Loreley's head. "Keep a close eye on her," she ordered Risa, like Loreley was a toddler who might run off.

"Yes, ma'am," Risa said. Loreley didn't say a word until Risa had helped her into the car and put her wheelchair in the trunk, at which point she turned to us and gave a forced grin. Dezy didn't see it, but Arcana later told her how the smile hadn't reached Loreley's eyes even remotely.

"Glad y'all could make it," she said. "Sorry 'bout my mom."

"We weren't paying attention," Arcana said quickly.

"Oh, yeah? My legs don't work, so she figures my brain doesn't either."

"A lot of people think that about us," Arcana said. "I mean, Dezy *is* kind of dumb, but—ow!"

"I'm not dumb," Dezy huffed, wincing at the pain in her own neck after she'd pinched Arcana's. She was lying to herself and her sister, and she knew it.

"I was just kidding," Arcana said, giving her braid a playful tug.

"Y'all are funny," Loreley giggled.

We didn't talk much on the drive there, but we noticed Loreley watching the high school as we drove by, turning her head to stare at the track for as long as she could.

Maybe our picnic would have been totally unremarkable if we'd had it any other day, or maybe, as Arcana suspected, it always would have turned out the same. It started off pretty well; we were lucky that the weather wasn't great, chilly and overcast, so there weren't a bunch of families watching us. We'd gone on a school day, too (Jewel said we could do our work when we came home), so there were even less people around. A butch woman in a small Southern town accompanied by a woman in a wheelchair and a pair of conjoined twin girls made for a pretty unusual sight, and none of us liked being stared at.

"It's kind of a nice day," Loreley said, resting her head in Risa's lap.

"Kind of?"

"I mean, it's cold…"

"We're warm," we said. Jewel had loaned us her fur coat.

"Yeah, well, you also look like Cruella DeVil," Loreley said, not unkindly. "What is that thing, anyway?"

"It's Jewel's. We don't even know if it's real," Arcana said, wrapping her arms tighter around Dezy.

"We don't know where she got it," Dezy added.

"I saw a PETA campaign—" Risa began, but was cut off by a voice we vaguely recognized, accompanied by Dezy gasping.

"Oh! You're my neighbors, aren't you?"

"It's Mr. Smith," Dezy whispered to Arcana. We'd already started calling him that and had no intention of learning his real name.

"Great," Arcana muttered.

"Hello," Risa said, smiling. Loreley, possibly sensing his creepy vibes, did not smile. (She once told us that the best thing about being in a wheelchair was not having to be polite anymore. Risa snorted that she was never very polite, and Loreley flipped her off.)

"Are these your friends?" Mr. Smith asked, walking over so we could both look up at him. He had a camera around his neck.

"Yeah," Arcana said cautiously. "Uh, Risa, Loreley, meet… our neighbor."

"A pleasure," Mr. Smith said. He didn't offer his name.

"You, too," Risa said.

"It's a little cold for a picnic, isn't it?" he continued.

"We didn't want people staring at us," Risa explained.

"Well, no one's staring at *you*," Loreley said softly. She was wrong about that; Risa got nasty looks pretty frequently in Eureka Springs, judgemental gazes lingering on her muscular, hairy legs, her unshaven underarms, her buzz cut.

"That makes perfect sense. People can be so nosey, can't they? I don't believe I've ever seen you two around."

"We don't live near the Garden girls."

"The… what?" There was a twinkle in his eye, though, like he knew exactly what our family nickname meant.

"People call us and our sisters the Garden girls," Arcana reluctantly explained, "'cause our last name's Gardner and our dad has a crazy rose garden."

"Oh, that's cute."

"We're kinda busy," Loreley said meaningfully.

"Of course. Enjoy your picnic, dears." With that, Mr. Smith walked away, and Dezy shivered.

"He seemed… nice," Risa said cautiously.

"He was looking at y'all the whole time, even when he talked to us," Loreley said to the twins.

"We know. We noticed."

We locked our window that night. In the morning, Dezy squinted suspiciously at it and whispered, "Did you hear anything last night? I thought I heard someone trying to open the window. Did you?"

"No," Arcana yawned. "You're paranoid."

"A sleepover?" Jewel asked, looking so shocked we felt a little hurt. We were asking her instead of Margaret because she was more likely to say yes.

"'Yeah," we said.

"Risa's a professional caregiver," Arcana said confidently, "so she'll keep an eye on us and make sure nothing goes wrong, plus Loreley's parents are gonna be home."

"I guess that should be fine," Jewel said cautiously.

"They live in town, so they're closer to the hospital anyway," Arcana continued, unaware that Jewel had already said yes.

"That's fine, yeah," Jewel said louder.

"Yay!" we squealed, Arcana hugging Dezy a little tighter.

Loreley's bedroom was huge, but very sparsely decorated. "It's kinda new," she explained. There was a couch up against one wall that pulled out into a bed, which was usually where Risa slept when she spent the night, but for our sleepover she stayed on an air mattress.

"We've never had a sleepover before," we admitted. We tended to speak in unison more when we were nervous, which freaked people out and made us more nervous. It was a vicious cycle that Loreley and Risa, being used to us, didn't contribute to.

"They're fun," Risa told us brightly. "Mrs. Washington made us cupcakes!"

"Mrs. Washington never really looks at us head-on," Arcana said, giggling to soften her words.

"She adores y'all," Loreley said confidently. "She told me the other night that she's super glad I'm making more friends and getting out more. I mean, she admitted that she's not used to conjoined twins—I guess nobody really is—but she really likes y'all."

"She seems sweet," Dezy offered. We'd quickly learned that the rumors about Loreley's parents loving her sister more were completely untrue. Having lost one daughter, they doted on the remaining one.

"Oh, yeah, she is. Kinda overbearing, though."

"Kinda?" Risa snorted.

"I don't think she wants me to move out," Loreley said, rubbing circles on her thigh with her thumb. She did this often, unconsciously, a test to see if she could feel anything in her legs yet. Still no. Always no. "I've been thinking I should get a GED, but my parents change the subject every time I ask. I didn't really… I was kind of scared to leave the house for a while. In cars specifically, I mean. I'm pretty much over it by now."

"You wanna go to college?" Risa asked. She kept her tone casual, but we heard the worry in her voice. Risa's family was dirt poor, and she never seemed to do much besides hang out with Loreley. She certainly didn't have any other friends, and we were never really sure why.

"Yeah. I want a job eventually." Loreley saw the nervousness in Risa's eyes and grinned. "I'm sure my parents would pay for your tuition, too, if you wanted."

"Really?"

"Yeah! I can't go on my own."

"Why not?" Arcana blurted out. Dezy wanted to kick her, but, lacking the coordination in her underdeveloped legs, settled for digging her fingernails into her neck as hard as possible. We both hissed at the pain, but Arcana kept talking, and Dezy wondered if she should start just physically covering her mouth. "I mean, a lot of paraplegic people live on their own."

"That's not really the only reason she's here," Loreley said. Her tone was suddenly cold, and Arcana wisely stopped asking questions.

"Can y'all do drugs?" Risa asked abruptly.

"*What?*" we squealed.

"I mean, if y'all smoked weed, it wouldn't, like… hurt you?"

"We've never tried," Arcana said.

"It's probably bad for our lungs," Dezy said.

"Damn," Risa muttered.

"Our lungs are fine," Arcana said, very confidently. "It won't kill us to try it once, Dezy, don't be a pussy."

"I don't know if that's a great idea," Loreley said cautiously. "Aren't you guys, like, fourteen?"

"Yes. And we shouldn't—"

"I wanna try," Arcana said. "You don't have to if you don't want to."

"She'll get high too, right? Not unless you both agree," Loreley said. Arcana and Risa both seemed a little upset, Arcana because she'd wanted to feel cool and mature, Risa because she, presumably, just wanted to get high and felt awkward doing it in front of us if we didn't join in.

"What else do people do at sleepovers?" Dezy asked hopefully.

"Jurt whatever, I guess. There's not an itinerary. We could watch a movie or talk or… I dunno." Loreley shrugged. "I haven't hung out with anybody except Risa in at least a year. Sorry."

"Can we watch *The Lion King*?" Dezy asked. Arcana pulled her hair, humiliated at such a childish suggestion, but Loreley lit up.

"Yeah! Oh, my God, I haven't seen that in forever!"

"I've never seen it," Risa chimed in.

"It's based on *Hamlet*," Loreley said cheerfully. "I think we have it on DVD, let's watch it in the living room…"

As it turned out, Risa did not like *The Lion King*. "This is just pro-monarchist propaganda," she announced halfway through, making Loreley roll her eyes and audibly groan. "I'm serious!"

"I *know* you are."

"What's that mean?" Dezy asked. Arcana was sitting sideways on the couch, leaning against the arm so we could both see, and she'd started paying more attention to our friends than the movie. They sat at the other end of the couch, Loreley with her arm around Risa.

"Monarchies are the most ridiculous, outdated system of government in the world," Risa began, talking over the movie that Loreley didn't bother to pause, "and, honestly, all of these people are assholes, but Mufasa and Simba are totally worse than Scar. Why the hell should Simba get to be king just 'cause he was born? He's a spoiled brat the whole movie, he shouldn't get to be in charge just by birthright. And Mufasa banished the *hyenas*—"

"Oh, God, here we go again," Loreley said with fond exasperation.

"—to *die*, as a species! What could they possibly have done to warrant that, huh? He's trying to commit genocide against the hyenas! Probably because he's sexist, honestly. Did you know spotted hyenas are matriarchal? The females are always bigger, stronger, and more aggressive than the males, and they have giant pseudo—"

"Risa," Loreley said, clearing her throat.

"What?"

"I didn't know you were this passionate about, uh, hyena rights," Arcana said, giggling.

"Spotted hyenas are my favorite animal. I've actually got a tattoo of a hyena skull on my thigh," Risa chirped.

"Seriously?"

"Yeah."

"I will say that if there has to be a king, it should at least be the guy who worked for it," Loreley chimed in.

"Scar killed his brother, though," Dezy said nervously.

"Well, his brother was a genocidal monster who eats his subjects," Risa said.

"They all eat their subjects," Arcana pointed out. "I think the moral is that lions shouldn't be in charge."

"Why's Scar a bad king, anyway?" Loreley asked. "It's not his fault there's a drought."

"The hyenas are overhunting," Dezy said.

"Because they're starving! And *why* are they starving? Because Mufasa tried to kill them all, because Mufasa is evil!" Risa exclaimed.

"So Scar should be king and also there shouldn't be a king. Understood," Arcana laughed.

"Vive la resistance," Loreley yawned, pulling Risa closer to her side.

Risa was sleeping on the air mattress when we fell asleep, but the next morning, she was in Loreley's bed. We watched them, before they knew we were awake. Risa was pointing to something on her phone and saying, a little too loud to be whispering, "See? I looked it up, and *The Lion King* actually might have had a negative impact on hyena conservation efforts in real life. They already had a bad reputation, but the movie really made them look worse!"

"Oh, that's nice, babe," Loreley muttered, still half-asleep. Arcana burrowed further under the covers, and Dezy patted her cheek. She thought it was kind of silly that Arcana had a crush on Loreley at all, since she didn't have a chance, but she didn't say that out loud.

We had our usual bi-monthly doctor's appointment a few days after Risa's birthday. All the medical bills added up after a while, which may have been part of why Tiff wanted to be a doctor. Margaret bought all our groceries for us, and Daddy, whether intentionally or not, we were never sure, kept us just below the poverty line so we could qualify for Medicaid. Our fairytale cottage had a leaky roof and rats in the walls, but we loved it anyway.

"How are you two doing?" Dr. Sansing asked us, smiling a little too wide. She'd been our pediatrician as long as we could remember, and her main job seemed to be referring us to various specialists who always looked like they wanted to dissect us. Dr. Sansing didn't like to touch us, but she was kind other than that.

"Good," we said.

"Actually, they've been having strange dreams," Margaret cut in. She still tagged along to all our doctor's appointments, and Dezy was glad to have her there. Arcana was not, but because it was *Margaret*, she didn't protest. "Do you want to tell the doctor about them?"

"No," Arcana said.

"They're not dreams," Dezy said.

"What?" Dr. Sansing frowned. "Are they happening while you're awake?"

"Well… yeah, but they're not hallucinations," Dezy said awkwardly. Arcana was sitting on the edge of the exam table, so she was facing backwards, and Dr. Sansing walked around the side to talk to her face to face. "We've just been hearing things at night lately, and I see a shadow on our wall sometimes."

"Clicking noises, too, and floorboards creaking, sometimes," Arcana added.

"And a breeze from the window, but we haven't heard any of that since we started closing it at night," Dezy concluded.

"That sounds… unsettling. When did this all start?" Dr. Sansing asked carefully.

"Maybe a month ago?"

"And were there any major changes in your life around that time?" We saw in Dr. Sansing's eyes that she, like Margaret, thought we were just having strange dreams, so we smiled and shook our heads and dropped the subject.

Loreley was laughing at something Risa had just said when she went stiff, very suddenly. We had never seen someone have a seizure in real life, so we may have panicked a little, unsure what was happening. "Is she okay?" Dezy yelped.

"She'll be fine," Risa said easily. "Don't touch her."

Arcana had turned to face Loreley fully, so Dezy didn't actually see her twitching, but she heard her inhale sharply when she came out of it, saw her lean forward and vomit all over her lap when Arcana turned back to the side.

"Fuck," Loreley said weakly. She wiped at her mouth and avoided eye contact with us.

"She's alright," Risa said softly.

"Happens sometimes. Sorry," Loreley muttered.

"It's fine," Arcana said quickly. "We totally get it. I have really bad migraines, and Dezy's basically a bunch of medical problems shaped like a person."

"Join the club," Dezy said weakly, then realized we weren't exactly in a club anyone would be thrilled to join, but Loreley laughed weakly anyway.

"Rose Red's grades are slipping," Jewel whispered at dinner, which Rose Red hadn't come out of her room for.

"She didn't even know Celeste that well," Dia said.

"Her friend was murdered," Jewel said sharply. "You don't know how well they knew each other, and it's not your place to speculate on their relationship, okay?"

"Okay." Dia said quickly. "Sorry."

"We should bake her a pie," Dezy offered, rather stupidly.

"I don't think that'll fix the problem," Arcana said.

Rose Red's grades continued to slip, and she could not be coaxed into eating.

"Our sister's in a mental hospital," Arcana informed Loreley. We were stroking each other's hair, more than a little nervous. We'd never known anyone who had to go to a mental hospital before. Arcana pictured Badlam, patients tied to beds, lobotomies and electroconvulsive shock therapy, while Dezy thought it would be more like Arkham Asylum, clean white corridors with evil doctors torturing the patients for fun.

"Which one?" Loreley asked.

"Which hospital? You know them by name?"

"Which *sister?*"

"Oh. Rose Red."

"Alice," Dezy clarified.

"I know who Rose Red is. That's rough, though, how'd she end up there?"

"She won't eat, and she cries all the time. I mean, she cried a lot before, but now she *really* cries over nothing. And her grades are bad," Arcana said.

"She's not turning in assignments anymore," Dezy added anxiously. "She's never done that before, never."

"She misses Celeste, but Dia says they just ate lunch together. She never came to our house, and we don't think Rose Red ever went to hers."

"How old is she?" Loreley asked.

"Sixteen."

"Even if you didn't know her all that well, imagine eating lunch with somebody every day and then she's murdered. That would be pretty horrific," Loreley pointed out.

"They don't know who killed her, either," Risa muttered. "Her poor parents."

"It's so *creepy.* Don't they think whoever did it was hiding under her bed?" Loreley shuddered. "Like something straight out of a little kid's nightmares, right?"

"How long is Rose Red gonna be in the hospital?" Risa asked.

"We don't know. Hopefully not very long, 'cause we can't really afford it," Arcana said, laughing weakly.

Risa had strong feelings about the military, the police, the law, and the United States in general. She hated all of the above. Loreley said Risa was an anarchist, but since we pictured anarchists as violent revolutionaries, we didn't quite believe her. (When asked about her own political beliefs, Loreley shrugged vaguely and said "Oh, I guess I'm a leftist, but I don't give it much thought. Risa reads a lot of political theory.")

"The idea that you should be loyal to a country just 'cause you were born here is insane," she ranted, brushing Loreley's hair even though she really could have done it herself. "I mean, you're expected to be willing to die for a country—for *nothing!* It's insane! What the fuck makes America different than France or India or Russia? Just because we were born here, we're supposed to love it? I can't buy alcohol, but I can go die in a war?"

"This has absolutely nothing to do with what I just said," Loreley told her.

"You were criticizing my fashion choices, and I'm defending them."

"I said you shouldn't wear your 'fuck the troops' shirt to your uncle's Memorial Day barbeque."

"I'm just expressing my constitutional right to free speech."

"Can you express it somewhere else? He's gonna beat your ass."

"You should come," Risa said, probably just to change the subject.

"No," Loreley said at once, pulling away from her.

"Aw, c'mon, it'll be fun! My mom's warming up to you from what I've told her, but I bet if she met you—"

"No. No way."

"She won't give you a—"

"I'm not going."

Arcana and Dezy looked at each other, feeling like we were intruding on something private. "Can we come?" Dezy asked hopefully.

"No," Arcana said before Risa could open her mouth. "People would stare."

"Y'all are more than welcome," Risa said gently.

"Is this illegal?" Dezy asked, wide-eyed.

"Grey area," Risa chirped. She'd invited us on what she termed an adventure, and Loreley just shrugged when asked what it was. ("Sometimes she goes places, and you just kinda have to go with her or stay home.")

"How do you... I mean, it seems kind of..." Arcana chewed her lip, staring at the grocery store dumpster Risa had brought us to. "Do you just reach through the side door things?"

"Nah, I usually climb in like a rat," Risa said brightly.

"And you do this because...?"

"Stores throw out perfectly good stuff all the time." We watched Risa grab the side of the dumpster and pull herself up, Arcana giggling while Dezy fidgeted with her hair, nervous about breaking the rules. Loreley was watching her legs, strong and thick, the hyena skull tattoo visible for a second when her athletic shorts rode up as she climbed inside. "My family doesn't have a lot of money, so when I was a kid, the only way we got, like, the fancy store cakes and shit was if they got thrown out."

"Aren't they *expired* if they're being thrown out?"

"Expiration dates are a suggestion!"

"Most things don't go bad the exact day they say, you just have to eat stuff really fast," Loreley elaborated.

"I found a teddy bear!" Risa yelled from inside the dumpster. "I think it's from Valentine's Day."

"We collect teddy bears," Dezy said hopefully.

"Have it, then, but you should probably wash it first!"

As it so happened, Rose Red came home just a few days after she was admitted to the psychiatric hospital. She wasn't cured, but she *was* prescribed a pretty high dose of Ativan and pulled out of public school. We were terrified of homeschooling with her until we realized that the Ativan kept her too sleepy and docile to yell at us.

This is the part where I would skip to the Louisiana trip if it was up to me, but I know how a good story should go. It wouldn't make any sense if I cut ahead, and just like real life, a story can't fast forward through the sad or scary parts. So: about a week after Jewel started homeschooling Rose Red with us, Loreley and Risa went missing.

They had been alone at Loreley's house while her parents were out of town. The police responded late to a noise complaint from the neighbor, who said she heard a woman screaming at around 10PM. The police came at 6AM. Different police officers gave conflicting reports on why they took so long, but an anonymous inside source said that everyone knew Loreley was physically disabled, everyone assumed she was intellectually disabled, too, and everyone assumed she was just screaming for the hell of it.

She wasn't.

Inside the house, they found signs of a struggle in Loreley's bedroom, most notably Risa's blood on the floor, already dry by the time they finally showed up to do their fucking jobs. It looked, the lead detective said, like someone had been dragged through it. The French doors that opened into the backyard from her room were left open, and the basement window was broken, which made the police suspect the attacker had entered through the basement while no one was home and taken the victims out through the French doors.

"It has to be the same guy," Jewel said, staring off into space while her omelet burned. "There's no way it could be anyone else, right?"

"What guy?" Rose Red asked. Margaret didn't let her read the news anymore; she was scared distressing things might send her into a tailspin.

"Don't worry about it," Dia said quickly. She glared at Jewel. "Take your medicine."

"It makes me tired."

"Yeah, well, you can take a nap if you want, how 'bout that?"

"But I just woke up—"

"Alice. Please." At the use of her real name, Rose Red shut up and swallowed her pill obediently. She had become very docile since she started taking Ativan.

"Does it bother you?" Arcana whispered in our dark bedroom, after triple-checking that the window was really locked.

"Of course it bothers me. Somebody was murdered, and now our friends—"

"That's what I mean. *Our* friends. Rose Red knew Celeste. We know Loreley and Risa. Doesn't that freak you out? With the clicking and the shadow, too?"

"We've probably just been imagining that," Dezy said nervously.

"I think it's a creepy coincidence that all the dead girls knew somebody in our family."

"Loreley and Risa might not be dead. The police are looking for them."

"Not very hard."

"Yes, they are! They were late that one time, but that's it!"

"I don't *want* them to be dead," Arcana said defensively.

"Girls," Jewel interrupted, her voice thick with sleep, "y'all can discuss this in the morning."

Like Celeste, Loreley was found a week after she went missing. Unlike Celeste, she was still alive. The decapitated corpse found with her was immediately identified by the hyena skull tattooed on her thigh.

Chapter Five

Risa's head was not attached to her body, and the police couldn't find it in the surrounding woods. I only say that because it's true, and the police said it was "relevant information" when they talked to the reporters. I don't like thinking about it, and I'm sorry to tell you, because I'm sure you don't, either. The other relevant information is that Loreley's tongue was cut out, and her hands were broken. The doctors said her tongue was cauterized—the wound sealed shut with fire, or something very hot.

They were found in the woods, very close to where Celeste had been found. Very close, incidentally, to where the Garden girls played in the river every summer.

Margaret refused to take us to see Loreley. "When she's better," she said repeatedly, "when she's better, you can visit."

"But we miss her," we whined, and Margaret shook her head firmly.

"It would just upset you to see her right now."

We weren't very stealthy, but Jewel was distracted and clumsy in the aftermath of another local tragedy, and Margaret was getting slightly deaf as she aged. Two nights after Loreley and Risa were found, Arcana slipped out of our room (we went to bed early, not because we had an enforced bedtime, but because Arcana was naturally a morning person and Dezy was dragged along with her) and down the hall, where she stood, clutching Dezy tighter than usual, listening in on their conversation.

"That poor little girl," Margaret sighed. We heard a wine bottle being uncorked, liquid splashing in a glass.

"She's Tiff's age," Jewel said dully. Loud gulping; more splashing.

"Twenty's young to me. Hell, *you're* young to me."

"Uh, yeah? Watch it, old lady. I'm barely in my thirties."

"Exactly. Young. I just think she's been through so much already, and now… I mean, I can't even imagine. Car accidents happen, you know? It was a horrible tragedy, but they're not… this isn't normal. Loreley's lost a sister, lost her ability to walk, and now she's even *more* injured, and the things she must have seen—"

"I think you should let the twins visit her."

"It would scare them."

"They already know what happened."

"Seeing it in person is different."

"Is it? Loreley's their friend. Risa was their friend, too. They're going to her funeral, aren't they? If they want to?"

"If they want to," Margaret said slowly. "They need that kind of closure. Yes."

"Seeing Loreley would give them some kinda closure, too."

"Loreley isn't dying. Once she's out of the hospital, I'll be happy to take them to see her, but not yet. It would scar Dezy for life, you *know* it would."

"She's tougher than you give her credit for."

"How would it help them? Loreley can't speak; she can't write—"

"I always got the impression," Jewel interrupted, "that her caregiver was her only friend, and I'd bet you anything she watched that girl die."

There was a long, long pause. Margaret inhaled several times, like she was about to speak, then changed her mind. Eventually, Arcana got so sick of waiting that we went back to bed, but we couldn't sleep. Jewel stumbled in maybe an hour later and started snoring within seconds.

"Margaret said I can take y'all to see Loreley, if you want," she said the next morning, blinking tiredly at us when Dia came to get us ready for the day.

"We do."

I always liked Loreley, but I wouldn't really *understand* her until later. Arcana and Dezy had been born together, and while we were certainly sick, disabled and abnormal, we never considered our condition a bad thing. In fact, we never wanted to be separated at all until we had no other choice. Maybe Arcana would have been athletic if we were born separately. She liked watching women's basketball (although Dezy always suspected that was just a lesbian thing). When our heart started failing and we were hospitalized, we were distressed and scared to die, but it wasn't a surprise.

Being born able-bodied, growing up an athlete, being so good you got to go to college for free, and then having all that taken away—that, we couldn't imagine. We never had a normal life to lose, so we never really wanted to be normal at all, but we saw how much Loreley missed walking, how much she missed *running*. She wasn't interested in wheelchair sports, even though she still had an athlete's instincts and probably would have been good at them. She wanted to run.

We only drank alcohol a few times in our life (I say our life as in, our life when we were conjoined, before the surgery; after the surgery, it's *my* life), and the first time was with Loreley and Risa. None of us were technically old enough to drink, but Loreley's parents went out of town a lot, and Risa was more than happy to break into their liquor cabinet.

"They won't notice," Loreley promised, pouring us each a tiny, tiny glass of hard cider. "This is some kind of fancy cider, but the alcohol content's not very high, so it should be fine. You shouldn't have more than that, though."

"You're not our mom," Arcana said.

"No, but I'm an adult and y'all aren't, and it's my house. Cheers!" We all tossed our drinks back—Loreley and Risa were doing shots of tequila—and both twins immediately started gagging.

"It tastes *awful!*" Dezy squealed, making Loreley burst out laughing.

"It doesn't taste that bad, Dezy, don't be a pussy," Arcana said quickly. She had a bit of a crush on Loreley and wanted to seem cool in front of her. Both of us knew Loreley saw us as little sisters more than anything, but Arcana's fantasies were harmless.

"D'you need some water?" Risa asked, already filling a glass for us.

"No," Arcana said.

"Yes!" Dezy yelped.

As the night went on, Loreley and Risa drank quite a bit more, but we switched to regular apple cider. "Did I tell you about the first time we met?" Risa asked us, slurring her words slightly.

"No," we said.

"We met them at the library," Loreley reminded her.

"I mean *us,* Loreley, you and *me,*" Risa said in an are-you-stupid tone.

"No," Loreley said, suddenly seeming much more sober. "That's not… no, it was a long time ago. It's not important." Her eyes actually started welling up with tears, so Risa cleared her throat and quickly changed the subject.

"How 'bout how I started working here, then? I answered this ad on… like… at the library, actually, right?"

"Mhm."

"Yeah, at the library, one of those where you pull off the paper thing? Y'know? Asking for a caregiver, 'cause I took care of my grandpa 'fore he died, and then I came here." Risa nodded firmly. "And Loreley was such a total bitch."

"Uh-huh," Loreley giggled, looking a little proud of herself. She wiped at her eyes sheepishly.

"She didn't want anybody to help her with anything, and she thought I'd just leave if she made me miserable enough… right?"

"Right," Loreley agreed brightly. "I threw pillows at you."

"You threw anything you could reach!"

"It was mostly pillows."

"And a *book*."

"Paperback book," Loreley muttered.

"Anyway, she threw stuff at me and screamed at me and slapped me—"

"That only—that was only once!"

"It hurt, and it was definitely more than once!"

"It was *one time!*"

"She was awful, is my point, and then one day I came in and said, 'look, cunt, I need the money real bad, so either we can torture each other forever or we can be friends, but I ain't fuckin' leaving,' and that got through to her. Somehow."

"It was 'cause you called me a cunt," Loreley said after a moment's careful consideration. "A real nurse wouldn't of said that. And…" She looked at us, then away.

"What?" Dezy asked blankly, but Loreley didn't elaborate on that point.

"I wanted to run," she said instead, "and I still thought I'd be able to if I tried hard enough. All the doctors told me I couldn't, I was lucky to be alive, all this shit, but I still… I really, really liked running. I felt like nobody could ever catch me."

"We're sorry," we said softly. Loreley blinked at us, then giggled.

"*You're* sorry for *me?*" She threw her head back laughing, and Arcana was scowling by the time she stopped. "My bad, my bad. I shouldn't—I'm not laughing at you, just… y'all must hate being pitied as much as I do, right?"

"Yeah," we said.

"Then don't feel sorry for me, and I won't feel sorry for you."

It was true that Risa was Loreley's only friend. She'd had a lot of friends in high school, but they all went off to college or stopped talking to her after the accident. The dead girl's crippled sister was too depressing to think about, let alone talk to.

"I can't imagine," Margaret muttered as she drove us to the hospital. "I just can't imagine, after everything that poor girl's been through…"

We couldn't imagine, either. Loreley didn't talk about the accident, but we knew, everyone knew, that she was driving, her older sister was in the passenger seat, and the truck driven by a drunk old man crashed right into her sister's door, killed her instantly. They'd been on their way to a track meet, Loreley's senior year of high school.

She dropped out after the accident.

She didn't attend the funeral.

"I can," Arcana said quietly, so no one but Dezy could hear. "I can imagine a car crash, but not this."

"Not *both*," Dezy agreed.

Loreley's hospital room was stark white, and she looked like a child in the railed bed, or an old woman hooked up to so many machines. She was obviously on a lot of drugs, but she met Arcana's eyes when we walked in, smiled faintly and tilted her head very slightly to beckon us closer.

"Hey," we said nervously. Arcana sat down next to her bed so we could both look at her, and we determinedly ignored the nurse staring at us in mute fascination. Loreley smiled again, then opened her mouth wide and showed us the stump of her tongue, far back towards her throat, raised her heavily bandaged hands and made a guttural noise. Margaret gasped and hurried out of the room.

"We brought you this," Dezy said, and Arcana pulled a teddy bear from the plastic bag Margaret had set next to our chair when she left.

"It's 'cause Tiff used to bring us teddy bears every time we were in the hospital overnight," Arcana said quickly.

It was a stupid gesture. We both knew it was a stupid gesture. Conjoined twins being hospitalized overnight was routine; being hospitalized after being kidnapped, after your best friend was murdered, was not something that could be fixed or made better by a teddy bear. Still, we couldn't think of anything else to do, and Dezy was genuinely convinced it would make Loreley feel better.

Loreley raised her eyebrows, and Arcana set the bear on her chest. Slowly, she raised one arm and touched her wrist to the fur, then closed her eyes and laid completely still, breathing very, very slowly. We all sat in silence until we noticed the tears streaming down Loreley's face, at which point we both awkwardly touched her shoulder and left.

Loreley was in the hospital, and then in a physical rehab center, for over a month. She was never in a psychiatric facility, but when she was finally released, she was prescribed a cocktail of drugs that seemed designed to keep her borderline catatonic. Her parents did not take her outside or leave her alone, and no one but us was allowed to visit her.

"She really likes you," Mrs. Washington said anxiously, wringing her hands together and trying not to look directly at us. "It's so good for her to have friends, good friends, isn't it?" (Mrs. Washington was on some pretty heavy-duty psychiatric drugs herself.)

"Yep," we said, and she shuddered. She never touched us, and Arcana muttered that she probably had the maid wipe down every surface we so much as breathed near.

Loreley was always in the living room. After the car crash, her parents had moved upstairs and put her in the master bedroom, since it was the only one on the ground floor; after she was kidnapped, they put another bed in her room and took turns spending the night with her. "Are you ever alone?" Arcana asked her. Loreley blinked slowly, the drugs she was on slowing her process speed, then shook her head.

"No, no, of course not," Mrs. Washington said from behind us. "Never! We never should have…"

Dezy felt sorry for Loreley's parents. To have lost one daughter so suddenly, then almost lost the second, seemed like the worst thing in the world to her, especially since they so clearly blamed themselves for leaving Loreley and Risa home alone. Arcana, who had started volunteering to give Rose Red her Ativan so she could throw it away, had no sympathy for them at all and thought they were drugging Loreley into complacency so they wouldn't have to face what had happened to her.

"Rose Red's doing a little better," Arcana offered. Loreley smiled blandly. "We, uh… I've been reading a lot about the Labelle twins—"

"No," Dezy interrupted. "Not now."

"Well, we don't really do much."

"How about you? Are you doing any kind of speech therapy?" Dezy asked Loreley hopefully.

"Not yet," Mrs. Washington chimed in. "She's so stressed, we think it's better to just wait for now…"

"I bet being able to communicate would help her stress levels," Arcana said flatly.

"Deirdre," Dezy hissed.

"It's so nice that she has you two, of course," Mrs. Washington said anxiously. "So nice of you to visit, especially given your own condition—"

"Local news," Arcana interrupted, "is that, like I said, Rose Red's doing better. She's eating now, which is great, and Dia's been getting ready for a graduation party that she's totally psyched about. Tiff's coming to visit next week. Uh…"

"Our neighbor's having a block party," Dezy offered. "You met him, I think? During our picnic…" A few seconds after she'd spoken, Loreley's eyes lit up, and she leaned forward in her wheelchair, making a frantic, high-pitched noise in the back of her throat, shaking her head.

"Oh," she said, "oh, oh, oh!"

"Loreley!" Mrs. Washington shrieked, jumping up to stroke her daughter's hair back. "Loreley, baby, what's wrong?"

"Oh!" Loreley cried again, still shaking her head. Dezy was terrified, confused out of her mind and afraid she'd said or done something to upset her, but Arcana's eyes narrowed.

"The neighbor you met at the picnic," she said slowly. Loreley screamed, and even Mrs. Washington seemed to realize what was going on, because she kept petting Loreley but stopped trying to make her be quiet.

"Do you know him?" she whispered.

"What's going on?" Dezy asked, tears welling in her eyes.

"Did he do this to you?" Arcana asked, and Loreley nodded.

"Call the police," Mrs. Washington said at once.

In the immediate aftermath of Loreley's kidnapping/Risa's murder, no suspects were named. There weren't any fingerprints found in the Washington house, the neighbors hadn't seen a thing, and Loreley obviously wasn't talking. Not for lack of trying; she smacked weakly at people, screamed and moaned, made desperate, incoherent noises until the doctors started giving her sedatives, but the police never interviewed her.

"That poor little girl must be so incredibly traumatized," the lead detective told the papers. "I hope, for her sake, she's blocked it all out."

The fact that Loreley was twenty years old and would more accurately be described as a young woman did not seem to occur to anyone in the police force or the media.

"What can we do for you, dear?" a cop asked Mrs. Washington, smiling placatingly. Loreley's parents had quickly developed a rather paranoid reputation around town once it got out that they slept in the same room as their daughter and had stopped letting her leave the house. Mr. Washington's random crying jags in the grocery store didn't help his case, and Mrs. Washington's barely went outside herself.

"Well," she began, clearing her throat, "well. As you know—as you must know—Loreley can't communicate anymore, verbally, I mean, and until her hands heal she can't, um, write, write or use sign language, but of course in the future—"

"I know," the cop interrupted.

"Right. Yes. You know. So that's why you didn't interview her, of course, but she did *see*—she does *know* who—Deirdre mentioned her neighbor, and Loreley started screaming. I asked—we both asked—the twins' neighbor. That's who Loreley says—that's the man who—"

"He lives in that red brick house not very far from us," Dezy added. Arcana, rolling her eyes, provided the actual address.

"Thanks," the cop said.

"You should write that down. We don't actually know his name, but he's super fucking creepy and weird," Arcana told him.

"I appreciate your concern, but we're already looking into this case," the cop said.

"It's solved! Loreley told us-"

"How did she tell you this?" The cop smiled sweetly at Loreley, who glared at him.

"She, well, she started panicking, and when Deirdre asked if it was this man who, um, hurt her, she nodded," Mrs. Washington said meekly. Loreley nodded again, as if to prove she could.

"We'll have to give this some consideration," the cop said. "I'll make a note, of course."

"Are you gonna arrest him? Is he a suspect?" Arcana demanded.

"Young lady, we don't arrest people without evidence."

"The *only witness* just told you *exactly* who it was."

"The only witness is a profoundly disabled girl who has no real way to communicate."

"She's not *intellectually* disabled," Mrs. Washington said quickly.

"I'm sure. Tell you what. Let's have her come in for an IQ test, evaluate her cognitive function, and then we'll see about some kind of testimony in the future. Screaming and jerking her head doesn't count as evidence, I'm afraid."

"Fuck you," we said, Arcana confidently, Dezy a little stunned that the words had left her mouth. Mrs. Washington looked mildly scandalized, but didn't comment. Loreley just stared at him, lips pressed into a thin line.

"You ladies have a nice day," the cop said coldly.

"I'll talk to them," Mrs. Washington told us. "I'll… see what I can do, okay?"

Loreley made a horrible, broken sobbing noise, and Dezy hid her face in Arcana's shoulder.

That night, Arcana shook Dezy's shoulder after Jewel fell asleep. "I'm sure he did it," she whispered.

"Why?" Dezy asked.

"*Why?* Because Loreley would fucking know, wouldn't she?"

"No, I mean why'd he do it? I believe her, I just wanna know why he did it."

"How should I know? I'm not some kind of… of lunatic. I don't know." Arcana lowered her voice even further, leaning in to whisper right in Dezy's ear, "But he'll be at the block party this Saturday, right? I think we should go look for something incriminating in his house while he's gone."

"That's a bad idea," Dezy responded.

"Shut up," Arcana said lightly, and Dezy sighed, knowing she didn't have a say in the matter.

Loreley took an IQ test, and although her results came back above average, Mr. Smith was not arrested or interrogated. The police allowed her to give her testimony, but I heard it didn't go well. Later, after she regained some function in her hands and wrote out a full, detailed account of what happened, she mentioned how the police initially dismissed her, how they patted her head and offered her candy she couldn't taste anymore, how they all spoke to her father instead of her.

Chapter Six

The day of Mr. Smith's block party, Arcana woke up with a migraine. Dezy had a nosebleed, as she often did when her twin's migraines began, and she didn't speak as Dia carefully wiped her face clean. At the time, she was secretly a little glad we weren't able to break into Mr. Smith's house (what a crazy idea, she thought, *breaking into a house* to prove he was a serial killer), but later we both wondered what would have happened if we'd actually done it. If we'd found what we did sooner, maybe the police would have believed us, maybe everything would have worked out as well as it could, and maybe Rose Red would still be alive.

People must have come from all over the place, maybe some people from Mr. Smith's church, because we heard the noise from the block party all the way down the street. Arcana whimpered involuntarily and pulled a pillow over her ears while Dezy hushed her and rubbed her back, *shh shh shh*.

Dozens of people. Enough people that no one was really paying attention to Mr. Smith, a man who, even when he was hosting a party, tended to blend into the background, or Rose Red, who'd become very, very quiet after Celeste's death.

Dozens of people, and none of them saw a thing.

"Have you seen Rose Red?" Dia's voice was high-pitched, strung tight with worry. "I made her go to the block party, but I didn't see her after…"

"Where's Rose Red?"

"Has anybody seen her?"

"I'm calling the police."

Unsurprisingly, the police told Margaret to wait twenty-four hours before filing a missing persons report. When Margaret icily told them that was a myth, they took her information "with obvious reluctance", as she would later tell anyone who asked or stood still long enough.

Arcana was too out of it to hear or understand anything that was said about our missing sister that first day, but when her migraine finally eased, Dezy filled her in immediately.

"Rose Red is missing," she said quietly. "She went missing at the block party."

"Fuck," Arcana said. Then she threw up.

Nobody talked at dinner.

"He killed Celeste after a week," Arcana whispered that night, squeezing Dezy tight, like she might get up and run away if she didn't hold onto her. "Risa, too. We still have time, especially since the police are doing fuckall."

"They're not looking into him now?"

"They don't believe Loreley."

"What are we supposed to do, then?"

"I told you already."

"That seems like a really, really, *really* bad idea."

"Do you have a better one?"

"No," Dezy admitted after a long pause.

This next part was hard to write. Tiff says I shouldn't interrupt the story to say stuff like this, but it's true, and I want you to know, before I tell you the really sad part, that I loved Rose Red. Reading this back, I'm scared I made her sound like a bitch, but she honestly wasn't that bad. She wasn't bad at all, she just wanted things done a certain way. She wanted us to be safe, and we knew she loved us—really and truly adored us.

When we were newborns, Rose Red wanted to visit us at the hospital every day. She cooed over us, patted our faces with her tiny hands, and told every nurse she saw that we were "*my* baby!" Margaret tried to explain that we were two babies, once, but Rose Red just scoffed (as much as two-year-old can, I guess) and insisted, "Nuh-uh. My baby."

As we got older, she dressed us up like dolls and made us play house or teacher with her, which wasn't always fun, but it was her way of showing she cared. House was nice, most of the time, especially when we were still small enough to fit on her lap. I remember, I'll always remember, Rose Red rocking us back and forth, singing a soft lullaby Margaret used to sing to us, and when we both fell asleep I heard her whisper, "My babies."

Rose Red loved us, and I think it might have killed her to know that only one of us survived the separation surgery. When I woke up alone, I thought it might even be good that she was already dead, then I wanted to hit myself because it wasn't fair that she died so young.

She was supposed to be valedictorian.

Jewel didn't bother with school for the next few days, but she didn't let us out of her sight, either. Dezy always felt guilty about what we did to get away; Arcana thought the ends justified the means.

"Don't!" Dezy hissed, tugging sharply on Arcana's hair as she ground up two of the sleeping pills Daddy took (by the way, if you're wondering where the hell Daddy was while all of this was happening: he was home, but the lights weren't on, if you get what I mean).

"Ow! It's fine, Dezy! We just need, like, half an hour, okay? He's at work, so we should have time to go through his house. We'll go fast."

"What if they make her sick?"

"Jewel has absolutely done harder drugs than this in her life."

"That doesn't mean—"

"Shut up!"

Arcana dumped the powdered pills in a milkshake and fixed Jewel with puppy eyes until she drank it. "I'll get fat," Jewel muttered, taking a reluctant sip. She'd been lying on the couch, staring at the ceiling, for two hours, calling out to us every five minutes and jumping up in a panic if we didn't respond.

"No, you won't. I'm practicing for when Rose Red gets back," Arcana said. "She has trouble eating, so…"

Jewel chugged the milkshake in five seconds flat.

"Delicious," she said, voice trembling.

We slipped out the door as soon as she fell asleep, feeling rather stupid in our attempts to be stealthy. "If it's not him, we're going to jail," Dezy pointed out.

"First of all, it *is* him, and second of all, we're not going to jail 'cause I'm the only one committing a crime," Arcana said confidently. "They can't send *you* to jail if you're innocent!"

"How do you know we'll even find proof?"

"I don't *know,* but I *hope* we do."

No one stopped us when we opened the gate to his backyard and walked inside, up to his back door. Locked. "Maybe the key's under the mat?" Dezy offered.

"Fuck the key," Arcana said, carefully crouching down to grab a stone from the edge of a garden bed.

"Oh my God, Arcana. Deirdre, *no*…"

She chucked the rock through the window in his backdoor and cut her arm reaching in to unlock it. Dezy's whispered protests were ignored and fell completely silent as Arcana stepped inside, eyes wide, looking around the completely normal house. *Completely* normal—completely plain actually. There wasn't a single photo on the walls, no decorations to be seen, nothing at all to tell you a thing about Mr. Smith. The walls were beige, the carpet was grey, and the furniture was white.

"Should we check the basement?" Arcana whispered.

"No."

She checked the basement anyway, but it was totally empty, save for a padlocked freezer up against the wall. Dezy shuddered as Arcana walked closer to it, squealed in fear when she banged on the lid, but nothing happened. "There's nothing here," she whined, tightening her grip around Arcana's neck, "let's just *go!*"

"We'll look upstairs," Arcana said. She walked through the basement one more time, searching for hidden doors, but didn't find any. Upstairs, we found a room with the windows blacked out, tubs of mysterious chemicals sitting around that made Dezy cry from fear, but Arcana quickly reassured her it was just a dark room. "For developing photos. Jewel used to have one in high school," she explained.

We went into Mr. Smith's bedroom last, purely because it was the last room upstairs.

White sheets. White blanket. White dresser.

Black camera.

Dezy stared at the camera sitting innocently atop Mr. Smith's dresser while Arcana pulled all the drawers open, carelessly rummaging through everything—if she'd been wrong, we would have been arrested for sure—and continued to stare as Arcana turned around and opened his bedside drawer. We both put it together at the same time, Dezy looking at the camera and Arcana looking, with a gasp, at the stack of photos held together with an envelope.

"Dezy," she whispered. "It's us."

And it was. Even in the picture's dim lighting, it was unmistakably *us* in the first photo, asleep in bed and lit only by moonlight. The second photo, us again, us in bed. Us asleep. The third, us in bed. The fourth, Jewel, asleep. The fifth, us in Daddy's garden. The sixth, Dia and Rose Red walking down the street, taken from a window in Mr. Smith's house. The seventh was us in bed again, and there was a dried, off-white liquid crusted onto it that made Arcana gag.

The eighth was Celeste.

Dezy burst into tears, and Arcana gagged, had to fight not to vomit. She dropped the stack of photos, nearly fell over trying to pick it up again, and forced herself, with trembling hands, to look through. Out of context, maybe the photos wouldn't have been so scary; Celeste sitting with Rose Red, Celeste walking home from school, Loreley and Risa in the library, Risa driving home from Loreley's house, but knowing what we knew, they made us feel sick.

They went on forever, and Dezy started wailing halfway through the stack, even after she'd stopped looking. Arcana nearly threw up when she got to the last photo. It was our picnic with Loreley and Risa, taken at such a distance we hadn't noticed him until he walked right up to us.

Arcana shoved the photos in her pocket and hurried out of the house, nowhere near running—she could never run—but walking as fast as she could, Dezy bawling in her arms, back to our home.

Jewel was still asleep when we returned, but she woke up when she heard Arcana screaming into the phone. "I need the police! I need the police to come here, now! Our neighbor, we don't know his name, he lives at—"

"What's going on?" Jewel muttered blearily, stumbling into the kitchen.

"I found photos in his bedroom, photos of us and our cousin *sleeping,* and of the girls he hurt. You need to come here!"

"What the fuck?" Jewel demanded. As soon as Arcana hung up the phone, she leaned her head against Dezy's shoulder, sobbing. "Arcana! Arcana, sweetie, what's *wrong?* Did they find…?"

"We broke into his house," Dezy said, because Arcana, she thought, had run out of words, "and we found these photos. Arcana, give her the… give her…"

Jewel took the photos when Arcana thrust them into her hand.

Jewel turned very, very pale.

"You broke in?" the cop asked immediately, before even looking at the photos.

"Go to Hell!" Dezy shrieked, but she was the parasitic twin, she was the one who should have been cut away, she was half a person and entirely ignored.

"Look at these," Jewel said tiredly. We saw on the cop's face that he didn't want to, and when he took the photos, we saw that he didn't care.

"This isn't admissible in court," he said.

"Are you fucking psychotic?" Jewel snarled.

"Let me finish, please. *These* are not admissible in court, but we now have grounds to search his residence." He fixed us with a cold stare. "You two, however, are still guilty of breaking and entering."

"He's a serial killer," Dezy said.

"Actually," Arcana interrupted, right as the officer's partner, a woman, walked in from outside, "*I'm* guilty of breaking and entering. Dezy didn't do anything." She grinned crookedly. "You can't put an innocent person in jail, can you?"

"What's that?" the female cop demanded. She took one look at the photo, gasped, and handed it back to her partner.

"You *happened* to *coincidentally* find something, and these photos don't prove he's a murderer," the male cop snarled. "Breaking and entering, property destruction—"

"Why are we not getting a search warrant right now?" the female cop interrupted. "We don't have time for this, Frank. Move your ass."

"Dezy's innocent," Arcana repeated, giggling slightly hysterically. "Dezy's innocent!"

"We'll be back for further questioning later," the male cop finally muttered. "By the way, you look like hell. Maybe make yourself presentable before calling the police next time."

"Piece of fucking dogshit," Jewel hissed after the cop left. "'These don't prove—is he crazy? I mean, really, is he *crazy?* He was in our *room!* God, he watched us sleep!"

"I told you," Dezy muttered.

"Rose Red isn't in his house," Arcana said, and Jewel seemed to suddenly come back to herself.

"She isn't, that's- you went over there? Really? I mean, of course… Deirdre! What if he'd come home?"

"He murdered two people. He's going to murder our sister," she said, completely emotionless.

"He could have killed *you.*"

"Well, he didn't."

"Can we go to bed?" Dezy asked. She was suddenly very, very exhausted.

"As long as Arcana understands she can't just… you can't risk your life, your sister's life, like this," Jewel said. She seemed a little shocked, like she didn't know quite what to say in a situation like this.

"What else were we supposed to do? Loreley told them who it was, and they didn't listen! If she can't make them search his house, how else are we supposed to—?"

"You could have died!"

"*I'm tired!*" Dezy screamed, making Arcana flinch.

"Alright," Jewel said quietly. Dezy almost never raised her voice, so when she did, she figured it was important. "Go to bed, then."

"I need to shower," Arcana muttered.

"I'll help," Jewel said. She had never been willing to help us bathe before, but she did it without complaint that day, helped Dezy into a medical brief afterwards because she didn't trust herself to put in a catheter, and tucked us into bed.

When we woke up and went into the kitchen, Jewel had a stack of papers spread out on the table. "I just checked," she said breathlessly, "and that bastard was *lying*. Inadmissible evidence is when law enforcement goes in without a warrant, it doesn't apply to citizens. The photos are hard evidence."

"Yay," Arcana said dully. Dezy wiped at the blood running from her nose and fell back asleep on her twin's shoulder.

Chapter Seven

The photos were evidence. Loreley's testimony would have been evidence if anyone was willing to listen to her. Honestly, though, I don't think that would have been enough to convict Mr. Smith. His DNA, obtained with a warrant, was later found to be a match to the DNA found on and in Loreley's body, but Jewel said, and we agreed, that the police wouldn't have bothered with a second warrant at all if they hadn't found Risa's head in his basement freezer.

I guess I didn't mention that part earlier. We knew, but I tried to block it out. I thought it was too disgusting to talk about. Mr. Smith raped Celeste, Risa, Loreley, and probably Rose Red, too, but by the time they found her body it was impossible to know for sure.

Mr. Smith was arrested, and Dezy refused to hear anything about the trial or the ongoing search for Rose Red. It made her feel sick to her stomach, and even knowing Arcana was reading about it made her want to puke, so out of respect for her sister, Arcana stayed away from the news. We stopped going out in public, and all Arcana asked Jewel and Margaret, every day, was "Did they find her yet?"

The answer was always no.

Daddy didn't seem to notice she was gone at all.

Mr. Smith pleaded not guilty at first, and we would later find out from a drunken Jewel that the male cop who showed up when we called 911 was harping on endlessly, all around town, about how we had broken into his house to find the photos, with no proof but an interpretation of what Loreley might have been trying to say. He suggested that we were acting out, we were juvenile delinquents, we couldn't be trusted, and might have continued on that track forever if a bartender hadn't snapped, "You seem more pissed off at the kids who solved the case than the man who raped and murdered all those little girls."

When she told us that story, chuckling bitterly to herself, Arcana responded, "Loreley isn't a little girl."

Mr. Smith was charged with stalking, kidnapping, rape, and murder. He was given a life sentence. A month before his trial, a woman tried for killing her abusive husband was sentenced to death.

Like I said, we didn't pay very much attention to his trial, so I can't tell you much. What I *can* tell you is this: he did not say where he had committed his crimes, and Loreley, who had been locked in the trunk of his car when he drove to wherever it was, could not identify the location on a map. More photos were found in a metal box under his bed, graphic photos of what he did to the victims, but they all showed the inside of a cabin, no real identifying features.

Five months later a hiker found the cabin by sheer accident. It was almost fifty miles away. People asked each other why they didn't notice him leaving the block party with Rose Red, why she followed him, what he did to convince her, and no one knew. He wouldn't say. All he said, when told that Alice Gardner's body had been found chained to a bed in his hunting cabin, was that he didn't kill her.

"She was alive when I was arrested," he said.

Daddy didn't change at all after Rose Red's murder. Tiff stopped coming home to visit. Dia finished high school, just barely, and lost interest in everything except us. We allowed her to fuss over us, since we felt pretty lost ourselves. Jewel drank more, Margaret came over more often and cleaned more thoroughly, and the Gardner household received a call from the police, informing us that Mr. Smith had finally given a motive.

Because we were minors, they wouldn't talk to us, but Jewel immediately told us everything they'd said anyway. "He was obsessed with *you,*" she said, taking a long, slow sip of her wine. "He'd never seen conjoined twins before, and he was… fascinated. That's his word, not mine, *fascinated.* He wanted to be close to people who were close to you."

"Why would you tell us that?" Arcana asked.

"Thank you," Dezy said softly.

Dia took us to visit Loreley every time we asked but refused to come inside. "I'll just wait," she muttered. Arcana thought she hated Loreley for surviving when our sister hadn't; Dezy thought she resented her, which was different. It seemed impossible to hate someone as broken as Loreley.

"What's up?" we asked, sitting across from her with identical fake bright grins. She blinked at us, her lips twitched into something resembling a sort of smile, and then she sat back in her wheelchair, eyes fixed on the wall behind us.

"We have something to tell you, actually," Mrs. Washington said from behind us, clearing her throat. "We as in Loreley and I, and her father, of course. You know."

"Yeah?" Arcana asked. Dezy tugged her hair, scowling at her aggressive tone.

"We're not getting any younger," Mrs. Washington said, clearing her throat almost compulsively, "and we think… we can't keep taking care of Loreley forever. We've been thinking about speech therapy, too, and, um, other things… she's fine with it, I mean, she likes…"

"What are you saying?" Arcana asked, forcing herself to sound as polite as possible.

"Loreley is moving into a residential care home next month," Mrs. Washington admitted. "She wants to. We can't help her as much as she needs, and we can't be with her twenty-four-seven. It's not healthy to try."

"You want to?" Dezy asked Loreley, who nodded, maybe a little hesitantly. "Are you sure?" Another nod.

"You have to remember that she was… it happened here," Mrs. Washington said softly. Arcana opened her mouth to argue, but Dezy dug her nails deep into her neck and she closed it again.

"How far away is it? Can we still visit?"

"Not far. You can visit, yes, of course. It's about an hour and a half from here. We're going to come several times a week, of course."

"Of course," Arcana repeated, a little too sugary sweet.

We weren't sure about the care home at first, but Loreley actually kind of thrived there. Her hands healed up eventually—not perfectly, but pretty well—and she started sending us typed letters covering everything from her speech therapy progress to her slowly expanding collection of felt animals wearing top hats. *The top hats are important,* she wrote. *I don't know why, but they are. They're essential.*

She did not mention Risa, and she carefully avoided talking about why she was there in the first place.

The second time we went to visit Loreley in the care home, a woman we didn't know was sitting at her bedside, clenching the armrests of her chair with white knuckles. She didn't look up when we came in, and when we sat next to her, she didn't even do a double take. Arcana immediately realized she had to be Risa's mother—they had the same eyes, the same freckles on the bridge of their noses—but Dezy had no idea who she was at first.

"How do you know Loreley?" the woman asked quietly.

"We're, uh, her friends," Arcana said. We were so used to people being horrified by our appearance that we didn't know what to do when we were treated as unremarkable.

"I thought Risa was her only friend."

"Nope. We're her friends, too."

"That's lovely. Risa was my daughter. I'm Joan Burke."

"Nice to meet you," Dezy said.

"We're so sorry for your loss," Arcana said.

"Thank you." Mrs. Burke twisted her wedding ring around her finger. "Did Loreley tell you how she met Risa?" Loreley tried to sit up in bed, whining, and shook her head weakly.

"No," we said.

"They were on the track team together. Risa was pretty tomboyish back then—it wasn't long ago—and she still is now, I guess. Loreley here was very girly, very pretty, little miss popular. Kind of went out of her way to be feminine when she wasn't running. Risa joined the track team, looking like she did—you know, butch, I guess—and Loreley had a problem with it." Loreley whined again. "They never told you? She was *horrible* to Risa. It wasn't just name calling and gossiping, she made her life hell. Told everyone Risa was a lesbian, accused her of watching other girls change clothes, said all these horrible things to her face, online, didn't matter. Shoved her to the floor in the halls. Beat her up."

"Ahh," Loreley moaned, shaking her head again. She was starting to cry.

"That's—"

"Risa tried to kill herself," Mrs. Burke said. Loreley sobbed. "I think I would have murdered Loreley if she'd succeeded. We both laughed when we read about the car crash, then felt horribly guilty, of course, because her poor sister… but I thought it was karma. Risa moved on, finished high school, and then one day she comes home and says 'guess who needs a caregiver?'

"I thought she was crazy to take the job, and I think she did it… actually, I really don't know why she did it at first. Risa was a nice girl, she wouldn't have done it to hurt Loreley, even if the bitch deserved it. I figured she'd quit after a week, with all the stories she had; 'Loreley screams at me, Loreley doesn't want help, Loreley called me a dyke, she's horrible, she's worse than she was before,' all this stuff. But she didn't quit, and she finally got Loreley to calm down. No idea how. I didn't say anything, 'cause she was making good money, until—I guess about a year after she got the job—she told me Loreley kissed her."

"Ahhh," Loreley cried.

"I think she wants you to stop," Dezy said quietly.

"I'm not done. Risa told me Loreley was different, she was nicer, she was so, so sorry. She told me she liked her… *loved* her. I was completely against it, but they started dating. No idea if Loreley's parents ever knew." Mrs. Burke sighed heavily. "If Loreley hadn't been such an awful bully, I dunno if Risa would've taken the job. She said she showed up to the interview out of curiosity, expected Loreley to say something to her parents, but she didn't. And if Risa hadn't taken the job, she never would of been—if she hadn't—if she wasn't with *you*."

Loreley made a hoarse noise, and Arcana cleared her throat. "That's enough," she said.

"I almost lost my daughter because of her," Mrs. Burke said. "Almost, and then I really did."

"Please leave," we said. Arcana reached out and put her hand over Loreley's.

"Have a nice day," Mrs. Burke muttered. She shuffled to the door like a zombie, and when she got there, Dezy watched her turn back to us, her gaze focused on our friend's legs. "Loreley," she said, loudly and suddenly. "You're still *so* beautiful. I couldn't help but notice that. A lot of the orderlies here are men, they're supposed to take care of you, right? Bathe you, change your diapers, all the things Risa did? I hope they don't notice how pretty you are." She smiled coldly. "After all, you can't exactly tell them no, can you?"

She left without another word, and Loreley fell back against her pillow, crying softly. "Is that true?" Dezy asked.

"Desdemona!" Arcana hissed.

Loreley looked at us, bit her lip, and nodded.

"You're not that person anymore," Arcana said quietly.

"I'm sure Risa forgave you," Dezy added.

Loreley just closed her eyes and cried.

"Still like it here?" Arcana asked, looking around Loreley's room. It wasn't as hospital-y as we'd expected. She was always cold, and the huge pile of warm quilts forming a nest on her bed looked remarkably cozy. The art prints a nurse had hung for her were beautiful, and the top hatted felt creatures were utterly adorable.

"Ah," Loreley said, nodding. She held up a crooked finger, *one second,* and grabbed the tablet she'd started using to communicate when she couldn't make herself understood verbally or wanted to make sure she was completely clear. *"I hope this isn't inappropriate. Stop me if it is. I just wanted to say that I'm so, so sorry about Alice."*

"Not your fault," Arcana said stiffly.

"I know what it's like to lose a sister." Loreley gave us a smile that didn't meet her eyes, then, with shaking hands, typed, *"I watched my sister die. And I watched my girlfriend die. I know there aren't any words for what you lost, but I want you to know that I think I understand, and I'm sorry. From the bottom of my heart."*

"Thanks," Dezy whispered.

"We're sorry, too," Arcana said softly. "For… everything." She didn't say *it's our fault,* but we knew we both wanted to. Loreley nodded slowly. She never talked about Risa again, and we never asked.

"Where are y'all headed?" Margaret asked with forced cheerfulness.

"We were gonna visit Loreley," Arcana said, equally perky. None of us looked at the basement door leading to Rose Red's room, which, as far as we knew, no one had entered since her body was found.

"Again?"

"She's our friend."

Margaret bit her lip. "It's kind of a long drive," she said quietly.

"Not really."

"I don't mind," Dia added.

"Can we talk for a minute?"

"Sure," we said, hesitantly. Arcana sat down across from Margaret, leaving Dezy to stare at the armchair upholstery. She reached out to trace the floral pattern that Rose Red always liked, but everyone else thought was hideous.

"I was glad that y'all had a friend," Margaret began slowly. "Two friends. But I'm not sure… I don't think this is healthy. Loreley is a nice young woman, but she is… she's incredibly damaged, and I don't know if she'll ever get better. I don't know if you *can* get better after something like this."

"So we should just leave her alone and forget about her?" Arcana snapped.

"That's not what I'm saying. All I'm saying is, I think you're visiting a lot, and it might be better for everyone if you went less often."

"She's lonely," Dezy said quietly.

"Her parents go multiple times a week."

"She misses Risa," we said, and Margaret inhaled slowly. She didn't say anything else, but she must have gestured for us to leave, because Arcana stood up and walked away. We didn't say a word until we walked into Loreley's room.

Rose Red had a small, private funeral. She was cremated before we saw her body. Risa's funeral was public, but not very well attended. It was a closed casket funeral. Although Margaret had said we were allowed to attend, we refused; we were afraid her parents would see us and somehow know it was our fault, that if Risa hadn't known us Mr. Smith never would have known or cared about her.

After her head was found, they dug her back up to bury it with the rest of her body.

Chapter Eight

We used to celebrate our birthday with a massive amount of fanfare. Every year was another victory, another milestone, and we were always a little thrilled, a little shocked, a little scared. There was always the sense that we weren't supposed to make it this long. On our tenth birthday, Dezy looked at our cake and burst into tears, exclaiming that we were cheating. *The doctors said we're not supposed to,* she wailed, *we're gonna get in trouble!*

After that, Margaret warned doctors to be very, very careful with what they said in front of us and how they phrased it.

Our fifteenth birthday was barely celebrated at all. Dia, as usual, made a point of scream-singing *HAPPY BIRTHDAY TO YOU!* right outside Daddy's door and Margaret baked a cake, but no one was in a particularly celebratory mood so soon after Rose Red's death. Tiff called and left a voicemail apologizing for not coming in person, finished it by mumbling that she had so much homework and loved us, wished us well, sounded like she might be about to cry when she said good-bye. In the dead of night, Arcana whispered that everyone knew we didn't have long to live, and no one wanted to think about how our birthday meant they were one year closer to spreading our ashes like Rose Red's.

"Anything in particular y'all wanna do?" Jewel asked, popping a stick of gum in her mouth. She'd stopped smoking when she moved in with us, but she still had an oral fixation, and since the funeral she'd had something in her mouth pretty much constantly. Sometimes she sucked her fingers in her sleep. "Pretty big milestone, right?"

"Sixteen's the big one," Arcana said. "Still gotta make it one more year."

"Oh, I'm sure you will. Strong girls, strong heart, et cetera." Jewel hummed. "Shit, I'll be thirty-four next year."

"That's cool."

"I feel like I'm getting wrinkles," she huffed.

"We'd love to—" Arcana began, but Dezy scratched her harshly. She knew what her twin had been about to say: *we'd love to live long enough to get wrinkles.* It used to be a sort of dark joke, but there was no way Jewel would take it well in the wake of Rose Red's early death.

"Oh, yeah, I got you a present. Happy birthday, ladies!" Jewel forced herself to grin as she handed Arcana a book, unwrapped. "I forgot to…"

"It's fine. This is great, Jewel, thanks."

"What is it?" Dezy asked.

"It's about the Labelle twins."

"Fantastic," Dezy muttered. She wasn't usually sarcastic, but sometimes it just came out.

If Jewel hadn't remembered Arcana's morbid obsession and bought the biography at a library book sale, we almost certainly would have stayed home all summer. We would have stayed home for a year, until our heart began to fail and the doctors said we only had one option, it was risky but we'd both die otherwise. Until they began to say, finally, *Desdemona is killing Deirdre.* They'd always thought it, they said it when we were babies, but they didn't actually say it to our faces until Arcana started passing out, until we began to have trouble breathing.

But we had the book. We had a distraction.

"Welcome still exists," Arcana said, re-reading her book for the third time since Jewel gave it to her.

"Yeah, I know. Yippee," Dezy said into her shoulder.

"They've got a little motel outside of town, and the Labelle house is still standing. Totally abandoned, but it's there."

"And infested with alligators, probably."

"We're not doing anything this summer."

"We are *not* going to a creepy-ass ghost town to trespass in—"

"I'm gonna ask Jewel," Arcana said loudly. "She wants to get away, too."

"What's in Louisiana?" Jewel asked blankly.

"Welcome," Arcana said. "The town, I mean. Welcome, Louisiana. Where the Labelle twins lived."

"Oh. I thought that all happened a long time ago."

"It did, but their house is still standing, and there's a motel we could stay at right outside of town. Just for a little while. For the summer."

"Dia and Loreley would miss us," Dezy argued weakly.

"We'll email and text and stuff. Please, Jewel?"

"Is there a hospital nearby?"

"Yeah."

"Maybe not close enough," Dezy said, sensing a way to change Jewel's mind.

"It's just a few miles away. We'll be fine."

"Why don't you wanna go, Dezy?"

"Because I don't care about the Labelle twins," she snapped.

"A vacation might be nice, though." We could see that Jewel was already convinced, so Dezy sighed and slumped her head against Arcana's shoulder.

"Whatever. Nobody vacations in fucking Louisiana," she muttered.

"Daddy?"

We almost never spoke to our father, but Arcana braved the rose garden to approach him after we had Jewel's permission. "What?" he asked, not looking up from watering his rosebushes.

"Can we go to Louisiana with Jewel for the summer?"

"Sure."

We were pretty positive he hadn't even heard the question.

So Jewel booked a long stay at the Welcome Inn, and we started to pack our bags for our first ever vacation. Medical bills had eaten up all our money, and our fragile health made it risky for us to travel anywhere without a nearby hospital, but Jewel seemed more reckless than usual after Rose Red's murder. We got the feeling she would have taken any excuse to get away from home, however slim.

Arcana was buzzing with excitement, but Dezy became sullen and withdrawn, muttering bitterly in her ear about how selfish she was being. While neither of us particularly wanted to travel before Arcana got her idea about the Labelle twins, Dezy was actively afraid to leave Eureka Springs. We had only ever slept in our house, Loreley's house, or a hospital; motels were completely foreign to us.

"Aren't they dirty?" Dezy whined. "Our immune system isn't very strong. We shouldn't stay at some cheap, dirty motel."

"We'll be fine," Arcana said. She had made up her mind to go, and no force on Earth could have stopped her.

"I've heard there's some beautiful nature down there. And I've never been on a train before!" Jewel exclaimed, pouring white wine into a water bottle.

"I hate trains," Dezy said.

"You literally know nothing about trains, so shut up," Arcana snapped. "It's gonna be great."

"We never do what *I* wanna do."

"You'll love it. Louisiana's great."

"If you try to break into the Labelle house, I'll scream at the top of my lungs."

"I'll cover your mouth."

"Why can't we just stay here? We could go on a ghost tour at the Crescent Hotel if you wanna be all obsessive about dead people."

"Desdemona, *stop.*"

She stopped.

I think I should warn you right now that the rest of the story might not sound real. I told Loreley what happened when she came to visit me after the separation surgery, when I became *me* instead of *we*, and she just laughed at me. She tried to apologize, but I quickly told her it was fine, I knew it sounded crazy.

"I must be high," I said weakly. "I'm on a lot of painkillers, you know."

But I wasn't high, at least not high enough to forget what I saw, and I'm not crazy. I'm not misremembering or exaggerating. Everything I'm about to tell you, everything about the Labelle twins, about the alligator farm, about Welcome, is true. Everything about Liliana is true.

I want you to remember that what I tell you about Liliana, in particular, is very, very true.

We went to Louisiana by train because Dezy was afraid of air travel, and Jewel thought airports would be bad for us. "Too crowded, everybody staring, super stressful," she declared. "Plus, flights get canceled all the time and I don't even know how we'd figure out seating—actually, I don't think the seatbelts would fit you girls at all…"

"What if the train crashes, though?" Dezy asked in a last-ditch effort to get out of the trip.

"Don't be stupid. Train crashes are super rare," Arcana scoffed.

"I got us a sleeper car, so we'll have privacy," Jewel added.

The Amtrak station was a nightmare. There weren't many people there, but all eyes in the building turned to us as soon as we walked in, stayed on us when they realized why Arcana was carrying Dezy, why we were sharing a dress. (We used to laugh about the musical *Side Show,* about Daisy and Violet Hilton, particularly "We Share Everything" sung by two singleton actresses pretending to be conjoined. Arcana often sang the titular line in a deliberately wobbly falsetto when we got dressed.)

We sat next to Jewel in an astonishingly uncomfortable plastic chair, Dezy able to make eye contact with everyone trying to stare at us behind Arcana's back, but it didn't really do much. When Arcana held eye contact with adults, they usually looked away, ashamed, but Dezy barely registered as human in most people's minds. She was, by definition, *not* a parasitic twin; that didn't stop people from thinking of her as one. The train was almost three hours late, and the woman who took our bags looked like she might throw up when she saw us.

"This isn't really how I pictured trains," Jewel said sadly as we got settled in our sleeper car. We all sat on the bottom bunk, looking out the window, and we all jolted when the train started moving. "That's fun!" Jewel exclaimed.

"It's cool," Arcana said. The train picked up speed, and Dezy held on tighter. "I used to have dreams about being in the ocean, and it felt like our bed was moving. This is like that, right, Dezy?"

"Sure."

We had never left Arkansas before, so even though we dozed off an hour into the trip, Jewel shook us awake when we crossed the state line into Texas.

"It's just another place," Dezy groaned.

An hour outside of New Orleans, the train stopped suddenly, not at a station. We waited patiently for half an hour, until Jewel finally got up, closing the door carefully behind her, to see what the hold-up was. "I hate trains," Dezy announced.

"Bet you'd hate planes even more," Arcana said, unwilling to admit that our vacation was off to a rocky start.

"Bad news," Jewel said when she returned, her lips drawn into a tight frown. "The train hit somebody."

"What?"

"They wouldn't give me any details, but it's pretty clear the person didn't make it." Jewel cleared her throat awkwardly. "We'll be here for a few hours, at least. There's some stuff that needs to happen with the police, apparently."

"How could they not hear the train coming?" Dezy asked blankly.

"They jumped," Arcana guessed. "I read an article about train engineers who've had people jump in front of the train. They say they feel like they murdered somebody, 'cause they can't stop it in time. It takes a really long time for trains to stop after you pull the brake."

"Maybe they just fell onto the tracks or something," Jewel said.

"Doubt it."

"Seems like a bad omen," Dezy said, but no one responded.

When we got to the Welcome Inn, it was pouring down rain. Louisiana was humid and hot as hell, and even Arcana was clearly starting to regret dragging us there. Jewel blatantly poured more white wine into her water bottle in the backseat of the Uber.

"Where, uh, where are y'all from?" the driver asked. He was clearly trying not to stare at us in the rearview mirror and had politely avoided mentioning our conjoinment.

"Eureka Springs, Arkansas," we said. If the driver was uncomfortable with our speaking in unison, he didn't say anything.

"I've never been up that way. Never been too clear if Arkansas's North or South."

"South," Jewel said firmly.

"I guess anything that's not *Deep* South is North to me," he laughed. "Y'all been down here before?"

"No, sir."

"What brings you here? There's not much over this way. Welcome's a borderline ghost town."

"I'm interested in the Labelle twins," Arcana said. "You heard of them?"

"Oh, sure. Everybody 'round here has." We could tell he was just itching to pry, but he restrained himself, so Arcana decided to take pity on him.

"We're conjoined twins," she said, addressing the elephant in the Uber, "which I guess is why I'm so fascinated by them." Her word choice made Dezy flinch, remembering how Jewel had said Mr. Smith was *fascinated* by us.

"That must be very… that must be a very unique life experience. Good to have all kinds of perspectives, outlooks, you know," the driver offered.

"Yep."

"Well, while you're in Welcome, you should know that there's two restaurants. One of them's called Welcome Restaurant and the other one's called Virginia's, and you wanna go to Virginia's. Welcome Restaurant used to be alright, but the cook's getting on up there in years, and now everything's burned or half-frozen. Virginia's, though, they make some of the best food you've ever had. The owner's named Cheryl now, but Virginia was her mama. Family recipes. There's a little general store where you can get whatever you need, and the Welcome Inn has a microwave in the hall to heat food up."

"Did you grow up here?" Jewel asked.

"No, ma'am, but my wife did. Some of the folks still speak Louisiana French."

"Is that different than French?" Jewel asked.

"It's a dialect, I s'pose. Don't think anyone from France would understand a word of it, but it's basically French with a Southern accent and a bunch of random words from other languages tossed in. Your Labelle twins would've spoken it, maybe not as a first language."

"That's cool," Arcana said eagerly. "Do you speak it at all?"

"Oh, a little. You don't need to know any to get by. *Cher* means 'my dear'. The wife likes that one," he said, laughing brightly. "What's Eureka Springs like?"

"Beautiful little town up in the mountains. There's a huge, haunted hotel that kind of overlooks the whole place," Jewel said.

"You believe in ghosts?"

"I've known people who worked there, and they swear up and down it's really haunted. I don't know if I believe *them*." Jewel giggled. "There's a morgue in the basement. Nonfunctional, of course, but the building used to be a hospital run by a psychotic doctor."

"He wasn't actually a real doctor," Arcana chimed in.

"Well, that's true. Quite a few people died there. It went through several phases, actually, wasn't it a college at one point?"

"I think so."

"They kept the morgue?" the driver asked.

"Being haunted is their big selling point," Jewel explained. "Well, that and being gorgeous. It really is one of the most beautiful buildings I've ever seen."

"I'm scared to go inside," Dezy admitted.

"Some folks say the Labelle house is haunted," the driver said, lowering his voice to a dramatic whisper. "Not sure how much I believe in ghosts, myself, but it's definitely spooky. Don't go out there at night, though, it's still got the gator pools just behind it. Well, a ways away, I guess. Can't be safe, though."

"Are there still a bunch of alligators?"

"Oh, yeah. They'll walk right across Main Street sometimes."

"Is that safe?" Jewel asked anxiously.

"I mean, you wanna avoid 'em, but it's not like they go in people's houses," the driver said.

"Huh."

"What else is there to do in Welcome?" Arcana asked.

"Not a damn thing. It's the restaurants, the Labelle house, and gator sightings. No jobs, either. Did y'all really come here just 'cause of the twins?"

"Yep."

"Good to have a hobby, I guess."

The Welcome Inn was cute, clean, and air conditioned. "Thank God," Jewel sighed, lifting her hair off the back of her neck. She'd always dyed it platinum before, but when she turned thirty she started going for a darker blonde. The desk clerk dropped our keys twice and stammered out every word she said, staring blatantly at us. Dezy disliked her immediately; Arcana appreciated her lack of false politeness.

"Which bed do you want?" Dezy asked Jewel as we walked into our room.

"I'll take the one by the window." Jewel did not trust windows anymore, for obvious reasons, and had actually rearranged our bedroom so we were further away from ours. She triple checked that the window and door were locked before we fell asleep that first night, but once she was sure we were safe, she was out in seconds. The twins stayed awake a little longer.

"It's not that bad here, right?" Arcana whispered.

"It's hot," Dezy responded.

"But the swamp is beautiful. I love all the trees, don't you?"

"Arkansas's way prettier."

"Louisiana's a different kind of pretty. That driver was super nice."

"People are nice back home, too."

"We're not gonna be here that long," Arcana sighed.

"Everyone's gonna treat us like circus freaks."

"Okay, you're in a mood. Just go to sleep."

"This bed's uncomfortable," Dezy whined, sounding like she might start crying at any moment. Arcana hushed her, pressed our foreheads together and stroked her hair until she finally fell asleep.

Jewel checked her phone first thing in the morning and flinched at the long list of missed calls, all from Margaret. "She is *pissed,*" she said, whistling through her teeth.

"Why?" Dezy asked suspiciously.

"Oh, I didn't tell her we were leaving."

"*What?!*" We were yelling, but we figured it was justified. How could Jewel have forgotten to tell Margaret that we were leaving home, going to hang out in a creepy Louisiana ghost town for the next two months?

"Ask for forgiveness, not permission," Jewel said weakly. "I knew she'd say no and make a huge-ass deal about it, so I just told her last night. I called from the train while y'all were asleep."

"We thought she knew!"

"She does now."

"What the fuck?" Arcana said.

"Look, your dad's your legal guardian, and he said it was fine."

"He's crazy," Dezy pointed out.

"Margaret'll get over it, I'm sure," Jewel said, waving a hand flippantly. "I'm gonna call her back, and then we can go check out that Virginia's place for breakfast."

Chapter Nine

Dezy hated Louisiana because she hated being away from home, but she had to admit Welcome was a cute town. Nowhere near as cute as Eureka Springs, of course, not nearly nice enough to make up for being gone so long, but fairly pleasant in its own way. Arcana saw her looking around and smirked, so to save face, Dezy announced, "It'd almost be nice if the air wasn't so sticky."

"You love it," Arcana said brightly.

"*Love* is a really strong word."

"I don't see any alligators yet," Jewel remarked. Her arms were crossed carefully over her breasts; she ran back to our room to take her push-up bra off as soon as she stepped outside and felt how hot it was, then immediately became self-conscious about her nipples showing.

"Jewel, can you put your arms down? You look angry," Arcana said.

"If I—"

"Everyone knows you have nipples. Literally everyone except us has nipples," Arcana said, rolling her eyes.

"I see you're really leaning into being a teenager," Jewel muttered. We didn't run into anyone else on Main Street (which was actually the *only* street in Welcome), and there were only three patrons in Virginia's, an old lady at the counter and a stunningly beautiful young woman sitting across from a little girl in a booth. The old lady was chatting with an even older woman we figured had to be Cheryl, and they all turned to look when the door opened.

"Whoa," the old woman at the counter said out loud, then blushed and looked down at the counter.

"Hi," we said, because they were staring, and because we always liked to establish that Dezy could speak right off the bat.

"Y'all from outta town?" the woman behind the counter asked.

"Yep," Jewel said, putting a hand on Arcana's shoulder to guide us into a booth. The only employee brought us menus right away, smiling nervously, unable to take her eyes off us.

"I'm Cheryl," she said with an air of forced cheer, "and, uh, I run this place. You can come by whenever for… food. I mean, yeah. It's… we got food."

"I should certainly hope so," Jewel said, sounding so much like Margaret we almost laughed out loud.

"We're thoracopagus conjoined twins," Arcana said, technically to Cheryl but loud enough that the entire restaurant could hear, "if y'all were wondering. We're joined at the chest."

"Oh, no, I wasn't—"

"It's fine if you were. Everybody always is."

"Nice to meet you," Cheryl said weakly before scurrying away like a mouse. She returned a few minutes later when she realized she hadn't taken our drink orders. We ordered ice water, and Jewel, who had already started drinking white wine from her water bottle, said she was fine.

"I wanna go to the Labelle house today," Arcana said at once, quietly. "Can we?"

"Sounds good," Jewel said. She squinted at the menu. "I think I need glasses."

After a few minutes sitting in awkward, sleepy silence, watching the fan move slowly overhead, Dezy noticed the little girl stand up at the other end of the restaurant and practically run over to us. "Hey!" she said brightly, like we knew each other.

"Hello," said Dezy.

"Where are your parents?" asked Arcana, who hated children.

"I'm Lili," the girl chirped. "I heard you say something about the Labelle house?"

"Yeah," we said, glancing at each other. Arcana had been whispering, and the restaurant couldn't possibly be so quiet she'd heard us from across the room, but maybe she just guessed where we were going. After all, there was no other reason to visit Welcome.

"Is it because they were Siamese twins, too?"

"Conjoined," Arcana snapped. "Do we look like we're from Siam, kid?"

"It's called Thailand now," Jewel reminded us.

"I'm from England," the girl said, even though she didn't have a British accent. She didn't have a Cajun accent, either; we couldn't have told you where she was from, hearing her speak. She was short and skinny, with long black hair tied into an elaborate braid crown.

"When did you move here?" Dezy asked, trying to be polite.

"A long time ago. I could tell you a lot about the Labelle twins, if you're interested? My grandmother knew them."

"You just told us you're from England," Arcana said, rolling her eyes.

"Oh, yes! Well, I was born in England, but my mother is from Welcome originally." She pointed to the woman sitting alone at a nearby table. "My sister was born in New Orleans."

"Did your mom travel a lot?" Dezy asked.

"Mmm. Where are you three from?"

"Arkansas," Arcana said flatly.

"I've never been, but I hear it's beautiful." Lili stepped aside so Cheryl could bring us our food, then smiled politely, bowed her head, and said, "I'll leave you alone to eat, but I have some things that belonged to the Labelle twins, if you'd like to have a look. I'll ask my mother if you can come over after breakfast."

"Hold on—" Arcana began, but Lili was already walking away. "Is she telling the truth?" she demanded of poor Cheryl, who clearly wanted us to eat and leave as fast as possible.

"Yeah. That fam'ly been here a while," she said reluctantly. "They come and go, but her gramma definitely knew the twins when she was a little girl. Think they move between here and New Orleans a lot."

"I wonder what she has," Arcana murmured, looking back over at the sisters. Lili was talking softly to the woman, patting the back of her hand.

"Her sister's beautiful," Jewel commented. "Even prettier than Loreley, huh?"

"Maybe you shouldn't be drinking so early," Arcana said.

As soon as we finished eating, Lili, who hadn't ordered anything in the time we were there and was almost certainly loitering, trotted over to our table with her gorgeous sister in tow. It was a little strange, the little girl leading the grown woman by the hand, but we didn't comment. "This is Lina," she said, gesturing to the woman, who frowned and blinked at us. She was so gorgeous it was kind of shocking up close—like an airbrushed supermodel, but real and right in front of us. She was the most beautiful woman we'd ever seen. "Actually, I didn't catch your names earlier?"

"Dezy and Arcana," we said.

"Mama," Lina said, dragging both syllables out, *maaaa-maaaa.*

"We're going *home* now," Lili told her slowly, tilting her head back to smile up at her. "*Home.* We are going *home.*"

"Mmm."

"Is she okay?" Dezy asked. Arcana pulled her hair sharply.

"Oh, she's… fine," Lili said with a sad smile. "Just a little slow. Our mother is coming to pick us up, she'll drive us out to our house. We can wait outside, if you'd like?"

"No," we said quickly. "It's way too hot."

"You're very synchronized," Lili said, raising an eyebrow. "The Labelle twins were like that, too. They often spoke in perfect unison."

"You must read a lot," Jewel remarked, "to be so well-spoken at your age. How old are you, honey?"

"Ten." Lili smirked, close-lipped, as she said it. "Lina's nineteen."

"Mama," Lina whined again.

"We're going home very soon, dear."

A middle-aged woman with her hair dyed a lurid green pulled up outside a few minutes later, and Jewel whistled through her teeth at the sight of her. "*She* looks interesting," she muttered under her breath.

"This is my mother, Stella. She's very into the goth trend," Lili said cheerfully.

We followed our strange guides outside, and Stella—who, despite the unbearable heat, was dressed entirely in black—glowered at us silently as we got in the backseat of the car. She didn't even seem to notice that we were conjoined. Her face only softened when Lina hugged her clumsily; she wrapped her arms around her older daughter and murmured a greeting, rubbing her back in soothing circles before Lili urged her into the car and buckled her seatbelt for her.

It was a slightly uncomfortable car ride, squished next to Jewel in the backseat with Stella glaring at us in the rearview, but we didn't complain. Dezy was exhausted from the humidity and just wanted to peel our clothes off and pass out, but Arcana was excited to see what this strange little family could show us about the Labelle twins.

"What's y'all's last name?" she asked eagerly, clearly hoping the grandmother had been mentioned in the biography she'd been reading over and over again.

"Oh, uh, Jones," Lili said quickly. "Yours?"

"Gardner."

"Everyone calls us the Garden girls," Dezy mumbled sleepily.

"How adorable!"

"Weird kid," Jewel said under her breath.

The Jones family lived in a small but well-kept house a little ways outside of town, just far enough that Dezy began to worry we were being kidnapped before we finally arrived. Lili led the way inside and practically ran down the hall to show us a library, dusty and smelling of mold. "This was my grandmother's," she explained. "There's a trunk over here that may interest you. Sage Labelle collected porcelain dolls, and she gifted my grandmother quite a few before her death. Here."

"Whoa," Arcana breathed, staring raptly into the open trunk. "Can I touch them?"

"I don't see why not."

Arcana picked them up, showed them to a completely uninterested Dezy. They were obviously antique, but kept in very good condition, and she laid them back down almost reverently.

"This is what will interest you most," Lili said, gesturing for us to follow her to a shelf, which she climbed to grab a huge, crumbling, leatherbound journal. "Florence Labelle's diary. I have Sage's sketchbook in a drawer, if you'd like to flip through that as well?"

"You're joking," Arcana said. Her eyes were so wide Dezy thought they might pop out of her skull. "How?"

"My grandmother took it from their home the night of the accident. Her handwriting can be a bit hard to read at times, but it's a fascinating piece of—"

"Can we borrow it?" Arcana blurted out.

"No. You may read it while you're here, and you're more than *welcome*—" Lili giggled "—to stop by whenever. Right, Stella?"

"Sure," Stella grunted.

"You call your mom by her first name?" Dezy asked.

"Oh, she's kind of a hippie."

"Can I start reading it now?"

"Be my guest."

After the surgery, Lili was kind enough to lend me the diary. She said she doesn't care if I publish this, because no one will ever believe me. So here it is, Florence Labelle's life in her own words.

Once upon a time, a woman from New Orleans fell in love with a man from a small town in Acadiana. She left her glittering city of sin and sex and song to move into his family estate, a huge mansion turning to rot just a decade after being built, surrounded by monsters on all sides. Her husband raised monsters for their meat and leather, and she hated them, but she stayed for love of her husband.

The woman quickly fell pregnant, and she sewed lightweight baby clothes to keep her son or daughter cool in the hot Southern summers. She painted a mural of the French

Quarter's skyline on the nursery wall and daydreamed of home, cooped herself up in her room to stay safe from the monsters that she feared would invade her husband's home to eat her baby. She became paranoid and distrustful of everyone, even her husband. She stopped attending Mass.

She went into labor in the dead of night, a Southern summer night, with air so thick it was like breathing underwater. The stench of blood carried through the heavy air and permeated the whole house, and the woman died before she ever saw her baby.

Her babies.

The woman from New Orleans had given birth to a monster. The townspeople whispered that God was punishing her for the sins she must have committed in the big city, and the new father locked his progeny up in the house, only allowing it out to feed the monsters in the swamp, because it had more in common with them than any human.

The monster was almost a girl, but it had two heads with two temperaments. They called it Florence-and-Sage or Sage-Florence; Sage was sweet and quiet and good, while Florence was mercurial and mischievous and evil.

The monster's father, however, claimed it was really two girls, two normal girls who happened to be Siamese twins. I am Florence; my sister is Sage. I love fairytales; Sage loves painting. I used to break her dolls to make her cry, so the maids started telling people I was the evil twin. They didn't know Sage dug her nails into my hip until I bled. We have a pet monster, a two-headed alligator hatched four days after our birth, and each head has its own personality, just like us.

We call her Ally-Ally. Left Ally is more playful, while Right Ally mostly likes to eat and sleep. She doesn't fight herself. Like us, she has learned to cooperate. We alternate feeding days, because when it's my turn, I want to break the chicken's neck first, but Sage wants to watch Ally-Ally kill it.

I'm writing a diary because Sage draws for at least an hour every night, and I've grown bored of listening to the radio.

"She writes like her life is a story that happened to somebody else," Arcana said.

"It's a very unique diary, isn't it?" Lili asked. Dezy squinted at her, wondering if we'd talked like that when we were children.

Once upon a time, a little girl named Adelaide befriended Sage-Florence by sheer accident. Her parents owned Welcome Restaurant, so they often went to the alligator farm to buy meat, and Adelaide was dragged along because she needed friends. She had a beautiful name, but she was not a beautiful girl; she was very short, very round, and very nearsighted. She cried easily, a trait Sage-Florence mercilessly exploited.

Florence would throw bugs at Adelaide, pull her hair, scratch her face, break her toys (even though they were the two-headed girl's toys in the first place) and threaten to feed her to the alligators, and then Sage would comfort her when she cried, tell her she would keep Florence under control, kiss her forehead and wipe her tears away. The good-twin-bad-twin routine was Sage's idea. She always had the best ideas.

Adelaide liked playing house, but Sage always wanted to play hide-and-seek, and because she wanted to stay on Sage's good side so she might keep Florence under some sort of control, Adelaide went along with whatever game she wanted to play. On a stiflingly hot day in mid-August, Florence told Adelaide she'd never pick on her again if she could hide for an hour without being found.

Sage-Florence counted to ten, and Adelaide ran away. The two-headed girl searched her entire house, but couldn't find Adelaide anywhere, so after an hour had passed Florence yelled that Adelaide won, it was safe to come out now. Adelaide did not reappear. Sage repeated the same information, thinking she might be scared of Florence; still, she did not reappear. The two-headed girl went back to playing by herself, bored of looking, under the assumption Adelaide would come back when she was ready.

Adelaide did not reappear.

The police were called, and Sage-Florence was practically interrogated. The cops didn't trust her. Sage could make herself cry on command, which she started doing to make them go away, but they weren't moved by her tears and started screaming at her to tell them where Adelaide had gone. Her father stepped in then, told the cops his daughter had done nothing wrong, and they left, furious and disgusted.

It was so, so hot that day, so humid you woke up sweating and were sticky all day long, and the next day was even worse. Around noon the day after Adelaide disappeared, Sage-Florence noticed a bad smell in her room, but ignored it at first. As the day went on and got hotter, the smell got worse, and finally Sage pointed out that it was coming from the trunk at the foot of her bed.

Florence was afraid to open it, but Sage said she wouldn't speak to her again if she didn't. She was silent for an hour before Florence started crying for her forgiveness and agreed to open the trunk. The lid was so heavy the two-headed girl couldn't open it on her own, so she called for her father in two voices and asked for his help. He opened the trunk, screamed, and slammed the lid shut again. The police were called. Sage-Florence was not allowed back in her room all day.

Adelaide, of course, was dead. Officially, the police figured she must have hidden in our trunk during hide-and-seek but been unable to open the lid from the inside. Unofficially, they made it clear they suspected us of murder, but they couldn't prove it because the lid wasn't locked. I thought we might be a little guilty since Adelaide was hiding from me more than anything; Sage said it wasn't our fault at all, and she was just stupid.

But it's Sage, not me, who sees her ghost.

"I read about Adelaide," Arcana said. "The biography didn't mention anything about the cops suspecting the twins, though. It made it sound like everyone just knew it was a horrible accident."

"Well, all those girls were eight years old at the time," Lili said. "They couldn't justify putting little girls down as official suspects, and Adelaide probably could have fought the twins off if she wanted to. They weren't very strong."

"Mama," Lina whined, startling us. She'd been sitting on the floor, playing quietly with dolls, while Arcana read the diary (Florence wrote in sprawling cursive that took quite a while to puzzle out), and we'd completely forgotten she was there. "Mama. *Mama!*"

"Shh," Lili soothed, patting her head. "I'm terribly sorry, but would you girls mind coming back later? Lina's not so good with strangers. You can come back tomorrow, if you'd like?"

"That works," Jewel said quickly.

"Oh- alright," Arcana said, disappointed.

"You girls?" Dezy muttered.

Coincidentally, at the same time Arcana started reading Florence Labelle's diary, Loreley emailed us saying Risa's little sister had brought her *Risa's* old diary after reading it cover to cover twice. *She said she thought I should have it. She found it under her bed when she was cleaning out her room, in a shoebox. I've been reading it over and over again lately. I don't have anything else that belonged to her.*

We loved Risa, and she died because of us. I told Loreley I wanted to tell her story here, and Loreley gave me her diary right away, even though there are parts that make her sound really terrible. I didn't include all of it, just the important parts about her and Loreley. Tiff said I should split it up into sections so I don't have to stop the whole story; here is the first entry of another dead girl's diary.

Dearest,

I think "dear diary" sounds too cliche, don't you? Like I should be lying on my bed kicking my legs and drawing hearts around some guy's name in a little pink notebook. "Dearest" sounds more… dignified. Actually, it sounds kind of Jane Austen, doesn't it? I think Jane Austen was a lesbian. She never married, but she was proposed to once, and she said yes but then literally ran away in the middle of the night. Wish I liked her books more. She never wrote a single scene without a woman present.

My new tattoo hurts like hell! It's only been a day since I got it, so I figure it'll settle down pretty soon, but it's my first one so I'm kind of freaking out about it. Mom says it gets easier every time. She got drunk at my graduation party and offered to pay for my first tattoo, and she stuck to it when she sobered up. It's a spotted hyena skull. I fucking love spotted hyenas, they're so completely bizarre. And they're matriarchal!

I kept a diary for years when I was a kid, but I kind of stopped in high school because I had so much other shit going on. My aunt gave me this really nice journal as a graduation present, so I figure I might as well put it to good use, right? There's still a lot going on in my life right now, but the main thing is that I have a job interview tomorrow. It's probably a bad idea to go.

I saw one of those help wanted ads on the library cork board with the little pull-off things at the bottom asking for a caregiver, and I grabbed one without really thinking because I took care of my grandpa for a while before he died, then when I was walking back out of the library I looked at the ad again and realized who it was about: Loreley Washington. I should have just thrown the paper away and gone home, but I kept it, called her parents, and the interview is tomorrow.

Loreley was a year ahead of me in high school, and we were on the track team together. She was the fastest girl on the team and probably the prettiest girl in school, and also a complete fucking cunt. I have literally never met a meaner human being. She did a bunch of shit I don't want to think about anymore, but to make a long story short, she decided she hated me as soon as she met me. The worst part was that nothing made me feel good about myself except running, but I had to see Loreley on the track team, and she was better than me at everything.

After I talked to Mrs. Washington, I sat in my car thinking about how I tried to kill myself in high school. I'm not gonna say it was totally Loreley's fault, because that would give her too much power over me (I've been reading a lot of books written by therapists), but she was definitely a major contributing factor. I guess word got around town, because when I came back to school, Loreley came up to me and said, "It's pretty embarrassing to fail at dying. Why don't you use a gun next time?"

I guess I should mention that the whole reason Loreley needs a caregiver in the first place is she was in this horrible car crash last year and broke her spine. Her sister died, too. I actually laughed out loud when I read about the accident in the newspaper, then I wanted to kill myself all over again because how horrible is that? Her sister sounds really sweet, from what I've heard. It's a tragedy that she died so young. I tried to tell myself it's sad that Loreley got hurt, but I've never been able to feel bad for her. At all.

To be completely honest with you, I'm only going to the interview because I want to see her. I haven't seen her once since the accident. I know she's paralyzed, but I don't know how bad it is. I'm sure she'll whine to Mommy and Daddy that she doesn't want me, I just need to know what her life is like now.

Love,
Risa

Chapter Ten

"What a weird fucking kid, right?" Jewel said as soon as we were back in our motel room. "She sounds so formal!"

"There's probably not many other kids her age around here, so she must read a lot," Arcana said.

"Are we really going back tomorrow?" Dezy asked.

"Of course we are! Are you kidding?"

"How do you know it's really Florence's diary?"

"Why would she lie? It's obviously old."

"I dunno. She's just weird, and it's weird that she has it."

"There's, like, ten people in Welcome," Arcana said, shrugging. "Somebody was bound to have a connection to the Labelle twins."

I know it might be a spoiler, but I hate mysteries, so I'll tell you now: yes, it really was Florence Labelle's diary.

"Margaret's pretty furious," Jewel told us that evening, picking at her PB&J. She had come home from the general store looking rattled and refused to talk about her experience there beyond muttering that the owner was a creep. "I told her it's perfectly safe, but she's threatening to call the cops. Apparently your father had to get involved."

"Daddy got involved in something?" Dezy asked, stunned.

"Yep. He told her she's not your mother." We could just picture him, probably covered in dirt from the garden, coolly telling the woman who he resented for keeping us alive that she had no say in what we did.

"Maybe we should of talked to her about it a little more," Arcana said, squirming guiltily.

"There's no way you could have convinced her." Jewel opened a screw top bottle of wine and started drinking straight from it, and we wisely decided to drop the subject.

Rose Red was an insufferable sister, but we privately thought she was always Jewel's favorite Garden girl. As long as everything stuck to a routine she understood and everyone followed the rules, she wasn't a hard child to babysit. Once, when we were very young, we sat under the Christmas tree and watched Jewel teach Rose Red how to wrap gifts.

"You want to make sure you get your corners right," she said gently, folding the paper over a book intended for Tiff. "Like this, okay?"

"Like this," Rose Red muttered. She was in her repetition phase at the time.

"Very good! Now you get your tape…"

Christmas was Arcana's favorite holiday, but Dezy preferred Easter. Margaret would spend the night for these holidays and wake us all up early in the mornings to make us stand at the end of the hall so she could take our photo, before allowing us to run into the living room for presents or Easter baskets. On Christmas, we all got three gifts each; one from "Santa", one from Margaret, and one from Jewel. Santa apparently favored knock-off Barbies, while Margaret always gave everyone a book and Jewel came up with the most random shit imaginable. Garden gnomes, earrings shaped like Rubik's cubes, action figures from superhero movies we hadn't seen, mysterious Norwegian candy. Easter meant little baskets with chocolate bunnies, itchy dresses, and an egg hunt in the backyard.

Holiday morning memories had a warm glow for us, giggling on the floor with our sisters, Margaret and Jewel watching from the couch, and feeling, always, like we had beat the odds by surviving another year. Arcana always said she wanted to see one more Christmas; for Dezy, it was one more Easter. Neither of us measured time by our birthday.

Lili had given us Stella's phone number, so Arcana texted her at 10AM the next morning, which she considered the earliest acceptable time to ask if we could come over. Stella's response was a curt *Fine*.

"I get the feeling Stella doesn't like us," Jewel said. The Jones family didn't live very far from the Welcome Inn, so we walked the ten minutes there, panting in the heat, rather than asking Stella to come pick us up again.

"I think she's just grumpy," Arcana said. Dezy twined her sister's hair through her fingers, watching a frog hop across the path behind us.

"*Welcome* back!" Lili cheered, throwing the front door open before we were even on the porch. "It's so good to have you again! We never see new people, you know."

"Hello," Stella grunted. Lina, who was clinging to Lili's hand, just blinked at us.

"How many people live in this town?" Jewel asked.

"Oh, about a hundred, maybe a little less," Lili said. We followed her down the hall to the library, where Florence's diary was already lying on the table. Arcana sat down facing it fully, which meant Dezy was stuck staring at the shelves behind us, but before she could settle into a daydream Lina walked up to stand over us. Without warning, she put her hand between our necks and touched the place where we joined together, mumbling something as she did. Dezy instinctively reached to slap her, while Arcana jerked away.

"Don't touch us!"

Startled, Lina fell back, and Stella yanked her away from us, pulling her into a hug and shoving her face into her shoulder absurdly fast. Lina's shoulders began to tremble, and we heard her sobbing, but Dezy thought that might very well have been because Stella snatched her away so abruptly.

"I'm so sorry," Lili said. Stella practically dragged poor Lina out of the room. "She was just curious, and we can't… we don't really have a way to communicate with her. She meant you no harm."

"Okay," Arcana said slowly, "but, like, she *really* can't do that. We're not a freak show."

"I understand. I'll make sure it doesn't happen again."

Arcana turned back to the diary, but Dezy kept staring at the door Stella had dragged Lina off through. When Lina touched us, she had mumbled something under her breath; it was hard to make out, but Dezy was pretty sure she'd said *Sage.*

Once upon a time, a little girl died in Sage-Florence's bedroom, and everyone in town quietly believed the two-headed girl was responsible. Her father told her not to think about it, offered to let her move rooms, but she refused. Florence wanted to leave; Sage wanted to stay. The two heads argued for weeks about it, Florence saying it was creepy, Sage saying she wanted to keep playing with Adelaide, and finally she decided to stay because Sage always won in the end.

Sage spoke to the dead. No one believed she could do this except Florence, who felt cheated by her lack of second sight.

It seemed to her that Sage had taken every good quality and left her with nothing, so she insisted to anyone who asked that she was one person with two heads, one soul in two minds, because otherwise she knew she had very little to offer.

Sage-Florence never visited Adelaide's grave. Florence felt too guilty, and Sage thought people would judge her harshly, whisper that she was gloating. Florence was very sorry that Adelaide was dead; Sage was thrilled to have a permanent playmate, one who never seemed to leave our room.

Lately, Sage has been taking to Adelaide more and more. She sits on the end of our bed for hours, chattering with thin air, and I just have to let it happen. If I try to interrupt, Sage just sneers, "She doesn't like you." If I wanted to be cruel, I would tell her she's too old for imaginary friends, but I believe that, at the very least, Sage believes she's talking to a real ghost. When we were children, I really thought her ghosts were real, but now I just think that if she's insane there are worse ways it could manifest.

Dearest,

I had my job interview today. It was pretty intense, honestly, and I think I feel like more stuff happened than really did, but short version, I got the job. Long version, it was crazy, and I feel crazy for going at all. I feel even crazier for ACCEPTING the job. I woke up thinking I'd made a huge mistake, but I made myself get up anyway and go out. The Washingtons live in this huge old house on a hill, which I remember very fucking distinctly (there was a track team sleepover in high school that I never want to think about again) and kind of hate them for.

Mrs. Washington answered when I rang the doorbell, which isn't really surprising, but I guess I was kind of expecting a maid to answer. Like Downton Abbey, even though their house isn't anywhere near that big or fancy. She didn't recognize me, thank God, just invited me in all sweet and nervous. I think she's on lithium or some other 1950s housewife shit like that. She kept saying it was so kind of me to answer the ad, and it's been "so hard for Loreley" (which I almost snorted at), and she's having a lot of trouble finding someone to be a full-time caregiver.

"Can I ask why she needs a full-time caregiver?"

"She's paraplegic, and she has some trouble... she hit her head pretty hard in the... she has epilepsy now, but that's it. She's not retarded." Mrs. Washington said it so defensively I figured Loreley probably was retarded, and told myself I wouldn't take the job if she was, because I don't know if I could be nice to her. (Turns out she's not.) "And she's lonely."

I was thinking that Loreley deserves to be lonely when Mrs. Washington sat down across from me in the living room and started telling me all about Loreley's condition and how my job would be to help her get around, monitor her for seizures, make sure she wasn't in one position for too long, and generally spend time with her. She told me Loreley's incontinent, and I had to bite my lip so I wouldn't laugh, which made feel pretty guilty. Then she asked me a bunch of questions about myself, my experience, why I wanted the job, et cetera. I must have answered them all right, because the next thing she did was tell me to wait while she went and got Loreley so we could see if we liked each other. I wanted to tell her, "Nope, we sure don't!" but managed to keep my mouth shut.

It took a pretty long time to get her, but eventually Mrs. Washington brought her out and we both just stared at each other for a long time. I was waiting for her to say she knew me. She never did. She looks pretty terrible, to the point where I just felt sorry for her. She's lost a ton of weight (and she was never anywhere close to fat), she looks kind of grey and tired, and there are huge dark circles under her eyes. Mainly, though, she was so skinny. I could tell she was super underweight even though she was wearing a sweater and a long wool skirt (in June). I think the wheelchair also made her look smaller than she was.

"Hi, Loreley," I finally said. She didn't say anything back, just kind of stared at me with this freaked out deer-in-headlights expression that made me think "yeah, she's definitely brain damaged". I was about to say I should leave when she cleared her throat.

"Hello," she said.

"This is Risa Burke," Mrs. Washington told her. Loreley's eyes got wider, and she looked even more scared, and then I realized she wasn't retarded or crazy at all, she was just scared of me. Me, in particular.

"You're pretty young," she said, sounding really nervous and kind of pissed off. "Do you have any experience in… this field?"

"I took care of my grandfather when he was dying."

"You're, like, eighteen," Loreley snapped. "You're younger than me. I don't—"

"Risa's a sweetheart," Mrs. Washington interrupted. "I think she's perfect. Come back tomorrow at eight, okay, honey?"

I should have said no, but I nodded. "Yes, ma'am," I said. I guess I'll tell you all about my first day tomorrow.

Love,
Risa

"Do you girls want anything to eat?" Lili asked, jerking Arcana out of her intense focus on Florence's diary.

"Uh, no," Arcana said awkwardly.

"Yes, ma'am," Dezy said, then felt stupid for calling little Lili *ma'am.* "I mean, uh, yes, please. Sorry."

"It's quite alright, dear," Lili laughed. "Do you like soup? We have a lot of canned soup. Stella's a bit picky about textures, so it's all potato. There's also some ice cream in the fridge! It's very colorful, I believe it's unicorn themed? Lina picked it out."

"Sure," Dezy said.

So Lili brought us potato soup and unicorn ice cream, and Arcana kept reading Florence's diary.

Once upon a time, Sage-Florence's father taught her how to feed the alligators. He showed her how to open the gates, told her to drop the chicken carcasses in the dark water and leave, to be very, very careful standing on the piers. "Reptiles can't feel love, and they're not smart enough to understand that we feed them, so if you fall in, they'll eat you. They don't have loyalty to their owners. They're not pets, understand?"

He was wrong, though. He was wrong about a lot of things, but he was particularly wrong about alligators and his daughter. Sage-Florence swam with the alligators at night, when no one was watching. She slipped out of the room Adelaide died in to walk the moonlit swamp trails and slide into warm, stinking water to play with her monstrous pets. Ally-Ally was her favorite; Ally-Ally nuzzled at her like a dog.

Sage-Florence was a strong swimmer. Sage liked to float on her back, scratching Ally-Ally under either of her chins, while Florence liked to dive underwater and swim to the bottom of the pool, run her hand through the mud and grass. The alligator pools were naturally occurring sections of swamp water that her father's father had fenced off. Sage thought the alligators loved her because she was a witch; Florence thought they loved her because she was a monster.

I used to threaten Adelaide with the alligators when she didn't do as I said. I told her I'd throw her in the deep end of the biggest pool, and Sage couldn't stop me. I told her the alligators would rip her limb from limb and eat her bones. It was stupid of her to believe me, since I obviously couldn't do anything without Sage's cooperation, so I didn't feel bad when she cried in fear.

Just like Sage talks to Adelaide, I talk to Ally-Ally. I like Left Ally better, but Right Ally is sweet in her own way. This morning, Sage told me I've been wasting time talking to our pet, and I reminded her that she talks to thin air for hours every night. She fell into one of her long, stony silences, and wouldn't speak to me again until I swore I believed she really talks to Adelaide and promised not to spend so long with Ally-Ally from now on.

"This is really fascinating," Arcana mumbled, more to Dezy and herself than anyone else. "The biography said Florence was always unstable, but she makes it sound like Sage is completely unhinged."

"Sage was a very unique young woman," Lili agreed, despite not actually being part of our conversation. "I don't think she was insane in the traditional sense, but she definitely saw the world through a very different lens than most people."

"That reminds me of the thing with Dia's friend," Arcana said, giggling. "Remember?"

"Yeah," Dezy said. We were thinking of the time Dia had a handful of friends over in middle school, and one of them actually passed out when she saw us. Dia didn't bother to wake her up, just stood by and let her friends do it. When the girl came to, she asked if we were an alien, and Dia coldly said *you can interpret reality however you want.* She never invited those friends back, but it became a running joke in our house, repeated anytime someone was blatantly wrong about something. "Sage interpreted reality however she wanted, huh?"

"Can I look at the sketchbook?" Arcana asked hopefully.

"Of course," Lili said, pushing it towards her. "Some of her drawings are rather graphic. I hope that doesn't bother you?"

"Not at all."

Sage's drawings were more than *rather* graphic. For the most part, they were somewhere between self-portraits and medical studies; she drew herself and Florence cut open autopsy style, their shared organs depicted in loving detail, limbs stripped down to the bone. On the sixth page, she abruptly switched to swamp landscapes that looked completely normal unless you looked closely and saw two screaming faces hidden in the mist that rolled through the cyprus trees. Unsurprisingly, she was obsessed with pairs.

There were several drawings of a two-headed alligator that had to be Ally-Ally, a torn-out page here and there, and in the middle, a sudden, shocking drawing of a child's bloated corpse stuffed in a trunk. Arcana quickly flipped past it. The next several showed a little girl sitting atop that same trunk, the twins on their bed, Sage apparently engaged deep in conversation with her. (You could tell the Labelle twins apart easily: Sage was on the right and Florence was on the left.)

Arcana looked through the entire sketchbook, then flipped back to a particular page and held it up for Dezy's inspection. It was a nude woman, probably about forty years old, with noticeable wrinkles around her eyes and mouth. She was leanly muscular, very tall, very pale, with a high forehead and broad hips, black hair streaked with grey. A lot of attention had obviously gone into drawing out her thick, dark body hair, the veins on her sagging breasts, and the stretch marks on her belly. To Dezy, the strangest thing about the painting was that she was hanging from a tree by her knees, grinning upside down at the viewer as menstrual blood matted her pubic hair and trickled down her stomach; to Arcana, turning the sketchbook over for a closer look, the strangest thing was how much she resembled Lili.

"Is this your grandmother?" she asked.

"Yes," Lili said, smiling just like the woman in the drawing. "Sage was very talented, wasn't she?"

"Why's she upside down?" Dezy asked.

"Oh, she was playful like that. Very active all her life."

"There's a few drawings of her in here." Arcana flipped through to another portrait, Lili's grandmother fully dressed in a garden, cooing over a baby alligator, pouring herself a glass of whiskey. Every drawing made a point to show visible signs of age, but if anything, it only emphasized her beauty.

"She was very close to the twins."

"What was her name?"

"Liliana. Family name." Lili smiled at us. "Dezy and Arcana are unusual names."

"Our real names are Desdemona and Deirdre," Dezy explained, "but everybody in our family has a nickname except Jewel."

"I don't need one," Jewel drawled, not looking up from the book Lili had loaned her. "My name describes me perfectly."

Dearest,

First day on the job!!! I didn't expect anything walking in. Yesterday I expected Loreley to tell her mom she knew me, and she didn't. All I knew was that Mrs. Washington was going to show me how to do everything, and then just leave us alone. I still don't think Loreley actually needs a caregiver, but what do I know?

Mrs. Washington acted like I was a long-lost relative when she opened the door, which made me feel more and more like I'm making a mistake. It's been a year since the accident, and they've definitely had other caregivers, so the fact that they're hiring randos from the library cork board plus what I know about Loreley makes me think she's driven off all the other caregivers. I guess I still don't know that for sure, but after today, I'd be willing to bet money on it.

I'm not really a morning person, so I was still half asleep when Mrs. Washington brought me into Loreley's room, formerly her and her husband's room. "She said we could just move her into the office if that was easier, but this room's bigger, it has a bathroom, and there's a cute little patio, see? It's nice."

Loreley was awake when we walked in, and Mrs. Washington grinned at her, started babbling about what a nice day it was and how maybe we could go for a walk. Loreley just blinked at her and then very slowly said, "I don't want a hired caregiver."

"I can't do everything, honey, we've been over this," Mrs. Washington said.

"I don't want you here," Loreley told me.

"Be nice," Mrs. Washington said, and Loreley stopped talking, but she pressed her lips together really tight and glared at me like it was my fault she was paralyzed in the first place. Then Mrs. Washington pulled her blankets back (she had, like, ten blankets at least) and started explaining that they had tried intermittent catheterization but it wasn't working out, so they were just using medical briefs, and wasn't it great that I'd already learned how to change them when I was taking care of my grandfather?

If you had told me back in high school that Loreley Washington, who held me down and dug her knee into my chest, locked me in a closet before a track meet, told everyone I was a lesbian, grabbed me by the hair and slammed my head against a wall, would start crying from embarrassment in front of me, I would have laughed in your face, but that's exactly what she did. She kept whispering "stop it, stop it, shut up" while her mom talked to me, and when Mrs. Washington didn't stop, she hid her face in her pillow and cried.

I thought I'd feel vindicated, seeing her helpless and ashamed of her body, but instead I just felt sad. It wasn't like taking care of Grandpa—he was old, and you just kind of naturally expect old people to need help. Plus, he'd had a really long life. Loreley's my age, pretty much. It made me think it could have been me lying paralyzed in bed, needing my mom to take care of me again, and I kind of wanted to cry.

Then Mrs. Washington changed her, which was the most awkward moment of my life (especially since she started crying louder), helped her get dressed, and put her in her wheelchair. Seeing her naked really drives home how skinny she is. I can count her ribs. Mrs. Washington said we should go hang out on the porch while she made breakfast, and I said alright because I didn't know what else to say.

"How's it going?" I asked Loreley as soon as we were alone. It might have been the dumbest question ever, and she looked at me like she couldn't believe how stupid I was.

"Bad," she said. "What the fuck do you think?"

"Do you remember me?" I don't know what made me ask that.

"Yes," she said. Nothing else for a long time, then, "I want you to quit."

"I need the money."

"Go work at the Crescent Hotel or something. They're always hiring."

"They're always hiring because it's haunted and no one wants to work there. I'm staying."

"Why? You get off on this or something?" She sounded a little like herself again, and I rolled my eyes.

"You're obsessed with my sexuality, you know that? 'Risa's a dyke, Risa's watching me change clothes.' Seems like you're projecting something."

"Fuck off."

"I made oatmeal!" Mrs. Washington said, walking out through the French doors. We all ate quietly (I was really

glad Loreley can eat on her own, even if she barely took two bites), and then she asked us what we wanted to do (after failing to coax Loreley into eating more).

"I want to be alone," Loreley said immediately.

"No," Mrs. Washington said.

I won't bore you with the details, but basically, we spent the whole day on the porch, glaring at each other and barely talking. Loreley kept crying when I had to take her inside to lie down (so she's not sitting for too long in the same position) or change her, and by the time I left, I couldn't hate her anymore. I'm keeping the job, I guess.

Love,
Risa

"These are beautiful drawings," Jewel commented, glancing at Sage's sketchbook as we walked out. "That's your grandmother, you said?" The particular drawing of Liliana that had caught her attention showed her nude again, one hand on her pregnant belly as she waded through a swamp, alligators swimming peacefully around her feet.

"Yes."

"She looks just like you."

"An older version of me," Lili said quickly.

"You're not worried about wrinkles, are you? You're practically a baby!" Jewel laughed. Lili flinched, then smiled again, brighter than before.

"No, no. I don't have to worry about that, you're right. Thank you all for visiting again."

"Can we come back tomorrow?" Arcana demanded.

"Certainly!"

"We should go up to their house," Arcana whispered to Dezy, late that night. "It's still standing."

"We have no idea what condition it's in. What if the floor collapses or—"

"It'll be fine, Dezy. Don't be a pussy."

"I'm being *safe*."

"Pussy."

Chapter Eleven

The next morning, Arcana told Jewel and Dezy we were going to Lili's house on our own. Dezy didn't believe her; Jewel was extraordinarily hungover and didn't care. "We'll go to Lili's house right after," Arcana promised Dezy as she walked in the opposite direction.

"Sure," Dezy said.

Being conjoined the way we were meant we each had a very different first impression of the old alligator farm. Arcana saw the Labelle house in all its crumbling glory, a sprawling Greek Revival mansion overtaken by moss and climbing ivy, every window long ago broken, casting a huge shadow over the wild grass growing up to the porch. Dezy saw the swamp creeping up around the trees just outside and wondered if Arcana could outrun an alligator on land.

The front door was gone, so we walked right into the entrance hall. Dezy felt like we were walking into a dragon's mouth, squeezed her eyes shut so she wouldn't imagine faces in the gloom. The Labelle house immediately threw you into darkness, corners completely shadowed even on a summer day, and Arcana murmured that Southern houses built before air conditioning were supposed to preserve shade as much as possible.

"I don't trust the stairs," Dezy whined, but Arcana went up the grand staircase anyway, the rotting carpet runner squishing beneath her feet. We went straight to the twins' bedroom, marked on a little map in her biography, and stood in a fully furnished room fallen into total disrepair.

"Whoa," Arcana breathed. "I didn't know it was still…"

"Didn't some guy buy it after they died?" Dezy asked.

"Yeah. I guess he bought it furnished. Look, this is the trunk—"

"Don't open it!" Dezy shrieked, irrationally terrified of seeing Adelaide's ghost.

"I'm gonna, but you don't have to look."

"No! Stop it! *No!*" Dezy pounded her fist hard against her twin's back, bit her shoulder, pulled her hair, tried to get in her way as much as possible, but Arcana was bigger, Arcana controlled our body, Arcana pushed her head aside and heaved the trunk lid open.

"There's nothing here," she announced. "Moldy blankets, that's it."

"I told you not to!"

"I knew there wouldn't be anything. You're being a fucking baby, Dezy, can you calm the hell down?"

"It's dangerous!"

"It's *fine.*"

Ignoring Dezy's protests, Arcana began making her way around the room, starting with the closet. She gasped in delight at the dresses still on their hangers, dusty and moth eaten but still colorful, closed away in a closet for sixty-five years. "These are beautiful."

"They won't fit us."

"No, but they might fit Jewel. I'm not gonna take them, though."

"Why not? The twins are dead."

Maybe it only struck Arcana then, how strange it was to be going through the twins' untouched room decades after their deaths, touching the clothes they had worn, because she inhaled slowly, stiffened up. Dezy hoped that meant she was ready to leave, but instead she just dropped the sleeve she'd been holding and closed the doors.

She went to the desk next, and while she went through drawers, Dezy stared at the dollhouse behind her. It would have been worth thousands of dollars if it wasn't in such a state of disrepair, and as much as she wanted to leave the house, she had to admit it was beautiful. It was, she slowly realized, a perfect recreation of the Labelle house as it must have been in its prime, weathered enough from sun and humidity that it still eerily mirrored the real thing.

"Whoa," Arcana muttered. "Check out these photos." She held up a black and white photograph of the Labelle twins first, one Dezy had never seen before, which meant it wasn't online, or Arcana definitely would have shown her. They had been beautiful women, tall and slender with long light hair. Their faces were pressed together, cheek to cheek, their hands clasped in front of them. Both smiled at the camera, but Sage's smile didn't meet her eyes.

The next photo was just the twins cross legged on a picnic blanket, and Dezy was figuring they'd all be shots like that when Arcana showed her the next one and she almost yelped in surprise. It showed the twins completely naked, sitting on the edge of their bed with their legs spread, Sage's fingers parting their labia. Neither of them were looking at the camera—Sage had her head thrown back in laughter, and Florence was glowering at the floor.

Next up was a blurry motion shot, the twins feeding their two-headed alligator, obviously taken at quite a distance. There were several pictures of the swamp, nothing special and no one present, followed by more overtly sexual nude photos. The last photo showed the twins up against a wall, their legs wrapped around the waist of a tall, black-haired woman with her back to the camera. Sage seemed to be kissing her, but Florence's face was fully visible, and she was staring straight at the viewer with an unreadable expression. The woman they clung to was covered in bruises.

"I can't believe these are still here," Arcana said, whistling.

"Are any of them labeled?"

"They're all signed MD, I guess that's the photographer."

"Who the hell was taking these kinds of photos in the forties?"

"Maybe that woman they're making out with in the last picture. Could be a self-timer."

"Leave those here," Dezy ordered.

"No way." Arcana carefully slid the letters into her bag and turned to face the room again, immediately heading for the dollhouse. "This is pretty cool."

"It's a replica of the house."

"No shit, Sherlock. I think it opens… here."

The dollhouse was better preserved on the inside. Arcana sat sideways so Dezy could look into it, although she didn't particularly want to, and made an aborted squealing noise when she saw the two-headed doll lying face down on the kitchen floor.

"Is this what rich people did back in the day? Just have weird custom doll stuff built?" Dezy asked, irritated.

"It's so *awesome!*" Arcana grabbed the doll without thinking, then flinched and nearly dropped it. It had a tiny knife buried in its fabric abdomen. "What the fuck?"

"Put that down," Dezy said at once.

"Do you think the twins did that?"

"Who else?" The thought of Florence and Sage having a doll of themselves commissioned just to stab it in the stomach made Dezy shiver; even creepier, it had been lying like that for almost seventy years. "Can we leave now? *Please?*"

"Alright. Yeah." Arcana didn't want to admit it, but the stabbed doll had obviously freaked her out. We left the house quicker than we'd come. "I wanna explore more later."

"I don't."

"Yeah, yeah, I know."

Like yesterday, Lili opened the door for us before we even knocked. Stella hovered behind her, looking mildly furious, which we were quickly realizing was her default state. "Did you like the Labelle house?" Lili asked us cheerfully. "You mentioned you were going to go today."

"Did we?" Dezy asked, furrowing her brow. She hadn't been paying much attention to what Arcana said.

"It was really cool," Arcana said brightly. "I mean, creepy, but cool. Have you been there?"

"Oh, yes. Many times."

"Did you ever open their dollhouse?"

"Not for a long time, but I remember it being a beautiful work of art. Sage loved dolls, and she had little replicas made of all her friends and family. I believe most of them are still in a box at the bottom of that trunk."

"I didn't see that," Arcana said, obviously disappointed.

"Thank God," Dezy muttered.

"Did you see her doll room?"

"No."

"She had at least two hundred porcelain dolls. Started collecting them after her father's death, but Florence didn't like them, so she kept them in a separate room. Since the next owner never moved anything in the house, they should still be there. She only gave a few to my grandmother."

"I hate everything about that," Dezy said flatly.

"Can I read the diary again?"

"Certainly."

Once upon a time, a mysterious little family came to Welcome. Every newcomer was exciting in such a small town, but this family was particularly fascinating because they had a beautiful, beautiful daughter. She was the prettiest woman anyone in Welcome had ever seen, so gorgeous no one cared how strange she was. She had jet black hair hanging down past her hips, soft skin pale as porcelain, and the greenest eyes anyone had ever seen. Her eyes seemed to glow in the dark, in a face so perfect it might have been carved from marble.

Every man in town fell in love with her from the moment they met her, even though she was quiet, sullen, and uninterested in anyone outside of her family. She was polite enough to women but curt and often outright rude to men. While her open disdain for the opposite sex made women who might have seen her as a threat trust her a little more, she was still so intimidatingly perfect that no one dared to befriend her. Her name, Malina, sounded exotic to the people of Welcome, and being from New Orleans made her worldly.

Malina came to town with her grandmother and her little sister, and they were strange, too. Her grandmother, Svetlana, pretended to be deaf in public but communicated freely with her family, and her sister, Liliana, spoke and acted very much like an adult, though she couldn't have been more than eight or nine years old. They rarely went into town; they never went to church, but when asked, Malina said they were Roman Catholic. Liliana said her mother was dead, so Svetlana was raising them.

Because the two-headed girl was a monster, she wasn't afraid to approach Malina or her unusual family. Being too beautiful, Sage told Florence, was functionally the same as being horribly deformed in a town like Welcome. It made you unapproachable and left you all alone.

Last night, Sage sent Malina a letter inviting her over for dinner. She thinks we should be friends with her. She says she's getting lonely without Papa around. I told her she can't possibly be lonely when we're together every second of every day of our entire life, but she wants a third person to talk to sometimes. "A third living person," she said. "Adelaide can't leave our room."

"I thought your grandmother was in her forties when she knew the twins," Arcana called to Lili.
"Oh, no. She just had Sage draw her that way."
"Why?"
"Eager to grow up, I suppose."

Dearest,

I swear I spent all day long switching back and forth between hating Loreley and feeling crazy sorry for her. She cries all the time (I actually got worried about dehydration and tried to make her drink more water, which of COURSE she refused to do), especially when I have to help her with something, but then she'll turn around and call me every homophobic slur she can think of even if they don't apply to me.

Got there first thing in the morning, just like yesterday, did the whole morning routine without Mrs. Washington's help, which, on the bright side, seemed to embarrass Lorely so much that she didn't speak to me at all for an hour. It was raining, so we just sat in her room, and after I read a magazine lying on her dresser that she's obviously never even opened (twice), I got up and started looking around. I was kind of trying to make her say something, but I don't think she even noticed at first.

That one time I went to her stupid slumber party thing in high school, she had a ton of random little trinkets, posters, a big corkboard with photos of her friends, jewelry, all this shit, but her room's pretty barren now. She pretty much just has clothes and blankets. Frumpy clothes, too, stuff she never would have worn in high school. Same with her bathroom—I remember a LOT of makeup in high school, but now it's just medications and scentless body wash. For some reason, I thought it was weird that she only has shampoo, no conditioner.

The only real decorations are the track and field awards. They're on a shelf way too high for Loreley to reach, but it looks like someone's been dusting them pretty regularly. Over a dozen medals and trophies, all first place. I was staring at them when Loreley snapped, "Are you done snooping around my room yet?"

"Where's the second place medal?" I asked. I only saw Loreley lose (well, by her definition of losing) once. She looked pissed, and kind of shocked, like she couldn't believe someone at this other school was better than her. She stayed after practice for weeks after that to keep running, and the next time we competed, she beat that girl solidly.

"Threw it away," Loreley said.

"What, recently?"

"No. The minute I got home after the meet."

"Looks like you threw everything else away, too."

"My parents moved me down here after the accident. I told them to get rid of everything, but they put it all in storage instead. Mom thinks the medals and shit will make me feel better."

"Do they?"

"I used to be the fastest girl in Arkansas," Loreley said. That was it. She didn't speak again until I had to help her with physical therapy, during which she raked her nails down my face and called me a dyke.

When I left at four, I kind of hesitated before saying, "Bye, Loreley. I'll see you tomorrow." For a second, she looked like she might say something polite—her eyes were kind of soft—but then she just told me to go fuck myself. What a sweetheart, right?

Love,
Risa

"Wait, so, can I ask about your family tree?" Arcana asked Lili. "It's Svetlana, Malina and Liliana here, then Liliana had Stella, and then she had Lina and you?"

"That sounds about right," Lili said, shrugging. It occurred to us that we had started talking to her like an adult very quickly, and Dezy was a little uncomfortable with the realization. She didn't like Lili, she decided, she was too put off by the contrast between what she said and the child's voice she said it in, the way she carried herself and her tiny frame.

"And how long have you lived in Welcome?"

"A while. You two were born in Arkansas, weren't you?"

"Yes," we said.

"I don't want to live anywhere else," Dezy added.

"Oh, I can understand that! I miss my home every day," Lili said with an odd mixture of sorrow and eagerness. "Louisiana is about as different from England as you can get."

"What brought your mother to England?" Arcana asked.

"Didn't you move here as a baby?" Dezy muttered, too quietly for Lili to hear.

"School. Are either of you planning on college? How would you decide where to go?"

"Neither of us wants to go to college, so that's not a problem here," Dezy said. "Arcana used to want to be a fortune teller."

"That was a long time ago. You wanted to be a fairy princess, so you can't say shit," Arcana said defensively.

Once upon a time, a two-headed monster grew up in a castle protected by a moat full of alligators. She was her own and her only friend. Her father may have tried to love her out of obligation, but she knew he was scared of her, no matter how well he hid it. The maid was much less discreet about her disgust; she wouldn't be alone with Sage-Florence and never looked at her if she could help it. When her father held parties, the two-headed girl was told to stay in her bedroom, out of sight and out of mind.

When she was seven years old, Sage-Florence snuck downstairs during her father's Christmas party. She was tired of watching the guests arrive from behind a curtain, and she had to know what they were doing, what they were like, or so Florence convinced Sage. Sage would have happily stayed in her bedroom and played with her dolls all night, but Florence couldn't remember ever meeting anyone besides her father, the servants and Adelaide's family, so she insisted she be allowed to go watch the party as a Christmas present. Sage agreed on the condition that she promise to stay hidden and not speak to anyone.

So Sage-Florence slipped out of her room and down the stairs, and when no one was looking, she hid in a coat closet very close to the ballroom. It was December, but it was still warm enough that no one actually needed a coat, so Florence was able to watch party guests come and go through the cracked open closet door. She thought the women looked like princesses in their evening gowns, wished she could actually see into the ballroom and watch them dancing. She wanted to dance with them.

For an hour, Florence sat watching normal people walk in and out, normal singleton women on the arms of normal singleton men, until Sage said she was bored and it was time to leave. Florence refused, at first, until Sage threatened to stop talking to her. She only had one threat, but it always worked, so the two-headed girl left.

She'd been so busy arguing with herself, though, that she wasn't paying attention to what was going on outside the closet door and walked right into a normal couple. They stared at each other, the two-headed girl and the singleton woman on the singleton man's arm, until the woman screamed at the top of her lungs and passed out. Florence screamed, too, and Sage burst into tears; the child ran away.

That night, Sage-Florence hugged herself tightly in bed, both arms wrapped around her middle so each side of her could feel that she was loved by the other. Florence was haunted by the normal woman's face, the terror in her eyes when she looked at the two-headed girl, the fact that she'd actually fainted from shock.

When Adelaide came over the next week, Florence pulled her hair hard enough to yank a fistful out, hit her so hard her pale skin had already blossomed with a purple bruise by the end of the playdate, threw a heavy wooden block at her head, and threatened to drown her in the bathtub. When Adelaide cried, Florence laughed at her, and when she tried to get away, Sage-Florence stopped her, dragged her back to the playroom. Sometimes Florence felt guilty for hurting Adelaide, but not that day. Adelaide looked too much like the normal woman for Florence to care if she was hurt.

I didn't want to be a monster when I was a little, little girl. I thought I was normal, and I didn't fully understand why we couldn't leave the farm or why the maid was scared of us. I woke up with my cheek pressed against Sage's and fell asleep holding her hand, and I thought it was perfect. I was happy. By the time we snuck down to that Christmas party I knew we were different, but I didn't quite realize how different until the normal woman fainted dead away just from seeing us. We looked in the mirror for a long time that night, crouched down so we could only see our heads and pretended we were two singletons standing very close together. Our faces were perfectly normal looking.

I read <u>Frankenstein</u> for the first time a few years ago. As a child, I didn't have the words to explain why the normal woman affected me so strongly, why I tormented Adelaide so harshly in the following weeks, but years later Frankenstein's creature gave voice to what I had felt back then, felt so deeply it hurt my shared soul: "If I cannot inspire love, I will cause fear."

When we took our medication that night, Arcana marveled at just how different every set of conjoined twins is. "Daisy and Violet Hilton lived into their sixties without medical intervention," she commented, "and one of them lived for days after the death of the other. We're going to die at the exact same time."

"Don't say things like that," Jewel said quickly. Dezy muttered an apology, but neither of us thought Arcana was wrong to say it. We had known all our lives that we were going to die together, had always planned to hold hands and look into each other's eyes in the moments before our shared heart stopped beating. It was supposed to end at home, in bed, surrounded by our family, hands interlocked, foreheads pressed together, Arcana's other arm wrapped around Dezy; I thought my twin's face would be the last thing I ever saw, but I woke up after the surgery and she didn't. We knew we'd die young. We thought Rose Red would attend our funeral.

When we were babies, the doctors wanted to perform what's called a sacrifice surgery, but because we were not actively dying, they couldn't. If Margaret hadn't been so adamant that we both deserved a chance to live, they would have tried anyway. There are three kinds of separation surgeries. Usually surgeons try to save both twins, but sometimes one twin has already died, so they have to quickly cut the living twin away from the dead one. Then there are sacrifice surgeries, where doctors kill one twin to save the other. They only do this if both twins will die otherwise, and they only do this to newborn infants.

Mrs. Bradshaw, who attended Margaret's church, drove to Little Rock every week to protest outside Planned Parenthood. When Margaret brought us home from the hospital months after our birth, Mrs. Bradshaw told her she was a monster for telling the doctors not to separate us. "If they grow up at all, Deirdre will never be a normal girl," she snapped, trembling with the righteous rage that she so often felt and expressed. "But they'll probably both die tomorrow, because you wanted to play God."

She came to our house to say this. Jewel, who had just graduated high school and jumped at the chance to get away from her parents by moving in with us, got in her face and demanded, "Don't you hate late-term abortions more than anything? You know those are *only* done to save the mother's life?"

"It's not the same," Mrs. Bradshaw snapped.

"Damn straight it's not. You think it's murder to terminate a fetus, but killing a newborn is fine if it'll make her twin look normal."

"They're *both* going to *die*!" Mrs. Bradshaw screamed at her.

"Doesn't God decide who lives and dies? A woman can't get an abortion to save her life, but you'll kill an *actual* baby to save the stronger twin's life?"

Margaret cut in and told Mrs. Bradshaw she'd call the cops if she didn't leave, but Tiff, who was watching from the end of the hall, never forgot the story. She told it to us so much it felt like one of our own memories, and it made Dezy, in particular, love Jewel even more than she already did. The only thing Arcana couldn't understand about her was what it felt like to be the "parasitic" twin, the one who could not survive without her sister, the one who was almost murdered— because she thought it *would* have been murder if they'd cut us apart and let her die.

"Sacrifice surgeries" are the only medical procedure in the world where doctors knowingly and deliberately kill a human being to save someone else's life. In any other circumstance, it would be homicide. Dezy didn't believe in Hell, but Arcana privately hoped the few surgeons who'd performed sacrifice surgeries would all be condemned there as murderers. She held her sister tightly throughout every doctor's appointment and adored her completely, never blaming her for their situation, never complaining about carrying her.

Dezy didn't really like to think about upsetting things. She was distressed about being the "parasitic" twin, but she had no desire to examine that any further. Arcana, though, sometimes obsessed over it. After she read Florence's diary entry about being a monster, she made Dezy (who had been dozing off peacefully on her shoulder) wake up so she could read it to her out loud.

"Doesn't that sound familiar?" she asked eagerly.

"Not at all," Dezy said, deadpan.

"Yes, it does!"

"We don't wanna hurt anybody. I think Florence was creepy and crazy and probably killed all those guys who went missing."

"It's true that people think we're monsters, though," Arcana insisted. "*I* think that's why sacrifice surgeries are legal. Doctors think we're so deformed and fucked up that we're not even human, so it's fine to murder one of us to make the other normal. I totally get why she was so weird, don't you?"

"No."

"If we hadn't had our family, and everyone just thought we were a freaky two-headed monster, we would've turned out just like this," Arcana insisted.

"What, serial killers?"

"The Labelle twins weren't serial killers," Lili called from the armchair.

"How would *you* know?" Dezy muttered.

"My grandmother told my mother. They didn't actually kill anyone, they were just strange," she responded smoothly.

"They both sound like budding psychopaths," Dezy huffed, then hid her face in Arcana's neck and refused to say another word until we returned to the Welcome Inn.

Jewel didn't want to go back to the general store, so we went to Virginia's for dinner. It really was an adorable diner, straight out of the 1950s; formica tabletops, vinyl booths, checkered tile floor, and a little neon sign in the window reading *Welcome, y'all!* Apparently it was the place to be on a Friday night, because there were six people inside, the Jones family included. Like before, every patron turned to look at us when we walked in, but this time, Cheryl waved with a nervous smile.

"Come sit with us!" Lili shouted, sounding more like a child than usual.

"We can sit alone," Dezy said hopefully.

"No, no, we should make friends," Arcana argued.

"You hate kids!"

"Lili's not a normal kid."

We joined them in their booth, doing a little rearranging so the twins could sit sideways, which left Dezy squished next to Lina. "Tell us about yourselves!" Lili chirped. "Do you attend public school?"

"No. Homeschooled," we said.

"Do *you* attend public school? Is there even a school anywhere near here?" Jewel asked.

"I'm homeschooled as well," Lili said, smiling, "so we have that in common. And so was Lina."

"Where's your dad?" Dezy asked. Arcana tugged her hair, a little surprised by the blunt question—Dezy was usually much more polite than her—but sometimes she tried to use her status as the less developed twin to get away with ignoring social norms. Loreley once told her that if everyone was going to assume you were mentally deficient, you might as well take advantage.

"Dead," Lili responded immediately.

"I'm sorry," Arcana said.

"Our mom's dead, too," Dezy offered.

"I thought you were their mother," Stella said, frowning at Jewel. It was the longest sentence we'd heard from her thus far.

"Oh, no! I'm their cousin," Jewel said quickly. "I'm not old enough to have teenage kids! Besides, I'd be a terrible mother."

"I've heard it's very rewarding and emotionally fulfilling," Stella deadpanned. Jewel laughed, then trailed off awkwardly when the older woman just kept frowning at her.

"Mama?" Lina chimed in, reaching towards Lili. She looked excited to recognize what we were talking about.

"That's alright, darling," Lili murmured, patting her hand. "You're alright." Lina smiled at her, took a bite of her hamburger, then immediately scowled and spat it back out onto her plate.

"May I ask what condition she has?" Jewel asked, as delicately as possible considering she'd been drinking all day. Arcana was worried about her liver, but Dezy understood wanting to blur the edges of reality without Rose Red.

"None of your business," Stella grunted.

"She has a traumatic brain injury," Lili said softly.

"That's a shame. She's so beautiful," Jewel said. She sounded like the nurses we'd once overheard in the care home hallway, outside Loreley's room—*she's such a pretty girl, too, it's horrible...*

"Would it be less sad if she was ugly?" Arcana asked.

"That's—I just meant—" Jewel sputtered helplessly for a second before Lili took mercy on her and patted her shoulder.

"I understand. Thank you for your sympathy. Anyway, girls, what made you decide to come here? It's an awfully long trip just to look at an abandoned house. You couldn't have known you'd meet me, after all."

"We needed to get away from home for a while," we said. Dezy wasn't willing to elaborate, but Arcana added, "Our big sister died."

"I'm so so sorry," Lili said, her eyes widening. "How old was she?"

"Sixteen."

"She was really smart," Jewel added quietly. "Really, really smart. Top of her class. She'd been going through some things that… a lot happened."

"Her name was Alice, but we called her Rose Red after her favorite fairytale when she was a kid," Arcana said.

"That's horrible. I've ha—heard of several children who died quite young," Lili said sympathetically. "Illness, mostly, but sometimes in accidents—"

"She was murdered," Dezy interrupted. "So was our friend Risa, and a girl named Celeste who we didn't really know. She was Rose Red's friend."

"There was a man who lived down the street from us that got totally obsessed with *us*. Me and Dezy," Arcana whispered. "Because we're…"

"The police connected him to several cold cases in other states," Jewel added.

"He had—" Dezy looked at Lili and suddenly realized we shouldn't be saying all this to a child, but she looked completely unbothered. "Sorry, Lili. I bet this is kind of scary, huh?"

"Terrifying, but it's nothing I haven't heard before. So many men like to hurt little girls," Lili said quietly.

"Maybe we should change the subject," Jewel said quickly. She was just sober enough to realize we shouldn't be telling a ten-year-old about the serial killer who'd been sexually obsessed with us; we figured the only reason she hadn't stopped us sooner was because Lili spoke so much like an adult.

"It's fine, dear," Lili said.

"Anyway, yeah, that's why we wanted to get away," Arcana said awkwardly.

"Was this very recent?"

"Yeah. Just a few months ago."

"I'm so sorry for your losses."

"Thanks."

Chapter Twelve

We kept going to Lili's house every single day. Dezy thought Arcana's obsession was disturbing, but Jewel didn't see a problem with it. She told Margaret we were taking our minds off "everything back home" and refused to bring us back before the scheduled end of our trip unless we had some kind of medical emergency. "It's kinda nice here," she said absentmindedly, drunk and half-asleep on her unmade bed. "I might wanna move somewhere like this one day."

Once upon a time, a beautiful woman decided to be the photographer instead of the model. She had an artist's eye, and she made real life look like a dream. Malina set up a dark room in her house so she wouldn't have to deal with developers asking her uncomfortable questions about her subjects; she liked to photograph the strangest people and scenes she could find, so when the two-headed girl invited her to dinner, she accepted eagerly. She brought her family with her.

They showed up on our doorstep dressed in beautiful, outdated clothes from Svetlana's youth. Later, Sage told Florence that Liliana's dress, in particular, was a true antique. It was from the Regency era, she said, or at least made in that fashion and dyed to look older than it was. Florence thought it was strange to let a child wear such a formal old dress to dinner. Liliana stood between her grandmother and sister, and without being asked, seated herself at the head of the table.

The two-headed girl had two different opinions of the strange family. Malina told her their last name was Deloitte, but they were not Cajun or French. Malina spoke with an accent split between New Orleans and somewhere we couldn't identify, Svetlana's was almost Russian, and Liliana's was completely foreign. She said Svetlana grew up in Russia and immigrated to Louisiana as a young woman. Malina and Liliana both had black hair, but they looked nothing alike otherwise. Svetlana refused to talk to Sage-Florence. Liliana spoke like an adult and was treated as such by her family.

Because Sage quickly loved the strange trio, fascinated by how completely alien they seemed, Florence despised them. She knew how obsessive Sage could be, and she hated the thought of her other half's attention focused on strangers. Sage was the quieter head in general, but that night, Florence refused to participate in the conversation at all.

I don't trust the Deloitte family, and I don't like Sage making up stories about them. She invited Malina back over to photograph us next week—which I agreed to because I knew she wouldn't speak to me if I didn't— and seemed to adore them. She likes children, and she fussed over Liliana like a doll after dinner, but as soon as they left she told me that Liliana is not human or a child. "I don't know what she is, though," she said, watching them walk away from our bedroom window. I told her she's going to scare them away if she keeps talking like that.

"Was Sage schizophrenic or something?" Arcana asked.

"Oh, I don't think so," Lili said. "Why?"

"She thought your grandmother wasn't human."

"Well, Liliana was a highly unusual child, and Sage had a very active imagination. Remember, she thought she was a witch, too, and believed she could talk to ghosts."

"She was kind of old to be playing pretend that much, wasn't she?"

"The twins were very sheltered."

Dearest,

It's been about a week since I last wrote, so sorry about that, but I didn't have anything interesting to say. Loreley's been the same as ever (screaming, scratching, throwing whatever she can reach at my head…) unless her parents are around, in which case she's suddenly a perfect little angel. I saw her have a seizure for the first time the other day, and it was pretty scary, but Mrs. Washington had told me what to do and she was sitting in her wheelchair, so it wasn't like she was in danger. Still, it freaked me out. She was really quiet all day after that, even when I had to do stuff that normally makes her cry.

Something worth writing about finally happened today, though! We were sitting in Loreley's room like usual (she absolutely refuses to go anywhere except her house and her porch, and I damn near have to fist fight her to make her eat) when her phone rang. I didn't even know she still had a cell phone, but apparently it's been in her bedside drawer this whole time, because she got it out so fast she almost dropped it.

"Who's that? Why's your phone in a drawer?" I asked.

"Clara!" Loreley squealed, and for a second she looked so happy I almost thought she was cute. Then I remembered who Clara is and wanted to hit her with a folding chair. Loreley's best friend, Clara, was also on the track team with us, and she was this total sycophant loser who did everything Loreley told her to. She always had super sharp acrylic nails. I know they were sharp because they dug into my sides when she held me down so Loreley could kick me in the stomach.

"How's she doing?" I asked, but Loreley had already answered the phone by then.

"Hey! What's up?" she said. She was grinning. Her hands shake when she's stressed or excited, so she switched the phone to speaker and set it on her dresser.

"Loreley!" I winced at Clara's voice, she's always been waaaaay too high-pitched. I didn't really understand the phrase "nails on a chalkboard" until I met her. "How are you?" She was kind of yelling, and she was talking a lot slower than I remembered.

"Oh, uh, y'know, I'm... here." Loreley laughed like she was trying to make light of her situation. "You?"

"I'm doing great, sweetie! Are your parents' home?"

"My...? Well, yeah, but why—"

"Can I talk to them?" Clara sounded like a kindergarten teacher.

"Why?" Loreley started rubbing circles on her thigh with her thumb and giggled, kind of nervous.

"I want to tell them something. Oh, if you have a nurse again, I could talk to them?"

"You can talk to me," Loreley snapped.

"Don't be mean, Loreley. I have something important to say."

"I can talk to her," I said, then added, quieter, "I'll just keep it on speaker phone." Loreley looked like she wanted to kill us both, but I guess she wanted to know what Clara had to say, because she handed me the phone. "Hey, Clara."

"Hey! Are you the nurse?"

"Yep." I wanted to ask if she recognized my voice but managed to hold back.

"Awesome! Okay, so, here's the thing." Her voice was back to normal just like that, still obnoxiously squeaky but not talking-to-a-deaf-toddler slow and loud. "I'm coming home to visit my parents for a week, for my dad's birthday, and I thought I should visit Loreley when I do. Is that alright? Can she have visitors?"

"Yeah. She's paralyzed, not sick."

"Great, great! That's great! What should I do?"

"What do you mean?"

"What should I do?" Clara repeated. "I've never, like, talked to a retarded person before."

Loreley's eyes got really wide and watery, so I turned off speaker phone right away. "She's not retarded. She broke her spine. That's it," I said.

"No, she hit her head really hard, too. Her mom told me she has brain damage."

"It gave her epilepsy, but—"

"So I don't have to do anything special?"

"You need to treat her like a normal person-"

"Cool! Can I come over on the thirteenth?"

"I'll have to ask Loreley."

"She'll love to see me!" Clara hung up before I could say anything else, so I set the phone down and just kind of looked at Loreley.

"I'm sorry," I said.

"I think she visited me in the hospital," Loreley said. She was sniffling and wiping at her eyes, and half of me felt really bad for her. The other half was glad she wasn't screaming at me. "Mom told me she came while I was still in a coma. I think that's where she got the idea that I'm..."

"Well, she wants to come over on the thirteenth. Is that okay with you?"

"Yeah."

The rest of the day was better than normal. Loreley didn't fight me on anything, and she only yelled at me once. Progress!

Love,
Risa

Once upon a time, a photographer came to the alligator farm to capture the two-headed girl on camera. She wore her raven hair in a long braid and swept through the front door in a vintage dress that had belonged to her grandmother decades ago. Malina said her family collected clothes. Right away, she asked the two-headed girl to go outside so she could photograph her feeding Ally-Ally. Florence agreed because she hated watching Ally-Ally kill live prey, and she thought Sage would be less likely to throw her a living chicken with Malina watching. In front of strangers, Sage was the nice one.

Malina took lots of photos, inside and outside, of the two-headed girl throwing a dead bird into the alligator pool, walking down a swampy path, standing in front of her house, sitting with her back to the camera. Finally, Sage invited Malina to see her doll collection, which made Florence hate the interloper even more; no one else had ever seen Sage's doll collection. It was private, locked away for her eyes only. Malina eagerly accepted, and she used the last of her film to photograph Sage-Florence surrounded by dolls.

It took a while to stage the photo. Malina wasn't content to have her stand before the shelves, no, she insisted on taking the dolls down, arranging them on the floor, and having the two-headed girl lie among them. Sage wouldn't have agreed to it if she wasn't so fascinated with the pretty girl who wanted to be around her.

I don't give a damn about Malina's photographs, and I don't think they can possibly be all that impressive. Photographs aren't like paintings or books, you don't need any real creativity to make them. All Malina does is point her stupid ugly camera at something and press a button. I suppose some work does go into developing them, but you can't call that art. She's promised to show us the photos; I have no desire to see them.

"Do you have the photo of the twins with Sage's dolls?" Arcana asked Lili hopefully. "I found some when we went to their house, but nothing like the one she's describing here."

"I think so." Lili disappeared for several minutes, eventually returning with a faded photo. "Here we are! Lovely, isn't it?"

"Beautiful, in an eerie kind of way," Arcana agreed.

"Malina was extraordinarily talented," Lili said, sounding a little shaky. For a second, Dezy thought her eyes glistened with tears.

The photo showed Florence and Sage lying on a floral-patterned carpet, surrounded by over two dozen porcelain dolls. The women and dolls all had their long hair fanned out beneath them, and each twin had a baby doll in hand. Florence held hers to their chest, while Sage's arm was tossed over their heads, holding her baby doll by the ankle. Sage wore a dead-eyed, empty smile, and Florence was outright glaring.

Dearest,

Loreley was way worse than usual yesterday. She refused to eat anything, all day long, and when I finally just set a bowl of soup in front of her and told her she could eat or sit at the table all night, she literally pushed it onto the floor. I think we were both kind of surprised by that.

"What the hell? What's wrong with you?"

"A few things," Loreley said. At least she's funny. I cleaned up the soup and we sat there until it was time for me to go home. Mom thinks I'm crazy to keep this job, but at this point I'm kind of sticking with it out of spite. Today, I realized she was being such a jackass because it was the twelfth, and Clara was coming to visit on the thirteenth. Apparently Loreley experiences all emotions as anger and expresses them all through bitchiness.

She was completely impossible this morning. We had two fights in the span of ten minutes, both of which were so, so, SO fucking stupid. First, Loreley said she wanted to just stay in bed, and when I told her she can't be lying in one position for hours on end she yelled that she's not going to get bedsores from staying in bed for just one day. I only got her to cooperate after pointing out that she'd look more sick and disabled if Clara only saw her in bed. Then she had a total freak-out about her clothes, insisted I show her every single article of clothing she owns before she could decide what to wear. Normally she just tells me to grab whatever.

"Not that!" Loreley screamed for the hundredth time. She was sitting on the edge of her bed in her nightgown while I showed her this skirt, that skirt, this blouse, that blouse, these sweatpants, this dress... it was driving us both crazy.

"I'm sorry, I didn't know we were going to the goddamn Met Gala," I snapped.

"I need to look good," she said, and of course she started to cry again.

"This is pretty, though."

"It looks like something an old lady would wear. Don't I have anything nice?"

"You made your parents throw away all your old clothes, remember?"

"No, they're in the attic."

So I asked Mrs. Washington to watch her while I trekked up to the fucking attic. Finally, I found a pleated miniskirt and a tank top that she deemed acceptable, but then she started panicking because she hasn't been shaving and I had to go help her with that before she could FINALLY get dressed. Normally our morning routine takes about twenty minutes; today the entire process took an hour and a half and I was ready to strangle her by the end of it.

Then we pretty much just sat in the living room until Clara showed up at noon. Loreley looked like she was going to have a heart attack when she rang the doorbell, and I felt pretty nervous, too, for a totally different reason—if Clara told Mrs. Washington I'm the girl Loreley bullied in high school, she'd probably fire me. I couldn't really say why I took this job, so it's going to look like I'm here because I like watching her suffer, which isn't true. I don't know why I'm still here.

Luckily, Clara didn't recognize me, or if she did, she didn't show it. I guess all that heinous shit they did had so little impact on her that she forgot what I look like after a year, which, great. Really great. Surely that says nothing at all about her ability to feel guilt and empathy. She walked in holding a little stuffed cat and some flowers, and when she saw Loreley she kind of froze up and swallowed really hard.

"Hi, Clara!" Loreley said with way too much forced enthusiasm.

"Hello, Loreley," Clara said. She really over-pronounced every single syllable. "I brought you a present!"

"Oh, that's sweet." Neither of them moved, and I was starting to wonder if Clara would just throw the cat at Loreley and run away when she finally walked across the room and handed it to her. Their hands brushed when Loreley took it, and Clara jerked back like she thought paraplegia was contagious. "Thanks."

"How are you?" Clara asked, loud as hell.

"I'm fine. I can hear you."

"*That's good.*" *She obviously wasn't listening.* "*Well, uh, I just wanted to stop by and see how it's going, so—*"

"*You're leaving?*"

"*I've really gotta go hang out with my dad, he's getting older, you know…*"

"*I thought we could go out somewhere,*" *Loreley said. She sounded so hopeful it kind of broke my heart, just a little, before I remembered who she was.*

"*Oh, uh, no. No, sorry. Bad idea. I don't know how to deal with…*" *Clara coughed and gestured vaguely to Loreley's wheelchair.*

"*Risa will come with us.*"

"*Who's Lisa?*"

"*Risa, my… companion.*" *I had to admire Loreley's dedication to downplaying her condition.*

"*Nah, that's alright. I've got a whole lot of stuff to do today,*" *Clara said, barely glancing at me.*

"*Could you come back later this week, then?*"

"*Sure, maybe. Yeah. I mean, if I have time. It's so good to see you, though.*"

"*It's good to see you, too. I really miss you.*"

"*I miss you, too.*" *That was the most sincere Clara sounded in the entire short visit. She gave Loreley a quick smile, then turned to leave.*

"*Bye! Love you!*" *Loreley yelled after her. She didn't respond.*

"*Cute cat,*" *I said after the door had closed behind Clara.*

"*I like cats a lot,*" *Loreley said.*

"*Why'd she come over just to give you a stuffed animal and leave?*"

"*Maybe something came up. She'll probably come back over later, there's a whole week before she has to go back to college.*"

"*Probably,*" *I said, because I, unlike Loreley and Clara, am not the kind of person who kicks someone when they're down. I could tell she already knew that Clara wasn't coming back. "Why'd you call me your 'companion'? You sound like a Victorian lesbian trying to save face." I immediately realized what a terrible idea that joke was, had a borderline flashback to all the times she'd called me a dyke in high school, and expected her to lose her complete, absolute shit, but instead she just… laughed.*

"You wish," she said.

I thought that was the end of the Clara incident, but later in the afternoon, right before I was supposed to go home, Loreley pulled out her phone and opened Facebook. (For the record, I hadn't seen her on her phone once before Clara called her.) She started crying, and I was going to ignore her at first but then she was really sobbing, *so I came over to see what was wrong. She just showed me her phone when I asked if she was good, and I read a post Clara made earlier today.*

It wasn't exactly shocking to me. It was just a long paragraph about how sad it was to see her high school best friend (that was her phrasing, high school *best friend*) so helpless and broken. She's so skinny, and she doesn't have any idea what's going on around her, *Clara said.* I knew it would upset me, but my mom made me go visit, and I think it just made both of us sad.

"That sucks," I said, kind of awkwardly. "Not the meanest thing she's ever said online, though."

"Did she think I wouldn't see that?" Loreley wailed.

"I think she thinks you can't read anymore."

"I'm not fucking retarded!"

"I know, Loreley. I'm sorry."

"No, you're not! I bet you're having the time of your life! This must be just great for you, seeing my life fall apart, right? I hope it's fun for you!" Loreley was screaming at the top of her lungs and pounding her fists against her thighs, ugly crying like she didn't care that I was watching her. She was obviously getting more and more upset every time she hit

herself, and I had to grab her arms before she could actually get hurt. "Let go of me! LET GO OF ME!"

"You can't hit yourself," I said.

"I can't fucking feel it!"

She was so loud that her parents came running in, and Mrs. Washington tried to calm her down while Mr. Washington pulled me aside to ask what was going on. "Clara said something on Facebook about how Loreley's… retarded, basically."

"Oh. We'll talk to her. You can go home early?" He always looks like he has no idea what he's doing, and today was not an exception.

"Yes, sir."

I don't really know what to think about what Loreley said. I know that she didn't deserve to lose her sister. Her sister, who was named Iris, is never mentioned in the Washington household, and no one looks at her baby pictures hanging on the walls. I met Iris briefly a couple times, at track meets, and she always seemed nice. I think it's a horrible tragedy that she's dead, and I feel so, so sorry for her parents. That part, I could never wish on anyone.

But I have to admit, I don't know how to feel about Loreley's disability. I think it's pretty damn ironic, and maybe kind of poetic justice, that she has to depend on me for help. Sometimes I feel bad for her, but sometimes, like today, I feel like she got what she deserved. I thought it was almost funny, in a fucked up way, that she was so torn up about Clara's probably well-intentioned post; I deleted all my social media accounts after her and her friends—half the goddamn track team—thought it would be funny to post a selfie I took to that stupid "roast me" subreddit, print out all the highest comments, and put them in my locker.

I talked to the coach, five teachers, the guidance counselor and the principal, and they all told me I wouldn't get "teased" so much if I grew my hair out, shaved my body hair, and dressed like a girl.

Sometimes, though, I feel really bad for Loreley, so I have no idea what to think overall. I'm gonna keep the job and see what happens.

Love,
Risa

"How long have you lived in Louisiana?" Jewel asked Stella. She sometimes accompanied us to Lili's house and tended to just sit quietly off to the side, skimming whatever book she grabbed off the shelf first.

"A while," Stella said flatly. She did not elaborate any further.

"What was your husband's name?"

"John."

"I'm not married," Jewel said.

"Lucky you."

"Don't you miss him?"

"Not particularly. I don't like men very much."

"Why'd you marry him, then?"

"I was young and stupid."

"Oh." There was an awkward pause. "I like your hair," Jewel offered meekly. Stella just scowled at her.

Once upon a time, Malina brought her photographs to the two-headed girl for her inspection. Sage loved them all and asked to keep several, but Florence wanted to burn them, preferably in front of Malina. The beautiful woman had been coming to the alligator farm more and more often, taking more and more pictures, making Florence hate her more and more with each passing day. Eventually, she invited Sage-Florence over to <u>her</u> house, and Sage, of course, said yes.

The Deloitte family lived in a pleasant little cabin a little ways outside of town, not quite as deep in the swamp as the alligator farm but far enough away from everything that no one could hear you screaming. Florence sat in stony silence as Sage chatted happily with Malina and Liliana, and even Svetlana chimed in occasionally. Her English wasn't perfect, but she could certainly hold a conversation. Eventually, they all sat down to dinner, and afterwards Liliana invited Sage-Florence to see her collection of antique clothes. "Play dress-up with me," she said, eyes twinkling.

Sage fussed over the little girl for hours, putting her in at least twenty tiny dresses, each one more elaborate than the last. At the bottom of a trunk, she found a truly ancient garment that she was almost afraid to touch for fear it would turn to dust in her hands. "What is it?" she asked.

"A kirtle. I believe it was made in the 1340s," Liliana told her.

"How did you get this?"

"Oh, you'd have to ask Svetlana."

Sage did ask Svetlana, but the old woman pretended not to understand the question and refused to answer.

We were at their house for entirely too long. I would say we overstayed our welcome if it was true, but none of the Deloittes cared. In fact, they invited us to spend the night. Liliana, in particular, was insistent that we sleep in the guest room, and when I tried to say no, Sage spoke over me. She rarely tries to dominate me in public, preferring to maintain her image as the soft-spoken twin, the hapless victim attached to an unstable, uncaring bitch, but she wanted to stay. We stayed.

When we woke up, Malina brought us breakfast in bed. She had mixed chunks of rare beef into scrambled eggs, and the blood leaking onto the plate made me feel sick, or perhaps I was already ill. We both agreed that we felt weak walking home from their house.

"I don't trust these people," I told Sage.

"Malina is so beautiful," she responded, far away and dreamy.

"Do you still have that kirtle?" Arcana asked.

"Yes, I think so. It's buried in the attic somewhere at this point," Lili said. "I can look for it at some point, if you'd like?"

"That's fine, don't go to any trouble on our account…"

Once upon a time, the two-headed girl got in a physical fight with herself, and Sage won. She told Florence what she wanted to do, and Florence hated her idea, begged her to reconsider, screamed that she didn't need anyone else in her life and generally caused such a scene that both heads were glad she'd fired all the servants as soon as her father died.

Malina was invited over, and Sage-Florence offered her wine while Sage touched her hands, her hair, marveled at how stunningly gorgeous she was.

"You're perfect," she sighed.

"Physically perfect," Florence said with a bitter, jealous smile.

And then, "Photograph us again," Sage said, "but why don't we take our clothes off this time? Wouldn't that be interesting?"

"It… would be," Malina said slowly. She thought about it, sipped her wine, and finally nodded. Florence resolved to kill her if she ever got half a chance.

Sage-Florence led Malina upstairs to her bedroom, where she stripped slowly for the camera, each stage of undress captured on film until she finally sat on the edge of her bed, spreading her legs wide. Sage tapped Florence's knee to make her move, then reached down and held herself open with two fingers, laughing while Malina took the picture. Afterwards, Malina seemed nervous and a little ashamed, but

Sage approached her, smiling, reassuring. She asked for a copy of the last photo, which Malina immediately agreed to give her.

I hated taking those dirty pictures. I'm not a whore, and I don't understand why Sage suddenly wants to act like one. When I asked her, she just said it was fun, it was something she'd never tried, and she wanted to do it again.

"I don't," I said.

"Well, I do. I want Malina to see we have a normal body where it matters."

Once upon a time, Sage made Florence pose for a hundred pictures, and when she promised she was done, she turned around and told Malina to take a hundred more. Florence wanted to know what, exactly, Malina intended to do with the photos, filthy, horrible photos that showed Sage fondling her breasts and fingering herself while Florence looked away, but she didn't ask. She no longer bothered to play the wild twin; it was now clear to everyone that Sage was in charge.

The two-headed girl had noticed how Malina blushed behind the camera, and Sage giggled about it every night after she went home. "She's interested in us, can't you see that?" she demanded, poking Florence in the arm.

"We shouldn't do this in our room. Isn't Adelaide watching?"

"She goes away when Malina comes over."

"Does she, now?"

On a warm, clear night, under a full moon shining bright as the sun, Sage ghosted her hand over Malina's and asked if she had ever been sexually intimate. Malina, who was always milk pale, somehow turned even whiter and shook her head frantically, <u>no</u>.

"I saw my mother having sex once," she explained. "It was horrible, she was crying and couldn't fight him off. I've never done that. After I got him away from her, my mother

told me I should be careful, because lots of men want to rape little girls. She thinks I'm old enough to start dating now, but I don't want to."

"What does your mother being raped have to do with little girls?" Florence asked.

"What if you were dating a woman?" Sage asked. Malina locked eyes with her.

"I think I would like that much, much more."

So Sage-Florence took Malina upstairs, and out of respect for her sister Sage laid Malina down and worked her over with her fingers, allowing Florence to close her eyes and ignore them until Malina felt the need to start screaming like a dying cat and piss on our bed. Sage, who sometimes reads medical textbooks, says it was something closer to ejaculate; I say it's disgusting, and I don't want that bitch in my fucking house or bed or life.

"She drops her whole fairytale narration thing halfway through a paragraph, here," Arcana said, pointing to the paragraph in question for Dezy's benefit.

"I didn't need to read that," Dezy responded.

Dearest,

Well, I finally got through to Loreley. It was a horrible morning. She was pretty much either crying or screaming until noon, and then she wouldn't eat lunch AGAIN, and when we got back to her room I just kind of snapped. She was yelling at me about something stupid, and I couldn't take it anymore. I got in her face and yelled, "Listen, cunt, I need this fucking job, okay? We can either make each other miserable forever or you can stop acting like a fucking baby and let me help you, but you're not getting rid of me, do you understand?"

Loreley stared at me for a long time, looking really shocked, and I thought oh, fuck, she's gonna go crying to Mommy and get me fired, *and while I was trying to decide if that would be better or worse (because I do need money, but I could just get another job pretty easy), she said, "I am* not *acting like a baby."*

"You literally throw temper tantrums every five minutes," I told her.

"Don't call me a baby!"

"Oh, are you gonna cry?" I asked, then realized how bitchy I sounded and froze up. I sounded mean and mocking, like Loreley when she punched me in the face or said I was so ugly it hurt to look at me. I told myself I'm not a bully and I don't pick on people who can't fight back, even if the person in question is Loreley Washington. "I'm sorry. I didn't—"

"You can call me a cunt or a bitch all you want, but don't call me a baby. Or retarded," Loreley said firmly.

"Oh," I said. She was *crying, but she was meeting my eyes, and her jaw was tense. Not for the first time, I thought about how hard this was for her, being an adult reliant on other people for help, getting treated like a helpless child by her parents and doctors. "Alright, then." The logical part of my brain told me to drop it, but the part that still hated her made me blurt out, "You're a cunt. You were an evil fucking cunt in high school and you're a whiny, pathetic cunt now. You were cruel and homophobic, and you basically tortured me for no reason, and you're still a spoiled brat bitching at me and your parents when all we're trying to do is help you. You're a shitty fucking person, Loreley."*

I started raising my voice halfway through my little tirade, and when I finished, I expected her to burst into more dramatic tears, yell for her parents, and get me fired immediately. I expected her to call me a dyke and tell me to kill myself, but instead she just blinked at me. She opened her mouth, closed her mouth, opened her mouth. Finally, after a long, long pause, she said, "I'm sorry."

"You can tell your parents to fire me if... What?"

"I said I'm sorry. I'm sorry for what I did to you." Loreley looked me in the eyes, then looked down at her lap.

"I don't believe you."

"It's true. I thought about it after your job interview. You looked..." Loreley swallowed and didn't talk for a minute. "You looked good. Really good. I mean, you looked..." She floundered, waving her hands around. "Sexy," she finally said.

"What," I said, completely stunned. That was probably the last thing I ever expected her to say.

"You looked sexy. I've always thought you looked sexy. When you walked onto the track field for the first time, back in school, I thought you were gorgeous. And you were obviously a lesbian."

"Yeah?"

"My family disowned my cousin when he came out. When I was at a sleepover with Clara in middle school, I asked her if she wanted to practice kissing, and she said we'd go to Hell. I told her I was just joking. You..."

"Are you seriously saying you bullied me until I tried to kill myself because you had a fucking crush on me?"

"I'm sorry," Loreley repeated.

"Oh my God," I said. I couldn't think of anything else to say, and I guess she couldn't, either, so we both just looked at the floor for a long time. "Are you a lesbian?" I finally asked.

"I don't know," Loreley said. "How would I know?"

"Are you attracted to women?"

"I..." Loreley stared at me. "You look like a man. I don't know if—I don't think that counts."

"I do not look like a fucking man!"

"I think you do," she said stubbornly.

"I... Wait, are you saying I'm the only woman you've ever been attracted to?"

"Why don't we change the subject?"

"Am I?"

"No, I had a crush on Clara, too. Are you fucking happy now?" Loreley snapped.

"What about men?"

"I don't—no, I don't think I have." She chewed her lip. "Does it matter?"

"It kind of matters a lot to me, since you went out of your way to torment me for being a lesbian for years."

"A year and a half. It wasn't that long."

"Oh, fuck you."

"I am sorry. I am."

"Would you be sorry if I wasn't your caregiver?"

Loreley didn't speak for a long time, but finally she met my eyes and said, "Yeah, I think so. If I hadn't broken my spine, I don't know."

"I wouldn't be your caregiver if you hadn't broken your spine."

"No, I mean, I was in the hospital for a long time and there was a nurse who..." Loreley did this thing she does a lot, where she tries to adjust her position but just ends up squirming from the waist up. "There was a nurse who was really new, and she hated all the... there's a lot of... she didn't want to clean up vomit or anything else, but she was new, so the other nurses made her do it. And she got mad at me for throwing up or, um, having accidents—she got really mad. I just remember she was really rough and tried to do everything as fast as possible, and one time I started crying that she was hurting me, and she said she had a lot of other patients, she didn't have time to coddle me.

"She told me to stop making her life harder, but I couldn't help it. It's not like I wanted to be throwing up and shitting myself all the time. I started thinking about how unfair it was

that she was being so awful about something I couldn't control, and then I realized I'd been... unfair to you. About how you dressed and your being... you know."

"So it took a spinal injury and medical abuse for you to realize you were bullying me?"

"No, I knew I was bullying you when I did it. I liked it," Loreley *said, and I thought,* hell, at least she's honest. *"I didn't like thinking you were hot. I wanted to feel like I... like I was stronger than you."*

"Wow," I said.

"I'm sorry. I was a jackass."

"I know."

We didn't talk again for the rest of my shift. I started writing as soon as I got home, and I think I remember most of our conversation even if it's not exactly word for word. I can't believe Loreley actually apologized to me—and I REALLY can't believe she was so horrible because she was having some kind of internalized homophobia crisis—or at least I couldn't before I remembered how she sometimes looked at me in the locker room, and then looked away when I met her eyes and yelled that I was watching her change clothes. I just thought she was judging my body, and I guess she kind of was, but not the way I thought.

I don't know what to think about her weird little confession. I think I just won't *think about it, honestly.*

Love,
Risa

Chapter Thirteen

Margaret demanded to talk to us on the phone a week after we got to Welcome. We'd been guiltily avoiding talking to her, Arcana because she was scared Margaret would say some magic string of words to convince her to come home before our allotted time was up, Dezy because she didn't want to hear the disappointment in our surrogate grandmother's voice, but we agreed to it for Margaret's sake.

"I got a cat," Margaret said as soon as Jewel handed us the phone.

"What?" we asked.

"I got a cat," Margaret sniffed. "I've been sitting here feeling sorry for myself, and it wasn't doing me any good, so I went out and got a cat."

"What kind of cat?" Dezy wanted to know.

"Some longhaired breed. She's gorgeous, very fluffy, very sweet. Likes to sit on my lap. I'm still trying to decide on her name, but I figure it doesn't really matter since cats don't respond to names anyway."

"How about Muffin?" Dezy suggested.

"That's cute," Margaret said vaguely. "How are y'all doing down there?"

"Pretty good. We met this family who have a bunch of stuff that belonged to the Labelle twins," Arcana said.

"Sounds pretty lucky. How many people live in Welcome?"

"A little less than a hundred, I think."

"Very nice." Margaret cleared her throat. "What about your health?"

"We feel fine."

"I wanna come home," Dezy added.

"I'd like you to come home," Margaret said.

"We'll come home when we're done," Arcana snapped, then quickly added, "Sorry, Margaret. I just… I want to finish reading this diary—Lili has Florence Labelle's diary—and then we'll come home. Her handwriting's kind of hard to read, so it's slow going. Plus they've got an intellectually disabled daughter who gets nervous if we're there for too long."

"Okay. I can't force you to do anything," Margaret sighed.

"Jewel's taking good care of us."

"I'm sure she is," Margaret said, voice dripping with sarcasm.

"We'll see you soon, Margaret. Love you," we said.

"I love you, too. More than you know."

"Do you know what used to be here?" Arcana asked Lili, holding up Sage's sketchbook. Several pages had been torn out, some more neatly than others, and she was gesturing to a page that apparently used to be some kind of landscape— we could see treetops over the jagged paper edge.

"No," Lili said, glancing over at it. "Perhaps she tore things out if she wasn't satisfied with them?"

"Perhaps," Dezy muttered.

Once upon a time, the two-headed girl was in such furious disagreement that both halves of her started to feel like an individual person. Sage wanted to be with Malina, to fuck her and be photographed by her; Florence wanted to be one isolated unit again, away from outsiders like the Deloitte family. The two-headed girl and the two-headed alligator, alone past the edge of town, the monster hiding in her cave, the creature without his bride.

Finally, there came a night when Sage ordered Malina to kneel before her and rub her sex against her leg until she reached completion, and Florence watched them in disgust, her other half's hand twitching on her hip, obviously wanting to touch herself while Malina rutted against her calf like an animal. She watched Malina moan and gasp and shudder violently as a clear liquid trickled down her thighs, most of it catching in the thick black hair between her legs, some of it dripping onto the carpet.

"You look like a dog," Florence sneered, and Malina looked up at her with glassy eyes, sweat running down her horribly perfect face. "You are *a dog, you're a bitch, humping my leg and pissing on the carpet."*

"It's my *leg, not yours," Sage said. "Ignore her, Malina, darling."*

"Do you hate me?" Malina asked, blinking at Florence.

"Yes."

"Shut up!" Sage snapped.

"I don't understand how one of you can hate me if the other one loves me," Malina said, settling back to sit on her knees.

"Be quiet, *Florence," Sage demanded, and Florence fell silent, because she knew Sage would really hate her if she embarrassed her in front of pretty Malina.*

Pretty Malina, don't want to embarrass Sage in front of pretty, lovely Malina? Malina got herself off on our leg like a fucking dog! Malina lets Sage put things inside her, chunks of ice and eggplants and glass bottlenecks and the barrel of a loaded gun, Malina lets Sage blindfold her and tie her to our bed, why should I worry about embarrassing Sage in front of a woman who would prostrate herself on the floor before us if Sage commanded her to?

Malina was hesitant at first, sweet and nervous, a beautiful blushing virgin, but every night Sage and her silver tongue talked her into some new depravity. The promise of my sister's love keeps her coming back night after night, the solid knowledge that she'll get to curl up with her head on Sage's lap in the aftermath to be petted and fawned over. She's like a child, blindly seeking adoration, and I wouldn't care if only she would go looking somewhere else. Like a beautiful faerie, she's spirited my Sage away to another world, one I don't know, a world of mysterious carnal pleasures I've never cared for until now.

Tonight, right before I sat down to write this, I told Sage that I want a lover, too. "I'll let Malina touch us if I can take a man to bed," I said, and she agreed after a moment's thought. There's a dance hall in town where all the young singletons go to find partners; tomorrow night, we will dress up and dance with them.

"They keep getting weirder," Arcana informed Dezy as we walked home that evening.

"The creepy serial killer twins are weird? That's crazy."

"Lili says they were innocent."

"They don't *sound* innocent."

"Sage has some kind of unhinged lesbian dominatrix shit going on, and Florence is—"

"Arcana, I don't like them. I don't like this story," Dezy pleaded. "Go read the diary, but don't tell me about it."

Once upon a time, the two-headed girl put on her best dress and went out to the Welcome dance hall. She expected men to turn her away—Florence may have told Sage she wanted a lover, but really she just wanted to make her jealous, force her to see how unreasonable she was being with Malina.

Neither of her heads expected what actually happened. She stepped into the dance hall, holding her hands together, and everyone turned to stare. That, she had anticipated. The music stuttered, stopped and started again, and that, too, she thought was normal. Silence reigned, broken by the occasional whisper or giggle as Sage-Florence walked to the middle of the dance floor and stood completely still, two pairs of eyes looking around the room, looking for someone brave enough to dance with her.

She would have started dancing by herself if a young man hadn't walked right up to her and held out his hand. "Delphin," he said by way of introduction.

"Florence," Florence responded. Sage said nothing, so she added, "And Sage."

The two-headed girl danced with the normal boy, feeling very clever for having thought to practice dancing on her own so she could keep up with him. "I've heard of you, but I didn't think you ever came down into town," Delphin said. He didn't seem to know which head to look at.

"I don't," Sage-Florence said in two voices.

After they'd danced together for an hour, Florence leaned closer to Delphin and murmured, low and husky, "Would you come home with me?"

"Yes," Delphin said.

I didn't think he'd say yes. Honest. I thought he was dancing with us as a joke, and I expected him to run away when I whispered in his ear and ran my hand down his side, but instead he willingly followed us home, upstairs, to bed. Sage began to cry when he pushed into us, and I had to bite my tongue to keep from yelling in surprise and pain—I had no idea it would hurt so much. It doesn't hurt when Sage fingers us for Malina's photos. Because my sister was crying, I threaded my fingers through Delphin's hair, moaned the way Malina does, wrapped my leg clumsily around his waist, and told him to thrust harder. I figured if he tore something inside of us, Sage would lose interest in sex altogether, and Malina has nothing else to offer.

Delphin kissed me as his hips shook, then peeled himself off our body and sat back, panting, while Sage tried to press our legs together. I kept moving mine, so she finally resorted to preserving our modesty with her hand. "I've never done anything like that," Delphin said.

"Neither have I," I responded.

"I'd love to see you again," he said.

I told him to see himself out and have a good night but allowed him to write his telephone number on a scrap of paper. Sage wouldn't move until the sweat slicking our body turned cold, and when we finally sat up we saw that we were bleeding.

"Do you still want to be with Malina?" I asked, eager to hear her say no, of course not, she would never ignore me again, she understood, now, that we were one person with one set of desires and no need for anyone else.

"Yes," she said, and my heart broke.

Dearest,

Not much to report today, but I thought I'd check in anyway. Loreley's been quiet since our little heart-to-heart, which made me super nervous at first but now I'm only kind of scared she's going to tell her parents I called her a cunt and get me fired. Mrs. Washington keeps asking if we're going to start going on "outings" soon and suggesting all these different places we could go. "How about the library?"

"What if y'all went to the museum?" "They have ghost tours at the Crescent Hotel!" Do you girls wanna go get lunch sometime?"

I guess Loreley finally got sick of all the suggestions, because after I helped her get dressed today she said, "Let's go get the mail."

"Did you order something?"

"No. Mom's on my ass about getting out of the house, and the end of the driveway is technically... I don't know, somewhere. A place that isn't here." She was fidgeting a lot, doing the thing where she rubs circles on her thigh, so I didn't say anything, just nodded.

Actually getting her to the end of the driveway was a lot easier said than done. She was fine in the living room and entrance hall, right up until I opened the front door. The second I did that, Loreley froze and shook her head a little, started to push herself backwards then stopped. "You good?" I asked.

"Maybe we could just go hang out in the backyard," she said, really, really quietly.

"I think we should at least try to go get the mail, Loreley."

"Is anyone outside?"

"Not that I can see."

"Well, make sure!"

I made a big production of sticking my head out the door to look up and down the street. "Nope, coast is clear. Can we go now?"

"What about the neighbors? I mean, what if they're, like, looking out their windows?"

"I'm sorry, are you in the witness protection program?"

"I don't want them to see me," Loreley whined.

"They already know you're paralyzed. It's not exactly a secret."

"They don't need to see it!"

"Is your plan to never leave the house again?"

"Kind of, yeah!"

"Okay, but that's fucking stupid. You get how that's stupid, don't you?"

"Everybody's gonna laugh at me." Loreley sounded so convinced of this I almost closed the door, but then I decided that that was exactly why I had to convince her to go outside, even if we didn't get far.

"Did you laugh at random disabled people before your accident?"

"Sometimes," Loreley said. No hesitation.

"Okay, bad example. Decent people don't just point and laugh at disabled people existing in public."

"But they used to know me. They liked *me."*

I gallantly resisted the urge to make a joke about her neighbors having bad taste and said, "They'll still like you, Loreley."

"They might feel bad for me, but they won't like me!"

"How do you know that?"

"Because!"

"Because…?"

"I don't wanna go. I changed my mind."

"I won't bother you about eating today if you'll go get the mail with me." I immediately realized that encouraging her anorexia in exchange for a three-minute excursion was probably what you might call "bad caregiving", but it was just for one day and Loreley needs *to go outside more.*

"Really?" The way she perked up was pretty depressing. Meals are a huge pain in the ass for both of us, and she doesn't want to sit at the table for an hour any more than I do.

"Just for today, and I still want you to eat, but yeah, sure. We don't have to fight about it today."

"Okay."

That got her out the front door, but then she froze up again and I had to talk her down the driveway. About halfway down, she started shaking her head and saying she wanted to go back inside, and when I tried to coax her a little further down she screamed that she'd had enough. So we went back inside. I told her that, since we didn't actually make it to the mailbox, I still had the right to nag her into eating at least a few bites of food.

"Where all have you been since you got home from the hospital?" I asked, tucking her into bed so she could calm down after what should not have been that stressful of an outing.

"I've had a few doctor's appointments."

"Nowhere else?"

"No. Well—actually, my first caregiver made me go to the grocery store, but it… didn't go well."

"I heard about that." Everyone in school heard about that, Loreley Washington scream-crying in the parking lot while a hired caregiver yelled at her to shut up. "What happened there?"

"I didn't want to go. She said it was important to get out, so she made me, even though I told her I didn't want to. I slapped her and stuff, but she could still pick me up and push my wheelchair." Loreley shrugged. "I wasn't trying to make a scene, I just started freaking out. I think I had a panic attack."

"She shouldn't have done that."

"Yeah, my parents fired her the same day. I drove off all the other ones, though." She grinned at me when she said that last part.

"Good for you. You look way too proud of yourself."

Nothing else happened all day, but when I left, I told Loreley we were going to try going outside again tomorrow. She can't just stay inside all the time, she's obviously agoraphobic already. Not sure why I give a damn, but I don't like the idea of Loreley spending her whole life hiding from everything in her room.

Love,
Risa

"How's that diary coming along?" Jewel asked, spreading peanut butter on a slice of white bread back in our motel room.

"Strange," Arcana said, shrugging. "Sage was apparently into some freaky shit, and Florence is… I dunno. Jealous of her sister's lover. Plus, she switches back and forth between acting like they're two people or one."

"That's interesting. You girls have always considered yourselves two people. Even when you were babies, you had very distinct personalities. Arcana was very curious, wanted to explore things, and Dezy was much quieter and sleepier, but so sweet. I remember that Arcana would just kind of pat my face like she was trying to figure something out, but Dezy would grab my finger with her little hand…" Jewel trailed off, smiling.

"The Labelle twins *were* super different, that's the thing. The biography said Sage was quiet and polite—if she was ever willing to talk, which wasn't often—and Florence was really loud and rude and just did whatever she wanted, and then in her diary that seems true, too, but Florence insists Sage is really the one who's in charge."

"And she still thinks they're two halves of a whole person?"

"She keeps saying they're a two-headed girl with a two-headed alligator. I kind of thought that part had to be made up, but Malina took some photos of it and Florence talks about it a lot."

"Her," Dezy corrected. "Ally-Ally was a female alligator."

"Who's Malina?"

"Oh, shit, I didn't tell you? She was Liliana's sister, so Lili's great-aunt, I guess, and she was apparently this super beautiful young woman that everyone was in love with. Their mom was dead when they moved to Welcome, but Malina told Florence this awful story about how she walked in on her mother being raped one time, and that's why she was scared to date men, apparently."

"When did their mother die?" Dezy asked quietly.

"That's horrible," Jewel said.

"Yeah. She started hanging out with the Labelle twins to photograph them, and then Sage asked her to take nude photos, and it kind of escalated from there until Sage was sleeping with her. Or, like, doing weird sexual domination shit to her. Some of the stuff Florence describes sounds dangerous, and I don't really have any idea what Sage is getting out of it."

"You told me Sage thought she was psychic, right?"

"She called herself a witch. She thought she could talk to ghosts, and apparently said Liliana wasn't human but still wanted to play dress-up with her."

"So Florence was the normal one?"

"I wouldn't say that. Oh, yeah, that reminds me, in the entry I read today Florence insisted on going out and finding some guy to have sex with, and it was the weirdest shit I've ever heard."

"Don't tell Margaret you're reading this," Jewel said, whacking the lid of a grape jelly jar with a knife handle to loosen it up.

Once upon a time, an inhumanly beautiful woman came to the alligator farm and left with Sage's handprints bruised on her backside. She kept coming back, and eventually she was covered in bruises, rope burns, cuts and scratches, all down her perfect, perfect, previously flawless body. With the motion timer on her camera, Malina photographed herself crouched on the floor, back bent at an awkward angle, a hundred little injuries clearly visible.

"It's too hot for you to be wearing these things," Sage commented, frowning at the long sleeves and skirts Malina had taken to wearing.

"I don't want my mother to worry about me."

"Your mother is dead," Florence said at once, and Malina blinked, grinned sheepishly.

"I meant my grandmother. Sorry."

After the two-headed girl's tryst with Delphin, Florence allowed Malina to touch her, but Sage only wanted to be touched in very specific ways. Malina could kiss her or lick at her sex, nothing else. She was good at it, which both halves of the two-headed girl disliked; Florence hated thinking Malina could do anything useful, and Sage thought reaching climax weakened her in some way, so she ordered Malina to stop after a few minutes, which always left Florence frustrated and unsatisfied. After Malina left, Florence rubbed herself with her hand until she was spent. Sage said it was too overwhelming, but didn't stop her.

Sage ordered a cattle brand from a metalworking company, and because the two-headed girl had a reputation as a rich eccentric, no one at the company questioned it. Perhaps they thought it was for the alligators. On a fairly cool, rainy night, she had Malina lie on her back before the fireplace and branded her initials over her womb, SL surrounded by a heart. Florence thought it was funny at first, laughed when Malina screamed and kicked at her instinctively, then started crying when the smoke faded and she saw that her other half was trying to share herself with someone else.

"Don't I already belong to you?" Florence begged Sage that night, grabbing at her hair and face.

"Can't you share?" Sage responded.

That was yesterday, and after Malina calmed down she seemed to like the brand. Sage cleaned and bandaged it, cooed that she was so pretty, so sweet, and Malina snuggled up to her like a lazy cat afterwards, gingerly trying not to put pressure on her stomach.

I called her a fat, ugly cow before she left, but she just shrugged.

"Hey, Lili? What happened to your great-aunt?" Arcana called without looking up from the diary.

"Can't remember off the top of my head, sorry." Lili was distracted with Lina, who'd been clingier than usual that morning, tugging at Lili's hand and half-yelling *mama, mama, mama!* until Lili sat with her on the floor to play dolls. Dezy was reminded of the Labelle twins' dollhouse and looked away.

Once upon a time, Sage-Florence woke up in a cold sweat. She was shivering, and there was a sharp, stinging pain in the skin over her stomach, but only Sage was distressed; Florence just wanted to go back to sleep. It was late at night, and her bedroom was more humid than usual, which Florence was ready to ignore until Sage grabbed her hand, frantic, and whispered, "Why is the window open?"

The two-headed girl got up to investigate, because she always slept with the window closed for fear of mosquitoes, but it was wide open now. As she stuck her heads out to look around, Florence had a vision of the window suddenly slamming down and decapitating her. Sage-Florence's window overlooked the swampy alligator pools, Ally-Ally's pool in particular, which she loved. Sometimes she sat watching her pet for hours on summer nights.

"Nothing here," Florence yawned.

"Someone opened our window," Sage insisted.

"Don't be stupid, we live on the second floor. We must have opened it ourselves before we went to sleep and forgot."

"We've never done that. We <u>didn't</u> do that."

"I'm tired."

"Adelaide," Sage cried, and Florence rolled her eyes as she was dragged back to bed so her other half could talk to her imaginary friend, "what happened? You were awake, weren't you?"

"I'm tired!" Florence yelled, but Sage ignored her, staring at the empty air over her trunk.

"Adelaide says a child climbed through the window," she finally announced. "A little girl with long black hair." She looked down at herself, at the source of the pain she'd been too frantic to notice and saw little dots of blood on her white nightgown. She lifted it to find several thin, shallow cuts forming a heart, in the exact spot where she'd branded Malina.

Sage says Adelaide saw the child cut us, but I think one of us must have done it in our sleep. The heart shape is strange, yes, but there's no way a child could have climbed up here. The window being open is an eerie coincidence, nothing more. I don't listen to what "Adelaide" says; it's just Sage being paranoid. If she unconsciously hurt herself in imitation of Malina's brand, perhaps she feels guilty. She may have woken up before me and done it then, actually. I think that's most likely. If she was half-asleep, she might not remember.

Malina is still coming over. She took a photograph with us the other day, our legs around her waist, and showed it to Sage with inordinate pride. Her brand is, unfortunately, healing into a thick scar, I had hoped it would become infected and kill her. She continues to grovel at our feet like a dog and allow Sage to do anything she wants to her, although yesterday she hesitated before putting her camera aside.

"My mother says I shouldn't let you hurt me," she said.

"You mother is <u>dead</u>," I reminded her. Malina constantly talks about her mother, and I think she must be like Sage, a crazy woman who believes she can talk to ghosts.

"Forgive me. I meant my grandmother. She raised me, so I tend to think of her as-"

"I don't hurt you," Sage interrupted. I heard the smile in her voice. "You like it, don't you?"

"Yes."

"Then I'm not really hurting you. We're both enjoying ourselves, aren't we?"

"Yes, we are."

So Sage choked Malina until she passed out, then fucked her with her fingers and sent her home. I didn't care as much as usual, because Sage had agreed I could invite Delphin over after she was done with Malina, and he wanted us on all fours like a dog. Sage hated every second, started pounding her fist against my side as soon as he left.

"He hurt me!" she screamed, punching me hard enough to make us both gasp for breath.

"Tell Malina to leave, then," I managed.

"No! She's <u>mine</u>!"

"No! Mine!" I repeated mockingly. "You sound like a child!"

"I won't talk to you if you invite him over again, Florence! I'll never speak to you again!"

"That's not fair! You have Malina, I have Delphin, isn't that fair? You know it's only fair!"

Sage screamed and kicked our bed, then finally settled down and admitted I was right. She hates him, though, I know she wants him dead, and I know she'll get rid of Malina when she can no longer stand him. I'm sure of it.

"Whassat?" Lina tried to take the diary out of Arcana's hands, and Lili had to pull her back.

"No, no, we don't snatch things! Sorry, girls, she's very energetic today, and Stella's not feeling well…"

"We can come back tomorrow," Dezy said quickly.

"You're a good sister," Arcana said, smiling wistfully. "Our sisters always took care of us, too."

Dearest,

After four days in a row of almost getting down the driveway, we have, at long last, managed to go get the mail, but the excitement of our successful Great Mailbox Quest was pretty short-lived. Like I've said a few times, Loreley has a lot of problems eating, and she never really wants to talk about it. No one wants to force feed her, so there's only so much we can do besides not letting her leave the table until she's put some amount of food in her body, but then she has a seizure and throws up anyway.

She was really tired and out of it all day yesterday, and right after lunch she just passed out. I thought she was seizing and waited for her to come back online. She didn't, so I checked her blood pressure and it was crazy-dangerous low.

And then we spent all day in the hospital because Loreley won't fucking eat! I stayed with her past four (I'm SUPPOSED to go home at four) because she was obviously really scared and I didn't think it was helping her to just see her parents. If I were her, I wouldn't like hospitals either. I finally left at nine, and then at, like, 2AM, Mrs. Washington called me in tears, literally begging me to come to the hospital.

"Is she dying?" I asked, stupidly, because I couldn't think of any other reason I'd be summoned to go see Loreley in the hospital.

"No, no, no. No! She's asking for you."

I thought I might have misheard her.

"What?"

"Loreley wants you here," Mrs. Washington clarified. "She was crying for you, and she keeps pulling her feeding tube out— they had to restrain her wrists, they didn't want to sedate her…"

"Are you sure she wants me?"

"She was saying 'Risa, Risa' over and over again."

"Okay."

"I'll pay you overtime—"

"I'm coming."

So I left a note for Mom, and I went to the hospital at 2:36AM in the fucking morning because Loreley Washington was crying for me. Maybe it was because I was SLEEP DEPRIVED, but it felt a lot like a fever dream, and when I got there Mr. Washington hugged me so hard it hurt my ribs. Being her caregiver made me a "support person", apparently, which meant I could be there in the MIDDLE OF THE NIGHT.

I was pretty pissed off when I went in her room, obviously, and I don't know if I would have gone if Mrs. Washington hadn't offered to pay me extra, but as soon as I saw her I felt bad for being so annoyed. She looked tiny and fragile in the hospital bed, especially with the feeding tube in her nose.

"Risa," she said as soon as she saw me.

"It's late. Your mom woke me up," I said, and Loreley kind of smiled guiltily.

"Sorry."

"No, you're not. Why do you want me here?" I sat down next to her bed and undid the strap tying her wrist to the rails—if she tried to pull the feeding tube out, I was ready to grab her arm, but instead she just held my hand.

"Nobody was talking to me."

"You couldn't until morning to talk to somebody?"

"No, I mean nobody was talking to me. The doctors were all talking to my parents, even when I tried to say something, and the nurses talked to me like I was a baby. I had a seizure

earlier and they were all cooing at me after, like I was scared. I'm fucking used to it by now." She pointed across the room to a teddy bear lying in the corner. "One of them gave me that."

"How'd it get there?"

"I threw it at the door after she left."

"That checks out."

"I'm hungry," Loreley said. I think my jaw literally dropped, and she rolled her eyes. "Don't look at me like that. I've been hungry this whole time, but it's like... everything else, somebody can make me do. My last caregivers all just picked me up when they wanted me to move and took me where they wanted me to go. They decided when to give me a bath, and the doctors decide when I have to take my medicine. I can't even choose when I pee, and then my caregivers decide when I can get clean. The one before you would just leave me in bed for hours, and I hurt myself trying to get into my wheelchair on my own—it was a little too far from my bed, so I just fell on the floor, and then I couldn't get up. I can't control *anything, but Mom said nobody's allowed to force feed me. She's scared it would hurt me. I get to decide if I eat."*

"Oh," I said. We looked at each other for a minute. "I still don't understand why you wanted me."

"You didn't make *me go down the driveway," Loreley said, very, very quietly.*

"I want you to be more independent. I need you to eat more, and in the meantime, we'll work on other stuff, okay? I'll talk to your parents."

"Okay."

I stayed with her for the rest of the night. She's really cute when she's asleep—I hadn't noticed before, but she brings her hand up next to her head and tangles her fingers in her hair. It's sweet.

Love,
Risa

Once upon a time, a strange child let herself into the two-headed girl's house and walked into the dining room while she ate breakfast. Florence liked to eat in the fancy dining room, but Sage liked to eat in the kitchen, so she took turns deciding where to eat each morning.

"Hello," Liliana said, sitting across from Sage-Florence at the table.

"You didn't knock. You weren't invited," Sage said.

"Yes, I was. You invited me in once, and that's enough. I am welcome here."

"That's not how invitations work," Florence said.

"Malina has a brand on her stomach. She comes home from your house smelling of blood and tries to hide her injuries from me. Whatever she does with you, it makes her ashamed." Liliana, who was almost always smiling, glared at the two-headed girl. The hatred and knowledge in her eyes was out of place in her soft child's face.

"Malina likes the things I do to her," Sage said.

"Go home, kid. You don't know what you're talking about," Florence said.

"Stop hurting Malina. I don't care what she tells you. Lie with her as you will, but if you ever raise a hand to my child again, I will make you regret it."

"Your child?" Florence asked.

"Yes. My child."

Liliana stared at the two-headed girl, looking from one head to the other, then left without another word. "She's crazy," Florence said.

"She's not human," Sage said.

I still think Sage is just insane, but Liliana <u>is</u> a creepy little girl, I'll give her that.

"Do you know why Liliana calls Malina her child?" Arcana asked Lili.

"She may have meant her sister. Florence could also be embellishing the story for her own amusement," Lili shrugged.

Once upon a time, Sage heeded Liliana's warning and became a gentle lover to Malina, who seemed thrilled with the change. She had liked the attention before, even when it hurt, and she liked it much more now that it came without consequence. A few weeks after the shift in their relationship, Svetlana died of old age, and Malina asked the two-headed girl to attend her funeral. She wept at her grandmother's grave, but Liliana cried harder than anyone, a broken-hearted child wailing like a banshee.

"My baby," she sobbed, "my baby, my baby." She covered her face with her little hands the entire time, and when she pulled them away they were smeared with blood.

For every romantic evening Sage spent with Malina, Florence invited Delphin over to hurt and humiliate her, gladly submitting to him if it meant her other half had to do the same. The two-headed girl hated him completely and equally, but so long as Sage loved Malina more than she hated Delphin, Florence would keep inviting him back.

Delphin wanted us to get on our knees so I could suck his cock a few nights ago, and even though I was the one doing the disgusting thing, Sage threw up after. She says I'm torturing her; I don't deny it, but if she wants it to stop, all she has to do is get rid of Malina forever. Last night, Sage fell asleep as soon as Delphin was done with us. She sleeps deeply, always has, so before he left I called my lover to my side and whispered in his ear.

"Sage is sleeping with a woman," I told him, "the most beautiful woman in town. I love you, you know I love you, but

she *loves Malina Deloitte. You can never have all of me, not until Malina lets go of her heart."*
     And I think he listened.

Chapter Fourteen

There was a pair of men's shoes in the hallway when we stopped by Lili's house, and Jewel snickered, glanced at Stella and then the shoes. "Should we be quieter than usual?" she asked playfully.

"What?"

"So we don't wake up your *friend*."

"Oh." Stella didn't blush. "I guess so."

When we left the library, the shoes were gone, but none of us had heard the unseen man leave.

Dearest,

Loreley is eating again! Huzzah! Not much, but more than she was before, and I don't have to harass her into doing it anymore. Her parents think I'm a miracle worker, which must mean they've straight up never actually asked her about this. I'm starting to realize they don't ask her about anything, actually. Mr. Washington took her phone away after the Clara incident. I get that he's trying to protect her, and

Loreley says she was barely using it anyway, but I don't think it's fair to just take things away from her like she's a little kid.

"What are your hobbies?" I asked her after I'd dressed her for the day. Loreley just pointed to the trophy shelf. "You need a new hobby. There are sports people can play in wheelchairs—"

"No way. Mom showed me those, they're look like fucking freak shows."

"That's really ableist, Loreley."

"I'm not interested."

"Chess is a sport."

"Boring!"

"Knitting, perhaps?"

"I'm not a grandma." I was going to keep rattling off (increasingly ridiculous) hobby suggestions, but Loreley's lip quivered as she said that, so I sat down next to her. She seems to be in a better mood when I'm physically on the same level as her.

"What's wrong?"

"I'm never gonna have kids. I'm not—I'll never be a grandmother."

"Loreley, c'mon. Lots of people are still gonna be interested in you. You're beautiful, and I'm sure there's something tolerable about your personality somewhere." I booped her nose as I said it, and she laughed weakly.

"Thanks, asshole, but that's not what I meant. I can't have kids. I had a lot of surgeries after the accident, and one of them was a hysterectomy. I was on so many drugs I didn't even know what was going on, I didn't know it had happened until we got home, and I didn't get my period two months in a row. Mom told me they did it because I wouldn't be able to take care of a child and they thought periods would be too inconvenient. It was the doctors' idea, not theirs, but they said yes for me."

"That's horrible." I had noticed Loreley doesn't have periods, but figured it was related to her spinal injury or something. "I'm so sorry that happened to you, Loreley."

"I wanted to be a mom."

"I'm sorry. You should've been allowed to choose."

"I want to try embroidery," she announced. Sometimes she'll just randomly change uncomfortable subjects.

"Alright. I'll talk to your parents about buying some supplies, and I think there are lots of tutorials online."

"Sounds good."

It goes without saying that I think Loreley would be a terrible mother for reasons completely unrelated to her disability, but I still think it's fucking bullshit that they sterilized her without her consent.

Love,
Risa

Once upon a time, the most beautiful woman in the world moved to Welcome, Louisiana and fell in love with one half of a two-headed girl. She followed her around like a puppy, the circus freak controlling the heart of the freakishly gorgeous lady, photographed her and adored her and worshipped at her feet, until the other half got jealous and told a dangerous man a secret she should have kept.

Malina Deloitte was, apparently, found by her little sister on the side of the road, bleeding out in the mud. She was hospitalized, went home, and did not leave her house again. That was what most people in Welcome knew, but because Malina had been friends with the two-headed girl, Liliana invited Sage-Florence to her house to show her what had happened.

"I'm sure she'll be fine," Sage said. She reached to knock on the door, but Liliana opened it before she could and ushered her inside. The child did not speak as she led her

guest to Malina's bedroom, where Malina sat, staring, at the far wall. She brightened when Liliana walked in and stretched a hand out towards her.

"Mama," she said.

"Someone bashed her skull in against a rock," Liliana told the two-headed girl. "She would have died if I hadn't found her."

"Do you know who?" Sage-Florence asked. Half her voice trembled with fear, the other half with excitement.

"A man. He raped her there, in the ditch, and tried to murder her. I saw the semen and the bruises, but I don't know who it was, exactly. Do you?" Liliana turned her eyes on Sage-Florence, cruel and ancient eyes that frightened the two-headed girl even though she was twice the child's size.

"No," she said.

"So it could be any man in Welcome."

"Yes."

"Very well." Liliana smiled up at Sage-Florence, her face as empty as a doll's. "I'll start with your lover, then, just in case."

Sage cried on our walk home, but I don't know if she was sad about Malina's fate or sad that she'd lost her favorite toy. After the initial ecstasy wore off, I can't say I was thrilled. I wanted Malina dead or gone, and I'd hoped Delphin would kill her when I told him. I didn't think he would do it like this. I don't know how Liliana knows about my lover, and I don't like the way she looked at us. Maybe Sage was right that she's not human at all.

Once upon a time, Liliana came to the alligator farm with Malina in tow, silent Malina, confused Malina stumbling around with her hands out to touch everything she could reach. "I want you to draw me, as a grown woman," Liliana told Sage.

"I can do that." Sage was quiet and miserable after Malina's injury, so Florence had been entirely responsible for keeping herself alive. Sage moved only when Florence did and spoke only when spoken to.

"Make me look middle-aged. I want crow's feet and stretch marks."

"Sure."

"And grey hair."

"Alright."

"Draw me naked, with wrinkles and sagging skin."

"I will."

After that strange request, Liliana left, dragging Malina behind her. Sage stood on the porch and watched them until they were out of sight, then sat down and began sketching.

Delphin called us this afternoon, but I told him I don't need him anymore.

Once upon a time, a young man disappeared from Welcome, Louisiana. His name was Delphin, and he had bragged to all his friends that he was the only man to lay with the two-headed girl. He left work saying he had a date and was never seen again. Two nights later, a married man went missing. He told his wife he was called into work for an emergency. A grandfatherly old man at the general store vanished without a trace. Perhaps the men of Welcome should have started walking home in groups, but instead, to prove their masculinity, they became bolder. They walked alone and disappeared into the night.

The two-headed girl didn't care, at first because half of her was immersed entirely in drawings of an older Liliana, and then because the other half realized she had missed her cycle for three months in a row.

"We should see a doctor," Florence told Sage, watching her play listlessly with her dollhouse. She had recently ordered custom dolls of Malina, Liliana and a separated

version of the two-headed girl, one Sage and one Florence, alone.

"Why?"

"I think we're pregnant."

"That's impossible."

"We haven't had a period in months."

"That's impossible."

"I'm going to make a doctor's appointment."

"I won't go."

We haven't gone to the doctor. I know Sage is serious about not wanting to go, so I won't push her, but I know we're pregnant. She knows it, too, she just won't admit it. We're going to have a baby! I hope it's a girl. I asked Sage what she wants to name the baby, but she just said "Malina" to spite me. I want to name her Ally.

"These aren't dated," Arcana said. "It looks like months are passing between entries, though."

"Florence wasn't very organized," Lili said, shrugging.

"I didn't know the twins were ever pregnant."

"Wasn't there an autopsy?" Dezy asked quietly.

"No. Their father wrote a will for them when they were children, and they updated it when they turned eighteen, to say that they didn't want one. They were cremated pretty much immediately."

"Funeral practitioners don't often respect the pre-death wishes of such uniquely deformed people, but the Welcome undertaker was very eager to do what the twins had wanted," Lili said.

Dearest,

Loreley's started embroidering. I think it's good for her. She doesn't like to read or watch TV or do literally anything at all anymore. She's just been sitting staring at the wall for the most part, and actually having something to do is making her really happy. Sometimes she talks to me while she does it, too, instead of just bitching constantly.

Today, she asked if I'd draw her a bird to use as a pattern. "I used to see you doodling things in class," she said.

"You remember that?"

"Yeah."

"Alright, I guess." I drew a phoenix, since that seemed more fun than a raven or some shit, and Loreley's already finished with the outline and started filling it in.

"I used to have a pet parakeet," she said after an hour of silence.

"When?"

"In middle school. I named her Squeak."

"Creative."

"Fuck off. I trained her to perch on my finger." Loreley looked up at me and smiled. She's gained weight recently, and I'm only saying this because I'm not blind, it's not because I'm checking her out or anything, but she's really pretty again. She was kind of corpse-y for a while there.

"What happened to her?"

"One of my cousins let her out of her cage and she flew away."

"Oh."

"I'm sure a hawk ate her pretty fast, but I like to pretend she's just hanging out in the mountains. Maybe she made some bird friends out there."

"You like birds?"

"Sure, I guess. I like wolves a lot more."

"I like spotted hyenas."

"Aren't they scavengers?"

"Yeah, but they're hunters, too. They have the strongest jaws of any land mammal in the world, and the females are bigger and more aggressive than the males. Female hyenas are always dominant over males."

"Cool."

"They also have giant clitorises that function as pseudo-penises." Loreley gave me a what the fuck *expression. "They urinate and give birth through them, and in order to mate, the male has to—"*

"I don't know if you're autistic or what, but that was not a 'tell me more about hyena clitorises' look."

"Well, whatever. Spotted hyenas are so fucking awesome."

"I'll take your word for it."

"Would you want another parakeet?"

"Yeah. I don't think my parents will let me get another pet, though. They're really overprotective now."

"Oh, really? I hadn't noticed."

"They miss Iris." She's never talked about her sister before, and I never asked.

"Yeah. I can't imagine losing a child." I didn't tell her that my mother almost went crazy when I tried to kill myself, that she was holding my hand when I woke up in the hospital and bawling that she loved me, she'd do anything for me, she would make everything better. She took me to a pride parade that June and found a priest to tell me God had made me perfect. I appreciated the gesture, but it had a lot less to do with being gay and a lot more to do with the bullying.

"She was really smart. Head cheerleader. I think my parents wanted me to do cheer, but I wanted to run. They were proud of me when I started winning."

"Was she anything like you?"

"No, she was better. Nicer, I mean, and smarter. I bet you wish I'd died instead, right?"

"I've never wished you were dead."

"Really? Even in high school?"

"I wished you'd transfer schools, but I didn't want you dead."

"Do you think I deserved this?"

"I don't know. I go back and forth," I admitted. "If I'm being completely honest, I think it made you better. You think so, too, don't you?"

"Yeah."

"I wish you could've changed on your own."

Loreley nodded slightly, then went back to her embroidery. She started talking about how her dad was obsessed with Breaking Bad, *but she hated Walter White too much to get into it. Later, I helped her take a bath because that's what we do every other day, and I noticed that her body hair's grown back since we shaved it for Clara. It's really thick and dark, and it looks nice on her.*

"You're fuzzy," I teased her while I toweled her legs off.

"Shut the fuck up."

"No, no, it's a compliment. You look great."

"You're lying."

"I'm not. I think you look better this way."

"Whatever." She smiled at me, though.

Love,
Risa

"How's the diary going?" Jewel asked. She'd been to the grocery store in town to buy more sandwich ingredients and wine.

"It's kinda bonkers. The twins were pregnant at one point."

"Is that possible?"

"They shared a reproductive system, so yeah. Don't know if they actually gave birth or not, I'm not there yet."

"You're treating this like it's a soap opera and not someone's life," Dezy muttered.

"I'm almost done with it," Arcana said, ignoring her.

"I might move to Florida after this," Jewel announced.

"What's in Florida?"

"Beaches."

"But there's mountains in Arkansas," Dezy protested.

"I like beaches more. I love the ocean."

"You've literally never mentioned this before," we said, and Jewel must have been able to tell how upset we were from our voices, because she quickly backtracked.

"I'll probably stay home, of course. I'm just thinking about swimming a lot lately. I'd be scared to swim here, even in a public pool, wouldn't you? Alligators."

"Alligators," we repeated, nodding. Dezy thought we were all going insane.

Once upon a time, another man went missing, followed by another, another, another, another, another. People had always looked at the two-headed girl strangely when she went into town, but they began to look at her with hatred in their eyes, so she stopped going out at all and started paying one of the farm workers to bring her groceries. The only alligator she personally cared for was Ally-Ally, who was never slaughtered.

At the Labelle farm, alligators are raised for meat and leather, and are killed with a knife through the neck when they reach two years of age. Sage-Florence never killed an alligator herself, but she watched her father do it countless times. Florence cried watching it; Sage squealed in delight. Both heads made her father promise to never kill Ally-Ally.

We're four months pregnant now and it's impossible to ignore. I told Ally-Ally that we're going to be wonderful mothers. Our daughter (I'm sure it will be a girl) will grow up in a beautiful house with lots of money from the farm, and Ally-Ally is the best pet she could ask for. She'll love playing with her, especially Left Ally, who has a sweeter disposition. Sage has been drawing dead babies in pools of blood.

Liliana came for her old lady portraits last night. She admired them for a long time, grinning, while Malina wandered around in circles behind her. "These are lovely, Sage. Thank you very much."

"Why do you want to look older?" I asked.

"Have a good evening," Liliana said.

Sage kept us up half the night talking to Adelaide about Malina, until I finally said, "Why do you even care? You just wanted to control her."

"She was mine, not his," Sage said.

"Did you love her?"

"I think I did. Yes."

I don't know if Sage really loved Malina, or at least, I don't know if Sage loved Malina in a way normal people would consider real. I know she's upset about what happened to her, though, and I hate seeing her so sad, especially when we're about to become mothers. I think I should tell her what I did. I was going to keep it a secret, but I'm beginning to feel guilty. I never wanted Malina to be so horribly injured, I only wanted her out of my life. I will tell Sage tomorrow.

Dearest,

Big news on the Loreley front: I got her out of the house today, and not just out of the house, but all the way into town! It's been a few weeks since I've written, just because nothing worth writing about has happened until now. I'm so, so proud of her—it was HER IDEA! She asked me right after getting dressed, said she'd been thinking about it all night. "I want to go to the craft store in person," she said, kind of shyly. "I've got some ideas for my next embroidery project, but I feel like I need to see the different colored threads for myself."

"Say no more," I told her.

Mrs. Washington damn near had a heart attack when I told her we were going out, then calmed down and started saying yes of course that's wonderful here's some cash, all that stuff. I could tell she wanted to go with us, but she stayed inside. Kissed Loreley on the forehead and petted her like a puppy before she let us go.

The first obstacle was getting Loreley through the car ride. She didn't have much trouble with the driveway (we've been going to get the mail every day) and was alright when I put her in the car, too. As I set her in the car, I said, "You're better than lifting weights," which she didn't think was very funny. It's true, though—my arms are getting pretty toned from picking her up all the time, even though she still doesn't weigh much.

It was when I actually started driving that she freaked out a little. She goes to the doctor all the time, but Mrs. Washington gives her some kind of sedative before they get in the car, so in a way it was her first car ride since the accident.

"You're alright," I said.

"Can you drive?" she demanded.

"Of course I can drive."

"I mean, are you a good *driver?"*

"Yes, Loreley."

She squeezed her eyes shut the whole trip and I had to pull over a few times when she almost started hyperventilating, but we got there alright in the end. Then I had to sit in the car and reassure her that no one would laugh at her for about thirty minutes before getting her in her wheelchair.

"But what if I see someone I used to know?"

"You mean one of your asshole friends? I think most of them are in college."

"That doesn't make me feel better!"

"Everyone knows what happened, and everyone knows it wasn't your fault. It was a horrible tragedy that no one blames you for."

"I look so different," Loreley whined.

"So? You're still pretty."

"I didn't shave." She touched her face and got this stunned expression. "I'm not wearing makeup, either."

"You look better without it. Do you want to go inside or not?"

"I guess I do."

I unfolded her wheelchair and set her in it, which is usually a pretty simple operation, but this time she wouldn't let go of me. "Can I stand up?" I asked, since I was bent over really awkwardly with her arms around my shoulders.

"I don't think I want to go," she said.

"We are in the parking lot."

"I changed my mind."

"Let go of me, Loreley."

"I wanna go home."

"Let me stand up and we'll talk about this, okay? Come on, let go." I had to pry her arms off. "I think we should try going inside. We got all the way here, didn't we?"

"People are staring."

"No one's here."

"People are gonna stare!"

"We can go home if you want, but I'm gonna wait five minutes. I know you're real excited about that embroidery thing, so I want you to think it through before we just turn around and go home."

Three minutes in, she decided to go inside. That was obstacle two, and thank GOD, it was all smooth sailing after that! Loreley stared at her lap and let me push her until we were in the thread aisle (I think she was scared to see anyone looking at her, which, yeah, a few people did, but who cares?), then she spent like twenty minutes comparing thread colors. I'm glad she's got something to be excited about, I guess.

We made it back home without further incident, and that was that! The Great Thread Hunting Mission was a SUCCESS!

Love,
Risa

Chapter Fifteen

I guess Risa's diary might not seem like it has much to do with the Labelle twins, but I felt like I had to include it. I'm sorry if it seems out of place. We didn't go to Risa's funeral, and I always regretted that. Letting her tell her love story here is the least I could do for her when I know it's our fault she's dead. Plus, it's nicer than Florence's diary, isn't it? Even if Risa's life had a sad ending, she was happy for a little while, and I like reading about the person Loreley used to be. I like knowing that people can get better—I think if the Labelle twins had lived longer, they might have become better people, too. I don't think they were evil. I have a hard time thinking of any woman as pure evil.

I apologize for interrupting myself like this again, but I need to remind you that what I'm about to tell you really did happen. I know what I saw, and I'm not crazy. You don't have to believe me if you don't want to.

The last time we went to Lili's house, Jewel was hung over and told us to go by ourselves before pulling a pillow over her head and falling back asleep. "How much more of the diary is left?" Dezy asked, nuzzling her nose into Arcana's neck.

"She didn't fill the whole thing, but I haven't looked ahead much."

"It's a life, Arcana, not a made-up story." Dezy was bothered by everything about the Louisiana trip, particularly how casual Arcana sometimes acted about the Labelle twins. Despite telling her she didn't want to hear it, she'd learned an awful lot about them and thought they were horrible, sadistic people with a sad, short life.

"You have to admit it was a hell of an interesting life, though, don't you?"

"Whatever."

Lili greeted us at the door, chipper as ever. "Hot today, isn't it? Can I offer you girls something to drink? Stella bought some sweet tea!"

"Oh, sure," Arcana said, sounding a little disappointed. Dezy knew she just wanted to get to reading the diary.

"We have these cute little cups from Virginia's! Cheryl was going to throw them out because they're chipped, so I said we could take them off her hands. Here!" Lili skipped ahead of us, grabbed a pitcher of pre-made sweet tea from the fridge, and carefully poured it into two slightly chipped glasses for us, beaming. She had to use both hands to pour, a rare reminder that she was just a little kid despite her bizarrely adult speech and behavior.

Lina walked up behind her while she poured tea and started reaching for it, whining. "No, no, not for you, dear. This is for our guests."

"Mama," Lina whined, *ma-MAAAA.*

"I'll pour you a glass if you want." Catching Arcana's eye, she explained, "She forgets she doesn't even like sweet tea."

"Thank you," we said, taking the tea with a smile. Lili poured another glass for Malina, who took it with a grin, brought it to her perfect Cupid's bow mouth, and promptly spilled it all down her front when she tried to drink from it.

"Damnit," Lili muttered. Lina set her glass down, scowled, and then, apparently bothered by the sticky sensation, pulled her blouse off in one smooth gesture. Lili yelled, "Ah, shit!" and jumped forward, trying to cover her up, but it was too late. Arcana screamed, Lina blinked at her and threw the tea-stained garment aside, Dezy demanded to know what was wrong, and Stella came running in looking even more furious than usual. Arcana turned so Dezy could see, and everyone in the kitchen stood in horrified silence, all of us staring at Lina's stomach.

There, right over her womb, were the initials SL, surrounded by a heart.

"That's a brand," Dezy whispered. "Isn't it?"

"Sage's brand," Arcana said hollowly.

"Malina?" we asked, even though it was impossible for Malina to look so young all these years later. If she was still alive, she would be in her eighties. She looked up, though, smiled at the sound of her name.

"What should I do?" Stella asked Lili. We realized she was blocking the kitchen door, and Dezy clung to Arcana a little tighter.

"Go get Malina a new shirt," Lili said with a weak shrug. "I'll talk to the twins. Won't you sit down, girls?"

"I think we should go," Dezy responded. Arcana sat down.

"Let me go get Florence's diary," Lili said, smiling kindly. "If you want to leave while I do that, I encourage you to do so. Otherwise, I expect you to hear what I have to say, is that understood?"

"Yes, ma'am," we said. It felt appropriate. Dezy wanted to run away with every bone in her body, but she knew Arcana wouldn't go.

Once upon a time, one half of a two-headed girl was jealous, bad-tempered, spiteful, and wicked. The other half was quieter, not kinder.

Florence's only intention in coupling with Delphin was to make Sage miserable enough that she'd get rid of Malina. She never intended to get pregnant, but when she did, she thought it was a miracle, a lucky accident that would mend the divide between her and her other half, bring them closer together.

"It'll be like having a doll," she told Sage. "You love dolls! We'll dress her up in the prettiest little outfits, play tea party with her—"

"Babies scream and cry and shit themselves."

"We'll hire a nanny, then, and we can hand her off for all those parts."

"I don't like baby dolls."

I know Sage is upset about the baby, but she'll love her once she actually meets her. I think hiring a nanny is a good idea, too, especially since I don't really want to change diapers either. We'll have a little family, just the two of us, and everything will be perfect once I tell her about my mistake. No more secrets after tonight.

"That's it?" Arcana asked, flipping through the journal's blank pages. "Where's the rest?"

"Why hasn't Malina aged?" Dezy snapped.

Without a word, Lili handed Arcana an old, sepia-tinted photograph. It was a portrait of the Labelle twins, both of them smiling, sitting next to Malina under a tree. Lili hung upside down from the branch above them, grinning at the camera. "This is the photo Sage modeled her drawing after," she said.

"It's you," Arcana said blankly.

"Yes. It's me."

"Should I call you Liliana, then?"

"I prefer that."

"Can you *please* tell us what the fuck your deal is?" Dezy yelled.

"I thought you were more curious about the twins."

"I am," Arcana said quickly. Dezy wanted to punch someone.

"This entry was written on their last birthday. What Florence doesn't really mention in her diary—she wasn't aware—is that the people of Welcome suspected her and her sister were responsible for the disappearances around town. Delphin had been telling everyone they were together, I believe she says that somewhere in here, and he was the first victim, so they were the natural suspects."

"Did they do it?"

"Do you think they did it? Florence says they don't know what happened, doesn't she?"

"Why should I believe her?"

"Because I did it," Liliana said. She grinned at us, really grinned with her lips pulled back for the first time, and we saw how long and deadly sharp her canine teeth were. "I hadn't read Florence's diary yet, so I didn't know what she told Delphin, but I knew about Sage and Malina, I knew how proud he was of being the only man to bed the two-headed girl, I put two and two together."

"What about the other men?" Arcana asked.

"Are you a vampire?" Dezy asked.

"So I knew the twins were innocent," Liliana continued, "and, while I didn't particularly care for them, I didn't want them to die for a crime they hadn't actually committed. When I heard that the locals were planning to go out to the Labelle house and confront them that night, I went to warn them. As I told Florence, I had already been invited in once, so I was always welcome in their home. I went in through the back door and heard Florence yelling upstairs—she was saying she was sorry. For what it's worth, she sounded genuine.

"Sage told her she was hungry, didn't respond when Florence kept asking if she forgave her. I followed them to the kitchen, staying out of sight, and watched what they did. The way they moved together was fascinating. I could tell Sage was furious with Florence, but they still cooperated effortlessly. They started going through the pantry, acting very normal; I'll never forget how strange it all was, Sage looking so perfectly calm while Florence panicked. She was crying, saying she was sorry, she hadn't meant for things to turn out this way, and Sage just ignored her. I was so distracted watching them that I didn't even notice Sage had grabbed a knife until she stabbed herself—and her sister—in the womb."

"Stabbed herself?" Arcana repeated, stunned.

"Yes. They both screamed, but Sage pushed it in deeper, and Florence grabbed her hand, tried to stop her. She managed to pull it out, which, by the way, is the exact wrong thing to do for stab wounds—"

"Wait, she? Which one?"

"Florence. She threw it across the room, they fell down, and I figured they'd die on their own, so I left them there."

"You didn't try to save them?"

"No. It seemed like a fitting end. I stole some of their things and went home. It takes hours to bleed out from an injury like that, though. They were still alive when the concerned citizens of Welcome showed up, and I suppose the visual of literal blood on their hands was dramatic enough to make them seem guilty."

"So the ending is true, then? They were tied to a car and…?"

"Yes. An unfortunate way to die."

"*Why are you a kid?*" Dezy yelled. She'd had enough of the Labelle twins.

"Oh, I'm afraid it's not a terribly interesting story. I was born in the year 1338, in an English village that no longer exists. When I was eight years old, a stranger came to town and made himself useful in every facet of life. He was charming, well-mannered, very strong, and he had a particular fondness for children. He gave me flowers, and, once, a little lump of sugar. I had never tasted sugar before— I don't believe anyone in my village had. I felt extraordinarily special. After a few months of flattery, he led me into the woods to play a game with him. I did not understand what he did to me, but I remember feeling… hurt, in a way I can't quite put into words.

"It had rained the day before. I thought the grass seemed especially green, and I saw a flock of birds overhead as we walked into the woods together. In a clearing, he asked me to take my clothes off. He said we were going to pretend to be physicians, examining each other's bodies."

"I don't wanna hear this," Dezy said quickly.

"No? Perhaps you oughtn't ask questions if you can't handle the answers. He molested me in the woods, but did not penetrate me; he said I was too small. I felt filthy afterwards, and when I tried to bathe myself in the river, I found I couldn't rid myself of the feeling. I felt his hands on me for many weeks to come. He was so kind, though, so gentle when we met in the village, that I convinced myself I had misinterpreted our game. I had many siblings, so being his favorite child made me feel *important*. For two years, he took me into the woods on a near-weekly basis.

"Around the time I turned ten years old, he told me he had a very special gift for me. He asked if I wanted to grow old and die. Naturally, I told him no. Then he asked if I wanted a wonderful surprise, and I said yes. He raped me in the dirt, then bit his own fingers until he broke the skin and shoved them inside of me, where he had torn me open. I felt very hot, then very cold. I felt my heart stop." Liliana held her tiny wrist out, and we each felt for a pulse, but found none. "Later, I would learn that all it takes is a mingling of blood. I've heard of many people doing it by cutting their palms and clasping hands. At the time, he told me that was the only way."

"We're so sorry."

"I have eternal life," Liliana said with a bitter smile. "Isn't that wonderful? Kings and emperors have killed for immortality, and I got it for free. When the Black Death ravaged my village, we alone were spared. He took me away after I lost my last sibling, and we traveled together for a time, with me posing as his daughter. After twenty years together, I got away from him long enough to tell a local priest that my father was a heretic. I put on such a convincing show of distress that he believed me, and, what with us being outsiders, the suspicious villagers were all too willing to turn on him. They burned him at the stake, and I believe he stayed dead. I ran away the day of his execution.

"For three hundred years, I worked as a scullery maid in various houses, leaving before anyone noticed I did not grow. I tried not to feed on innocents during this time; I made it my habit to approach men in the street and offer them my body in exchange for some food or coin. I emphasized how young I was. Most turned me away in disgust, some asked where my parents were and even paid for lodgings when I said I was an orphan, but a great deal of them accepted my offer. I possess a kind of venom that paralyzes my victims completely, and it has usually kept me safe. There have been many times when I could not bite them before they raped me. When I could not find a man who I thought deserved to die, I resorted to taking small quantities of blood from well-meaning strangers who allowed me to stay with them for a night.

"Eventually, I realized that my life would be easier if I had a more permanent caregiver. I found a gravely ill prostitute in the streets, finished her off- it was a swift, peaceful death— and took her baby to raise as my own. At first, she was my little sister, then my elder sister, then my mother, and finally my grandmother. I raised her in isolation as much as I could, ensuring she was never close to anyone but me so that she never thought I was a monster, and she gladly took care of me all her life. Her name was Ingrid. When she got older, she adopted a baby girl, who would become my new family. I traveled around Europe for some time, raising daughters and watching them die."

"Why didn't you just turn one of them into a vampire?" Arcana asked blankly.

"I offered. None of them wanted it."

"*None* of them? You did this for centuries, and not a single person wanted to live forever? Seriously?"

"It's not as glamorous as it sounds. I'm very… tired. I don't quite understand the modern world—it all changes too fast for me to keep up. I watch empires rise and fall and everyone I love dies. My daughters saw the half-life I had, how I hated myself when I had to drink the blood of innocents, and decided they wanted no part of it. Additionally, I am a Catholic, and I raised my daughters in the same faith. Once they were old enough, I told them the story of my life and death, and they all agreed that I had no real choice in what I became, but to *choose* this might mean damnation."

"But isn't Malina a vampire?" we asked.

"Let me go at my own pace. I adopted Svetlana in Russia, and together we immigrated to America. Galveston, specifically, but we quickly moved to Louisiana because I spoke better French than Spanish."

"What's that have to do with anything?"

"Texas is basically Mexico," Liliana said. "At any rate, we ended up in New Orleans, where we adopted Malina as a baby." She paused, played with her hair. "I have always tried to raise my children as best I can. I want them to have somewhat normal lives, but by necessity, they've always ended up very isolated. Malina felt that most deeply, I think. Men were attracted to her from a very young age, too, which didn't help at all. She became afraid to go outside on her own, preferring to stay close to me or Svetlana in our apartment at all times. We decided to move to a rural town so she might feel more comfortable, and you know the rest."

"No, we don't, because she's a vampire now. Right?" Dezy said irritably.

"Shut up," Arcana hissed in her sister's ear.

"Delphin's assault on her left her near death," Liliana said. For the first time since she'd begun her story, her voice shook. "She had gone out for a walk, and I went looking when she didn't come home within the hour. At first, I thought it was lucky that I was the first one to find her, but now I think I made a mistake. I always tried to give my daughters a choice, and they *all* chose to die. I hadn't asked Malina yet. I saw her struggling to breathe, her eyes rolling in her head, and I didn't think. I couldn't. I bit my wrist open and turned her, probably a few minutes before she would have died. As you've seen for yourself, her mind was affected by the injury."

"If you knew Delphin did it, why'd you keep killing people?" Dezy asked. Arcana pinched her.

"Malina was lonely," Liliana said, which wasn't an answer. "She had been lonely all her life, no matter how much Svetlana and I tried to be everything she needed. Men treated her like a pretty object, and although she tried to befriend other women, our unique situation meant she could never get close to anyone. In a city like New Orleans, we might stay in one place quite some time, but we did not intend to stay in Welcome very long. She had a lot of secrets that no one would believe. She took up photography to keep herself sane, and when Sage took an interest in her, she was a little hesitant at first but quickly fell in love. A connection with another woman, particularly one in Sage's position, who could not judge her, was all she ever wanted."

"Did Sage actually love her?"

Liliana paused, chewing on her lip. "I don't know that Sage was capable of love," she finally said. "Florence certainly was, but it was a fierce, jealous, hateful kind of love. She only had room in her heart for Sage, whom she loved so much she thought they were one person. I think she would have died before being separated. What Sage felt for Malina was, I believe, not unlike what she felt for her dolls, but Malina didn't see that. She told me Sage adored her, Sage doted on her, 'oh, Mama, Sage gives me the most beautiful drawings', and she pretended to be unbothered by Sage's sexual desires. If a man had treated her that way, she would have brought him home for me to kill, but it was somehow different—in her mind—coming from a woman. I never quite understood that."

"She seemed upset after Malina's injury," Arcana offered quietly.

"Given time, she would have found another toy to break," Liliana said. We didn't argue, but later we would both agree that Liliana, while she definitely had understandable reasons to hate Sage, may have been too harsh. No one commits suicide over a lost toy.

"Can we go home?" Dezy asked meekly.

"Certainly! This is the modern age, dear," Liliana laughed. "Did you think I would kill you after telling you everything? Who would ever believe you?"

"Wait, is Stella a vampire?" Arcana demanded.

"No. Just my adoptive daughter."

"If Svetlana was dead and Malina was, uh, disabled, how'd you adopt a kid in the… seventies? It wasn't like you could just grab one off the street."

"We were living in New York at the time, in an abandoned tenement building. There was a little group of older homeless people there, and they all had their crosses to bear, but I told them our parents were dead and they took us in. I had one of the women watch Malina while I hunted. Back then, I went home with my victims very often- I would make it look like a suicide. One of the men I went home with had a five-year-old daughter whom he was clearly abusing. I had intended to call child welfare services when I left, but she walked in on me drinking her father's blood and called me an angel. I took her with me." Liliana laughed. "It's actually rather easy to 'just grab a kid off the street'."

"How do you eat in such a small town?"

"I meet men online." Liliana smiled coldly, Louisiana sunlight trickling through the window and glinting off her fangs. "Would you like to watch? I have a man coming over tomorrow night, if you're interested."

"No," Dezy said.

"Yes," Arcana said.

"Well, decide by five o'clock tomorrow afternoon. You are always welcome in my home."

Chapter Sixteen

*D*earest,

Just finished the weirdest week of my entire fucking life. Good weird, I guess, but I'm still kind of reeling. It started when I saw this photo of Loreley and her sister as little kids in front of a campfire—I wasn't going to ask about it, but Loreley saw me looking and said they used to go camping a lot.

"Did you like it?" I asked.

"Loved it."

"Really? You don't seem super outdoorsy."

"I used to be an athlete."

"Yeah, but you weren't competing in the woods."

"Well, I like camping."

She sounded sad, so I dropped the subject. It got me thinking, though, about how her birthday is coming up and I don't think she has any plans. Mrs. Washington asked if I thought she'd like a surprise party. I said probably not.

When I got home that afternoon, I started looking into accessible camping. There's technically ADA laws, but they can't do much about most campsites being fundamentally incompatible with wheelchairs, and I was worried about being out in the middle of nowhere if Loreley had some kind of medical emergency. Eventually, I came up with an idea that I privately called "close enough" camping—Loreley's parents have a bigass backyard, I figured we could set up a tent back there for a night and at least sleep outside.

"Wanna go camping?" I asked Loreley at around 3PM yesterday. Seemed like a good time, since she'd been in a better mood than usual.

"Funny," she said.

"No, I'm serious. If I set up a tent in the backyard, we could sleep outside, right? I'll get an air mattress, that'll be easier than a sleeping bag, and—"

"Why?" Loreley interrupted.

"Why not? Your birthday's coming up, and you told me you like camping."

She stared at me for a long time, and I thought she was going to say no, but then she swallowed and nodded. "Alright. Sounds fun."

"I'll stay the night, then."

"I'll ask Mom to pay you extra."

It actually hadn't occurred to me that the camping thing would be overtime, and when I realized that, I had to stop and think for a while. I'd just been thinking of it as a fun thing to do with Loreley, not a job, which means I'd stopped seeing Loreley as a job. I don't know exactly when that happened. Maybe it was when I realized how funny she is when I'm not the butt of the joke, or when she stopped fighting me on every little thing, or when she grabbed my hand at the end of the driveway the first time, we actually made it to the mailbox. Maybe it was when she wanted me with her in the hospital.

I set the tent up with some help from Loreley (I wouldn't have expected her to know how to set up a tent, honestly) and then we just hung out in her yard until sunset. It was a really beautiful sunset, too, this nice orangey-pink that wouldn't have turned out well in a photo; you had to see it in person.

"We live in a beautiful town," I told Loreley.

"I like it here," she agreed.

Before it got completely dark, I had to figure out how to actually get her in the tent. My solution wasn't exactly great, but it wasn't my worst idea ever—I picked her up, set her right inside, and then crawled inside myself and pulled her in as carefully as possible.

"This is stupid," Loreley complained.

"Do you want to go camping or not?"

It took some wiggling and cursing, but we got there eventually! As dusk fell, I zipped the tent closed and immediately realized that I was lying in bed, in the dark, with a beautiful woman. I decided to get as far away from her as I could, which wasn't far at all because we were in a tent, and then she reached over to me.

"Where are you going?"

"Oh, you know. Over here."

"Why?"

"I am... claustrophobic."

"Since when?"

"If you could go camping anywhere in the world, where would it be?"

"Alaska," Loreley said. Her arm was still stretched towards me, so I wiggled a little closer, and decided I'd made a fatal mistake when she pulled me in for a hug, trying to find a position we could comfortably snuggle in.

"What's up?" I asked. "You're not usually... clingy."

"We have, like, two inches of space in here, and it's cold outside. I'm bad with temperature regulation."

"It's seventy degrees."

"My temperature's not regulating," Loreley insisted.

"Alright."

I kind of cuddled up to her side and put my head on her chest, let her put an arm around me. I wanted to say she was a good pillow but thought she might take that the wrong way, so I didn't say anything and tried very hard to pretend my face wasn't right up against her tits. It wasn't a well-thought-out choice of sleeping position.

"Hey, Risa."

"What?" I asked.

"You're really stiff."

"I'm cold."

"I can warm you up."

I stammered at her for a few seconds, then finally demanded, "What are you talking about? Like, what are you saying, exactly?"

Loreley got quiet. She didn't let go of me or say anything, and I almost thought she'd fallen asleep until she said, "Can I kiss you?"

I definitely should have said no for about a million reasons. In no particular order: she used to be a horrible bully who tried to ruin my life, I'm her caregiver, her parents are paying me to be here, her family might disown her if they find out she's gay, she obviously has some kind of internalized homophobia shit going on, I have to see her five days a week even if we kiss and it's awkward, but I had a bunch of excuses ready to dismiss all those, too. She's a better person than she used to be, she's genuinely sorry for what she did, she's an adult capable of consenting. She's smart and funny and pretty.

"Yeah," I said.

Loreley has really soft lips, and she smells like talcum powder. I liked kissing her. I kind of loved it, actually. When we pulled apart, it was too dark to see her face, but she sounded happy when she said, "That was nice."

"Yeah."

"You're not just kissing me 'cause you feel bad for me, right? Or because my parents are paying you?"

"No. I like you."

"Would you ever want to do anything else?"

"Maybe, but not tonight."

"I can't feel anything down there," she said.

"I know. We can figure it out later."

"Okay."

"Can I kiss you again?"

In the morning, everything was really normal, except I kissed her good morning and she grinned at me. I don't know what exactly we are now, but I know I like her. It still feels weird to think about present-day Loreley and high school Loreley being the same person. I think I could fall in love with present-day Loreley.

Love,
Risa

"I don't wanna go," Dezy told Arcana flatly. "She's a literal fucking vampire, are you insane? She's a *vampire!*"

"I don't think she'll hurt us," Arcana responded.

"Of course she will! She's a vampire!"

"Can you stop yelling about vampires in public?"

"No one's here! This is a ghost town, because of the—!"

"The vampire, yeah, I know. I got that."

We were walking down Welcome's Main Street, arguing bitterly about Liliana's invitation. Arcana wanted to accept, and Dezy knew she was going to accept, but she'd be damned if she wasn't going to put up a fight first. "We could die, and nobody'd ever know what happened! All those men just vanished…"

"Then we'll see Rose Red and Risa and it'll be fine," Arcana said calmly.

"You don't get to decide that it's *fine* if we die!"

"It's fine."

"We're going to Lili's for dinner!" Arcana yelled over her shoulder as we walked out the motel room door.

"Have fun," Jewel called, swirling wine in her water bottle.

"Welcome back," Liliana said, grinning, as she opened the front door for us. "'Come freely. Go safely; and leave something of the happiness you bring.'"

"Hello," Stella grunted. She didn't look thrilled to see us, but then again, she didn't look as angry as usual. We assumed she'd been updated on the situation.

"Dinner should be here around seven. In the meantime, Stella made something called pasta e ceci for you."

"Can you eat normal food?" Arcana asked.

"You've seen me eat!"

"I mean, yeah, but does it do anything for you?"

"Oh, no. It doesn't taste particularly good, either."

Having dinner with two vampires and their human thrall was not as exciting as you'd think. Liliana started ranting about inflation, sounding very much like Margaret, and we were lulled into an easy sense of familiarity for most of the meal. Finally, Arcana cleared her throat. "Liliana?"

"—for a *dime,* these days you might as well just buy the whole pig- what?"

"Can I ask you one more question about the Labelle twins?"

"Ask me anything you like, dear."

"You said Sage stabbed herself and Florence?"

"That's what I saw."

"I read that they couldn't speak when the… the mob, I guess, showed up. Did they say anything that you heard?"

"Florence pulled the knife out right away, and then she just looked down at herself for a second before they fell. I think she said, 'I need to check on Ally-Ally'." Liliana shrugged. "Then she went into hysterics."

"What happened to Ally-Ally, anyway?"

"Oh, I'm sure someone let her and the other alligators out of their pools. Probably went off into the swamp and lived a nice long life."

I didn't like what happened next.

Liliana told us to go wait in the guest room with Malina right before the man showed up. Dezy was thinking of him as a victim in her head at first, but she was afraid Liliana would kill us if she screamed, so she stayed quiet as we went with Malina to the guest room. It occurred to her, waiting next to the door, how impossible this all was—vampires weren't *real,* but here she was in a vampire's house, a little girl who would never grow up or die, who drank the blood of adults who wanted to hurt her. A young child and a woman who would always need a caregiver; Liliana and Malina were the last people you'd expect to be monsters luring men into their house.

We heard the front door open, and then Stella's voice murmuring something we couldn't make out. She came into the guest room a few seconds later, her fists clenched tight at her sides, biting her lip so hard we thought she might draw blood. In the hall, a man's voice said, "How often do you do this kind of thing?"

"Um, maybe once a month?" Liliana responded. She pitched her voice higher than usual. "Can we do it in my room? I just got new sheets, they're super bright pink, and they *look* glittery but they're really not."

"That sounds great, honey."

The man's voice made our skin crawl. We held each other tighter, listened to their footsteps going down the hall, and waited.

Waited.

"Malina!" Liliana called a few minutes later, laughing. "Malina, darling, come in here!"

Stella led Malina by the shoulder, and we followed her into a child's bedroom that was obviously never actually slept in. A man in his thirties lay paralyzed on the bed, eyes darting frantically around the room, half-naked, while Liliana sat next to him with a wicked grin across her face. She wore a white church dress, her hair tied in pigtails with long pink ribbons, and when she gave us a two-fingered salute in greeting Dezy fixated on the fact that her little fingernails were painted baby blue.

"Watch," Liliana said.

She bent her head over the two tiny puncture wounds in the man's neck and latched on like a nursing infant, making quiet suckling noises barely audible in the completely silent room. Stella was distracting Malina, who'd started whining when she saw the injured man. After a minute, Liliana pulled back, licking her lips, and called, "Malina, baby, come here. Come here, please."

"No," Malina whimpered.

"It's fine, dear. He's not hurt. You won't hurt him if you drink a little bit. Come, now." Guiltily, Liliana glanced at us and said, "I'd cut his throat and let her drink from a glass, but it's not the same. It doesn't nourish you very well."

Finally, Stella and Liliana coaxed Malina into drinking the man's blood. Dezy gagged at the sight, but Arcana, knowing what we did about the dying man, thought it was almost beautiful. When they were both done, Stella petted Malina's hair and led her away, wiping her mouth with a sleeve.

"I hated that," Dezy announced, feeling like she might throw up.

"When I told him I was ten, he said he wished I was younger," Liliana said, very sweetly.

As we left her house for what we all understood would be the last time, Liliana gave us her phone number. "You may call me anytime. I've never been to Arkansas, you know, I'd love to visit you in the future. If you're amenable, of course."

"Why are you so nice to us?" Dezy asked blankly.

"I'm six hundred and seventy-six years old, and in all that time I've only encountered two pairs of conjoined twins," Liliana said with a grin.

"Are you serious? You think we're freaks?"

"Not freaks, no. Unique young ladies. I also thought it was a strange coincidence that I met you in Welcome, and when I heard you were interested in the Labelle twins I thought it must be fate." Liliana reached up to pat Arcana's head. "I must say, I quite prefer the two of you to them."

"Thanks," Arcana said.

"That seems like a really low bar," Dezy said.

We stayed in Welcome a few more days, ate lunch with Liliana's family at Virginia's several times—Cheryl had gotten used to us by that point—and, finally, went home. Liliana and company came to the Welcome Inn to see us off.

"So nice to meet y'all," Jewel said distractedly, rummaging in her purse for her phone.

"Have you been to the Labelle house since the twins died?" Arcana whispered to Liliana.

"No."

"We found this doll," she said, then hesitated. "Yeah, uh, we found this doll that looked like them—Sage had those custom dolls—and it had a little knife in its stomach. You didn't put that there?"

"No, I didn't."

Dezy and Arcana looked at each other but said nothing. We never mentioned the Labelle house or the doll again.

And that was it, that was the Louisiana trip. We were quiet most of the way home- Dezy was trying to convince herself she'd imagined everything, while Arcana was trying to remember every second. She said she should write it all down later, maybe not actually publish it but at least get it down on paper. Margaret met us at the train station when we got home, hugged us for at least five minutes before she started lecturing Jewel, and Dia took us to visit Loreley right away. Rose Red's room was still untouched.

We passed an uneventful year, triple-checking to make sure our window was locked every night and basically homeschooling ourselves since Jewel was so out of it. Dia threw us a bigger birthday party than usual when we turned sixteen, and Liliana (who had not been told our birthday or address) sent us a box of strange chocolates as a gift. Arcana started talking about college, Dezy tried to get into chess but found she was an unsurprisingly horrible strategist, and we almost stopped thinking about what we'd learned in Louisiana.

Then Arcana's fainting spells began.

Chapter Seventeen

I told you in the beginning that one of us is dead, but I bet you forgot all about that part, didn't you? Serial killers and alligator farms and vampires are a lot more dramatic than the inevitable death of a seriously disabled, deformed teenager who lived sixteen years longer than she was supposed to, but my twin's death is the whole reason I'm writing this story.

We'd been sick before, so Arcana, at least, was not very concerned at first. Dezy always got nervous when new medical problems cropped up, while Margaret fully panicked every time. We were hospitalized when Jewel woke up in the middle of the night and heard us struggling to breathe, but Tiff, still away at college, wouldn't come back to Eureka Springs until Maragaret told her this wasn't like normal. We always wondered what exactly she said to get her to come back and decided it was probably a reminder that we had lived too long already.

You'd think we would be grateful for doctors, but actually we always thought of them as enemies. No one could understand this except Loreley, who told us she'd only met one doctor since the accident that spoke to her like an adult. "He asked if I wanted my parents to stay in the room during the appointment, and when Mom said 'of course we want to stay' he told her he'd been talking to *me*," she said, still sounding a little shell-shocked months later. "They didn't like him, though, so they found a new specialist instead."

We were so severely deformed, so profoundly disabled, that we did not believe anyone in the medical field was capable of seeing us as Arcana and Dezy, the youngest Garden girls. In the eyes of every doctor we saw, we were a problem to be solved, and the solution was always to separate us. Margaret and Daddy wouldn't allow it, albeit for very different reasons: Margaret said it was inhumane to perform a sacrifice surgery when we weren't dying, and Daddy prayed for our deaths every night. He didn't want any procedures that might prolong one of our lives.

For the rest of her life, Dezy would remember how Arcana's eyes rolled back in her head and she fell as if boneless to the floor, limp and helpless, how she hit her head on the arm of the couch and could not be woken up no matter how hard Dezy slapped her cheek or how loud she screamed in her ear. For the rest of *her* life, Arcana would remember how Dezy began to feel very, very cold in her arms, how her fingertips turned blue, and her breathing grew shallow in the days before we were admitted to the hospital.

We always worried that every hospitalization would be our last, but this time we *knew* it. We'd exceeded expectations, lived so much longer than we were supposed to—lived, somehow, longer than our healthy sister—and now we were going to die. Arcana calmly accepted this fact, but Dezy, who had always been complacent before, did not.

"What if we had two hearts?" she demanded of the cardiologist who told us our shared heart could no longer support us.

"You might have a better chance then," he admitted. "But a procedure like that would be tricky, very complicated and completely unheard of. One of you would need a heart transplant."

"If we're going to die anyway, we should at least try," Dezy said.

"It would be a very expensive procedure," the doctor said.

"Go fuck yourself," Arcana whispered, pale and sweaty beside her twin. "We want to live." Later, she confessed that she didn't actually want the surgery that badly, and would have preferred to just die naturally, but she couldn't stand this doctor telling us that money was standing between us and life-saving care.

"There are lots of charities that are willing to help, I'm sure," Margaret told us.

"Surgeons from all around the world are reaching out already. It's a totally unique case, and they all want to be the ones to do it," Jewel added.

That night, we received a phone call from Liliana.

"Cheryl read an article about you two," she said, without a greeting. "She liked you quite a bit."

"What do you think we should do?" Arcana asked.

"Make whatever choice you both feel is right. If you want the surgery, I'll pay for it."

"That's sweet, but it's gonna be, like, a million dollars or more. Wait, does Stella have a job? How are y'all making money anyway?"

"I told you. I meet men online. Stella usually has them pay half a million dollars in advance, and they're told to bring the rest in cash, to be paid afterward. They're funny—so careful not to leave a trail, so suspicious, always very eager. They're all terrified of getting caught, so they go out of their way to throw people off their trail before—"

"We get it," Dezy interrupted, feeling like she might throw up.

"Stella also sells antique jewelry. Men used to wear much more jewelry, but the dead don't need finery."

"You'll pay for the surgery?" Arcana asked.

"Of course. I'll have Stella make an anonymous donation, assuming that's what you really want. Do you have time to think it over?"

"Not really."

"Give it at least an hour and call me back."

Usually, Arcana was the decision maker, but this time we made the choice together.

"I don't want to die yet," Dezy said.

"I'll do it," Arcana said.

As promised, the hospital received an anonymous donation that covered the full cost of the surgery.

It took a month to assemble a medical team, devise a plan, find a donor, and in that time Dezy started throwing up everything she ate. She was put on a feeding tube, and when she began struggling to breathe, we were moved to the ICU. Arcana's lungs were slightly stronger than her twin's, but she had a migraine all the time and we shared chest pain every second of the day. Dezy was put on a ventilator, and while it made her sleepy and confused, she still overheard two nurses murmuring in our room late one night.

"How much is this operation going to cost, anyway?"

"Somebody paid for it all. It's not really costing the hospital anything."

"It's costing us a bed. It's costing us *time*. The little one's not gonna survive the surgery, you get that, right? There's no way in hell."

"Keep your voice down."

"It's completely asinine to waste resources on an experimental surgery like this. You realize that if the goal was actually saving a life, we would have already separated them and given Deirdre the heart? I don't know why they didn't do that when they were *born*."

"They weren't dying back then."

"Well, they're dying now, and we're spending a billion fucking dollars pretending a parasitic twin is a person instead of just saving that poor girl's life."

"I've *talked* to Desdemona."

"I heard she's retarded."

"She's not very smart, but she's sweet. Not *intellectually disabled*, just not too bright. Anyway, IQ tests shouldn't decide who's human and who isn't."

"She can't walk, she has one arm, and look at all that shit keeping her alive. That thing wouldn't survive on her own."

"She might."

"We're spending two million dollars on 'she might'."

"You can't put a price on human life."

The day before the operation, Margaret, Jewel, Dia, Tiff and Loreley each visited us, one after the other.

Margaret sat next to us and stroked our hair back, murmuring that she loved us like her own grandchildren. "God made you incredibly unique. I think you were given a wonderful gift, and whatever happens here, I hope I was able to give you a good life," she murmured. She almost never cried, but there were tears streaking her cheeks that day even though her voice was steady.

Jewel forced herself to smile, winked, and said, "I'll take y'all out drinking when you turn twenty-one, huh? Remember how I used to promise that? I'm holding you to it."

Dia took a selfie with us but didn't post it anywhere. "I'll print this out and start a scrapbook. Last photo of conjoined Arcana and Dezy, but there'll be a fuckton of y'all two separate! I'm gonna take so many pictures it'll just be annoying, honestly."

Tiff said nothing, just kissed both of us on the cheek, squeezed our hands, and left.

Loreley glowered at the nurse who watched her typing on her tablet. *"I'm really glad I met you two at the library. It was Risa's idea to start going there, and she liked you guys a lot."*

"It's our fault," Arcana said hoarsely. "That guy, he said it was 'cause of us. He was obsessed with us."

"He was crazy. It's not your fault."

"It is."

"Well, I don't blame you. I'll see you both soon."

It was decided that Arcana would receive a heart transplant immediately, while Dezy would keep our heart, recover in the hospital, and be given another transplant a year later. "A transplant right away would be much too hard on your body," the doctor explained, patting Dezy's hand like she was a child.

We were taken into the operating theater. If we both woke up, we would be separate in a way we had never even imagined—we who had lived our lives with one heart between us, we who were born staring into each other's eyes, we who breathed in unison, would be able to sleep in two different beds. Arcana would walk freely, without the burden of her sister in her arms, and Dezy would spend her life in a wheelchair. We had already decided that we still didn't want to be apart, that we would never be apart if we could help it.

"I'll push your wheelchair, or carry you on my hip," Arcana promised. She couldn't imagine moving without Dezy's familiar weight.

We looked each other in the eye, held hands, and, for the last time, fell asleep together.

Twenty-six hours later, Desdemona woke up alone.

Chapter Eighteen

I had never lain on my back before. That was the second thing I noticed, once I understood that I was still alive. Arcana sometimes laid down flat for a few minutes, but we mostly laid on our side, and I did not lie on my back. She was heavier than me, it wasn't safe for her to lie on top of me. The ventilator was still breathing for me, making it hard to turn my head, and I could not see my twin.

I started crying, reaching towards the space where Arcana should have been, still a little foggy from the drugs. I understood that the surgery was over, and we had obviously been successfully separated, and once I realized that I expected a nurse to help me move, show me Arcana was in the bed right next to me; this did not happen. Several nurses did come to comfort me, but no one told me where Arcana was. I touched my chest and regretted every choice I'd made that led me here.

Jewel and Margaret came to see me together, one on either side of my bed. Margaret stroked my face, Jewel held my hand, and they both murmured quiet reassurances that we would be fine. Both of us. "You'll be fine, love, you'll *both* be fine."

After a week, they began to wean me off the ventilator. I took a second to relish breathing on my own, then said, "Deirdre."

"You can see her later," the nurse told me.

I asked Jewel the next time I saw her. I knew she would tell me the truth, no matter how much I didn't want to hear it. "Where's Arcana?"

"Alive," Jewel said instantly, "but she's on life support. You were just on life support, too, though, and they're taking you off the ventilator, so there's no reason to think she won't be just fine."

"Can I talk to her?"

"Well." Jewel coughed, cleared her throat, became very interested in getting herself a cup of water.

"*Can I talk to her?*"

"She hasn't woken up yet," Jewel finally muttered.

They took me to see my twin, sleeping in another room of the ICU. Another room! It felt surreal, being wheeled in to look at Arcana, my *other half* as Florence Labelle would say, alone in a hospital bed. She did not move when I touched her cold, clammy skin. A machine was breathing for her, and a stranger's heartbeat in her chest.

I wonder if that's why she died, sometimes. If our heart was perfect for us, and nothing else would work.

"I need to call Lili," I told Jewel.

"Will you come here?"

"Of course. It went well, then? I saw on the news that you're both—"

"Arcana's in a coma," I interrupted. "You need to come here *now*."

There was a long pause. It occurred to me that we'd never heard Liliana breathing, and I wondered how we hadn't realized what she was sooner. I guess you wouldn't know to look for that sort of thing in real life. "Why do you want me there?" Liliana finally asked.

"You know why."

"I won't do it unless she asks, and she can't ask if she's in a coma."

"She'll wake up. Please, Liliana, *please,* I need you. You're the only—I need you here, as soon as possible."

"I am not God, Desdemona. I don't perform miracles."

"I can't live without her!"

"Yes, you can. The things a person can survive would amaze you."

"I need you," I sobbed, and Liliana drew in a breath to very deliberately sigh.

"I will come," she finally said, "in case Arcana wakes up."

The next day, I was told that Arcana was brain dead.

Two days later, Liliana walked into my hospital room with a bouquet of white roses.

"Too late," I told her dully.

"I thought I might be. I'm sorry for your loss."

"I'm gonna die."

"No, you're not. You have your sister's heart. Don't waste it."

"I've never been alone before."

"Most people are born alone and die alone. You were extraordinarily lucky for sixteen years, and I imagine it will be very hard for you to learn how to be alone this late in life, but you'll manage. Everyone else does, after all."

"Didn't you turn Malina because you didn't want to be alone?"

"I turned Malina because I saw my child suffering and thought I could help her."

"I wish we'd died together."

"Weren't you the one who wanted the operation?"

"Yeah," I whispered, tears welling in my eyes.

"You wanted to live, Desdemona."

"I wanted to live *with my sister.*"

"You have the rest of your life to make her proud, and a long time from now you can tell her all about it. Dying young, not unlike living forever, isn't so romantic as you think. That might sound insincere coming from me, but I *am* dead. My heart does not beat. I draw breath only to talk. I died at ten years old, murdered in the forest by a monster who sought his pleasure with children, and I have had a half-life ever since. I have watched entire human lives and envied every second. You could get married, Dezy. You could have a child and grow alongside her, you could be a grandmother. Look at me."

I looked. I saw a little girl with old, old eyes boring into my soul.

"I will never grow up," Liliana whispered. "I am dead. Live your natural life, Desdemona, and make your sister proud. You don't really want to die young."

Beloved daughter, sister and friend Deirdre Gardner passed away this week on October 22nd, 2015, aged sixteen. She is survived by her elder sisters Tiffany and Diamond, her twin sister Desdemona, and her cousin Jewel Davis.

Deirdre and Desdemona were born conjoined at the chest, sharing one heart between them. Although they were given just hours to live, the girls surpassed doctor's expectations and then some when they not only survived but, in their own way, thrived. They could not be safely separated at the time, so Deirdre carried Desdemona, born with underdeveloped legs, for her entire life. Despite this challenge, Deirdre was a vibrant, happy girl, nicknamed Arcana for her love of tarot cards and strong belief in the supernatural.

She is preceded in death by her mother, Helen, and her elder sister Alice. In her short life, Deirdre made an impact on everyone who knew her, and she will be dearly missed by all who had the pleasure to be her friend.

Rest well.

I loved Rose Red. I didn't talk about her as much as I should have, because even though I loved Risa, too, she wasn't my sister. I can't write about Rose Red without crying, even though she got on my nerves sometimes, and we weren't even conjoined. I miss Arcana so much I could never put it into words. We shared a heart, we shared a *life,* and now she's gone.

I've been in the hospital for two months. I still don't know if I'll ever go home. I'm supposed to have a heart transplant later this year, but I don't really want to no matter what Liliana says. My sister walked into this hospital and never walked out; it doesn't feel right to leave without her. She was cremated, but she hasn't had an official funeral yet. Jewel says they're going to have it once I can leave the hospital; I kind of think they're waiting to give us a joint funeral. Either way, they gave me her ashes in a silver urn that sits next to my hospital bed.

I started writing this because I needed something to do while I wait to either get better or die. Arcana told me a lot about Florence's diary, but I never actually read it myself until now. After reading it, I don't know if I like the Labelle twins more or less. I don't understand Sage at all, and I think Florence was insane—still, I think I get her a little more than Sage. Like her, I was the less dominant twin, and like her, I didn't really want to be apart from Arcana. I just wanted to live a little longer. Unlike Florence, I would never have hurt my sister to keep her with me.

Jewel says that when I get out of the hospital, we'll spread Arcana's ashes together. She told me to think about where I want to do it, and I'm trying to get up the nerve to tell her I don't actually want to have her ashes spread at all. Loreley told me that there's a way to mix ashes into tattoo ink, and I've decided that if I live to eighteen, I want to do that. Arcana was with me all my life; I can't just throw her away in the woods somewhere. I'm going to get a tarot card tattooed over my heart, but I haven't decided which one yet.

By then, it won't even be *my* heart, will it? Right now I have our shared heart beating in my chest, but if I survive the heart transplant, it'll be someone else's, someone I never met. They're going to call our heart medical waste and throw it away like it never meant anything, the heart I shared with my sister and my soul mate.

Reading this back, I still don't know what to make of everything. I don't envy the Labelle twins, or Loreley, or Risa, but I'd rather be any of them than Liliana. I don't want to live another day without Deirdre, let alone forever.

About the Author

Iphigenia Strangeworth was born and raised in Houston, Texas, where she began writing horror stories as soon as she found out what death was. She now splits her time between Texas and Virginia and, when she's not writing, can be found reading, sewing, baking, embroidering, and being a little weird about her doll collection. She enjoys hyper-violent horror and sparkly pink unicorns in equal measure. Like most authors, she is semi-nocturnal and might scurry away if you encounter her in the dead of night; ask her about Monster High and give her a cookie to gain her trust. Should you find yourself without a cookie, she'll take a fun fact about spotted hyenas in a pinch.

You can find her online at:

iphigeniastrangeworth@tumblr.com, where she reblogs a great deal of *My Hero Academia* fanart, or, occasionally, in small-town antique stores, cooing over the most haunted porcelain dolls she can find.

OTHER HELLBOUND BOOKS

Snow White in His Glass Coffin

This Southern gothic, psychosexual horror story follows siblings Chastity and Jonathan Caldwell throughout their terribly troubled lives…

From spending their grim childhood in a ramshackle trailer with an unstable, cruel mother who prostitutes Jonathan out to fund her meth addiction, through a brutal murder that permanently alters their relationship, and into their adulthood, where Chastity begins to take increasing sadistic joy in controlling and tormenting her poor brother.

Told from Chastity's unique perspective, Snow White in His Glass Coffin dares you to empathize with two deeply disturbed people who commit and attempt to rationalize their unspeakable, brutal crimes.

A gut-wrenching tale most definitely not for the faint of heart.

The First Time I Saw Her

Anna and her mother are on the run after a tragedy shatters their world. A stranger has offered them protection in a private community hidden deep in the woods, and Anna and her mother have no choice but to abandon their life and belongings to take refuge until they can figure out their next move.

But the woman who helped them may not be what she seems, and the safe-haven community has its own secrets ... and its own dangers.

Anna is no ordinary girl, though. She can perceive things others cannot, impossible things. Now thrust into an unfamiliar setting with horrors unfolding all around her, Anna must figure out what she is and what she is capable of before she loses what little she has left of her life.

THE FIRST TIME I SAW HER is the first installment in the Gossamer and Pitch Trilogy, a series about love and hate, witches and demons, and the sheer veil between life and death.

Anthology of Splatterpunk: Vol 2

splat·ter·punk
noun
informal
noun: splatterpunk

Definition: "A literary genre characterized by graphically described scenes of an extremely gory nature."
Welcome once again, fellow gore lovers, to HellBound Books' second foray into the deliciously bloody, innards-strewn world of splatterpunk! Death, dismemberment, and destruction abound within these pages, as we bring to you nineteen perfectly ghoulish tales of terror that are definitely not to be read while eating!

Go on, we dare you!

You have short tales from: Shannon Blake Skelton, Juan Ozuna, Sarah Moon, Seaton Kay-Smith, S.C. Vincent, S. Michael Wilson, Carson Demmans, Diana Parrilla, Michael Errol Swaim, John Schlimm, P.J. Verfall, Karly Foland, W.L. Lewis, Caleb James K., Brian J. Smith, D.J. Tuskmor, Terry Grimwood, Dave Davis, and Paul Allih.

Anthology of Creature Features

Come on, admit it, we all love a gripping tale of our fellow creatures gone bad. Think *Jaws, The Rats, The Crabs, Pede, Them!* – the list is practically endless (hell, they even made a movie about killer bunny rabbits! *Night of the Lepus*, 1972, anyone?).

There's just something so inherently terrifying about the animals we see every day and take for granted are going to stay in their dens, burrows, nests, swamps, and crevices going on a murderous rampage of mayhem and outright slaughter against us poor human beings. Knowing what they are truly capable of has us keeping one wary eye on the critters, that's for sure.

And so, gathered within the pages of this skin-crawling, nerve-jangling anthology, you'll discover a collection of the most horrifying examples of Mother Nature gone psycho we could unearth.

We have killer goldfish, a murderous mantis, a hellish giant arachnid, giant lizards, turtles, something altogether indescribable with tentacles, and so much more. Heck, there's even a tale of butterflies we guarantee will chill you to your very soul!

Featuring zoological tales of terror from: *Tim Newton Anderson, R. D. Tyler, Chad Barger, Seaton Kay-Smith, Milan Kovačević, Julien Jayus, Robb White, Serena Daniels, Rose Strickman, Janna Layton, J. Neira,* and the amazing *Cliff McNish.*

Buds

"The love child of an 80's monster movie and a serial killer's wet dream."
Wildus Guidry, amateur scientist extraordinaire, invents time travel. To his bitter disappointment, he discovers his device only transports him mere fractions of a second into the past.
Inhabiting the new, alternate world of that fractional past is a variation of Homo sapiens that reproduce asexually by budding and uses sex only as a recreational pastime and as a means of feeding.

Disappointed by his discovery, Guidry and his entrepreneurial girlfriend decide to bring back some of the Buds and open the world's most bizarre and exclusive brothel - the Buds' unique appearance as grotesquely erotic conjoined twins, triplets, quadruplets (and more!) prove to be incredibly popular amongst the brothel's elite clientele.
Of course, all goes terribly wrong as the Buds turn out to be not as benign as first thought, and chaos and the end of the world ensues.
Buds is a unique, sexy take on the popular time travel trope, and a must for all lovers of conjoined twin tales.
Erotic, at times brutal and disturbing, Buds is a story told with lashings of dark humor.

The Horror Writer

"The most definitive guide into the trials and tribulations of being a horror writer since Stephen King's 'On Writing.'"

We have assembled some of the very best in the business from whom you can learn so much about the craft of horror writing: Bram Stoker Award© winners, bestselling authors, a President of the Horror Writers' Association, and myriad contemporary horror authors of distinction.

The Horror Writer covers how to connect with your market and carve out a sustainable niche in the independent horror genre, how to tackle the writer's ever-lurking nemesis of productivity, writing good horror stories with powerful, effective scenes, realistic, flowing dialogue and relatable characters without resorting to clichéd jump scares and well-worn gimmicks. Also covered is the delicate subject of handling rejection with good grace, and how to use those inevitable "not quite the right fit for us at this time" letters as an opportunity to hone your craft.

Plus... perceptive interviews to provide an intimate peek into the psyche of the horror author and the challenges they work through to bring their nefarious ideas to the page.

And, as if that – and so much more – was not enough, we have for your delectation Ramsey Campbell's beautifully insightful analysis of the tales of HP Lovecraft.

Featuring:

Ramsey Campbell, John Palisano, Chad Lutzke, Lisa Morton, Kenneth W. Cain, Kevin J. Kennedy, Monique Snyman, Scott Nicholson, Lucy A. Snyder, Richard Thomas, Gene O'Neill, Jess Landry, Luke Walker, Stephanie M. Wytovich, Marie O'Regan, Armand Rosamilia, Kevin Lucia, Ben Eads, Kelli Owen, Jasper Bark, and Bret McCormick.

And interviews with: Steve Rasnic Tem, Stephen Graham Jones, David Owain Hughes, Tim Waggoner, and Mort Castle.

**A HellBound Books LLC
Publication**

www.hellboundbooks.com